STONE COLD, STONE DEAD

STONE COLD, STONE DEAD

Margaret Duffy

This first world edition published 2018
in Great Britain and the USA by
SEVERN HOUSE PUBLISHERS LTD of
Eardley House, 4 Uxbridge Street, London W8 7SY.
Trade paperback edition first published
in Great Britain and the USA 2020 by
SEVERN HOUSE PUBLISHERS LTD.

British Library Cataloguing in Publication Data
A CIP catalogue record for this title is available from the British Library.

ISBN-13: 978-0-7278-8815-0 (cased)
ISBN-13: 978-1-84751-931-3 (trade paper)
ISBN-13: 978-1-78010-986-2 (e-book)

Typeset by Palimpsest Book Production Ltd.,
Falkirk, Stirlingshire, Scotland.

ONE

The man from MI5 was of short stature, somewhat rotund, and when he spoke, with a very slight stammer, chins wobbling, I found myself having to listen very carefully as his words came out in little more than a hurried whisper.

'There's no question of anyone wanting you to kill this man, you understand, merely to observe and monitor his movements. As you're probably aware, he was stripped of his knighthood while he was in prison, so is no longer Sir Julian. I also don't have to remind you that he was the co-conspirator in a plan to murder a very senior man in MI5 – your boss at the time.'

'I don't think I shall ever forget it,' murmured Patrick, my husband.

The man, who had introduced himself as Charles Dixon, continued, 'I understand that once released some six months ago he changed his name to Mannering, Julian Mannering, but this doesn't seem to have been done officially as there's no record yet of a deed-poll application. Unofficial sources appear to indicate that it's a stolen identity. We think there's every chance that—'

'Unofficial sources?' Patrick interrupted. If he was offended by the assumption that he would be prepared to remove someone from the land of the living without a blink, he gave no sign of it.

'What I believe you police call "snouts",' Dixon answered with just a hint of distaste. 'It seems that he's consorting with serious criminals, possibly with a view to making money by illegal means. And *that* suggests to us that he's thinking of using his considerable fortune, previously accrued by fair means or foul, no one knows but probably the latter, to either buy his way into what I'll call an existing crime set-up or is planning to start something of his own. We're involved because one of the people with whom he consorts was a member of parliament until she lost her seat at the last election. She was on several committees, one of which was involved with national security, and questions were being asked about her too. But she's out of politics now and the situation's changed. That's where you come in.'

'I no longer work for MI5,' Patrick said.

I have discovered over the past few years that this is actually debatable – that is, I think he does, sometimes, very, very quietly, the occasional little job. But Dixon need not necessarily know that.

Dixon impatiently shook his head. 'No, but developments point to the situation having become a police matter.'

'I don't take orders from MI5 either.'

Please see the above.

'I'm not giving you orders. Those will come from the usual sources – *your* usual sources. The deciding factor is that you've already met him when he and another man by the name of Nicholas Haldane endeavoured to enact revenge on your then MI5 superior Richard Daws. This was following some past action of Daws that caused the knighted banker huge resentment.'

'That dated back to the time they were both in the army and the illustrious gentleman was discovered to have been embezzling mess funds,' Patrick told him. 'Worse than that, and although there was no evidence, he was suspected of having then been involved in the death of the junior officer who found out and reported him and whose sports car went off the road after the brakes failed a short while later. Despite his protestations of non-involvement at the time – the brake pipes had been tampered with – Daws was so angry he threatened to have him shot. An accident on the firing range, naturally.'

'But I understand he subsequently admitted to the crime.'

'Yes, he did. When he thought he'd got away with it.'

'Major, eventually, weren't you?'

'Lieutenant colonel.'

'I understand Daws recruited you into his department in MI5 after you suffered severe injuries serving with Special Forces.'

'That's right.'

'And in the end Haldane *was* responsible for Daws' death, not that he lived to tell the tale, of course.'

'No, he just happened to be standing in the way when someone fired a couple of loaded cannon at Daws' castle – who in real life had been, as you must be aware, the Fourteenth Earl of Hartwood.'

Dixon had asked us – I work with Patrick on a part-time basis – to meet him in the Francis Hotel in Bath, just a few miles from where we live in the Somerset village of Hinton Littlemoor. I supposed it was good of him not to expect us to go to London but as it was a Friday I reckoned he might be hoping for a weekend away on expenses. I'm not usually so cynical but having worked alongside Patrick for D12, a small department of MI5, some years ago, I approach anything coming from that direction with extreme caution.

I had an idea that Patrick was of the same mindset but his general demeanour still gave nothing away and he sat relaxed in his chair in one of the hotel's lounges as inscrutable as a cat. Being pickled in self-control as a result of early Special Forces training was to his advantage right now as he was deeply grieving the recent death of his father. I shall never forget Elspeth, Patrick's mother, putting her head around the kitchen door that morning when we were having an early cup of tea and whispering, 'Patrick, I think John's dead.'

He had died in his sleep and it had been a week before Christmas.

'What are these developments you mentioned?' I asked Dixon.

'We've been informed that the ex-MP in question has been seen with people who, in view of her suspected continuing contacts with people in government, is worrying.'

'Criminals, you mean?' They were still watching her then.

'Yes, criminals. One of whom is Mannering. Another is a man who operates under the name of Herman Grünberg but there's no need for you to concern yourself with him right now.' He turned to Patrick. 'I think, *eventually*, it will become necessary for you to speak with Mannering. We would need to find out what he's doing – in case a foreign country's involved.'

Patrick said, 'There are several very large holes in any proposal regarding my getting involved with this. First, you say you want him watched, monitored, mentioning that I've met him. It's very difficult to get close to someone in covert fashion if there's a risk of them recognizing you, thereby jeopardizing the operation. And my days of disguising myself as down-and-outs, fencing contractors and general jacks-of-all-trades are definitely over. Second, any speaking to him regarding his intentions – and I take it we, or rather you, are talking about his possibly dabbling on the side in things like selling industrial secrets – is your job, as if there was a criminal sideline such as money laundering the police would probably be content for him to carry on with his activities for a while in order that he could be apprehended together with any lowlife cronies. My last reservation is the most important – that I was personally involved with the crime insofar as Mannering, or whatever the hell the man's calling himself these days, had kidnapped my young son and was responsible for rather a lot of assault and battery being inflicted on me personally. Police protocols will not allow me to do as you ask. Not only that, this man is little better than a common criminal and can be dealt with by any number of undercover cops. No.'

Dixon drank some of his coffee, possibly to plan his next move. It seemed unlikely that he had thought Patrick would be a pushover. When you have been headhunted by MI5 and then by the Serious Organised Crime Agency – before it was subsumed into the National Crime Agency – a certain reputation is involved. And now, with Patrick at an age when we had discussed his retiring not just from such a potentially hazardous job but retiring full stop, I guessed the last thing he wanted to do was get within spitting distance of the man I remembered as a ruthless and insufferably pompous bore.

'I think you *will* be given relevant orders,' Dixon said, finally.

Patrick sighed. 'I really don't think your superiors have hoisted in the present situation as far as I'm concerned either. As of the middle of last year I'm the NCA officer with the Avon and Somerset force – "embedded" they call it. What goes on anywhere else is not my concern unless it spills out into this area.'

'Oh, I didn't say, did I? This man now lives in the village

of Upper Mossley, which I believe is some miles from here but still just about in Somerset.'

'And he's consorting with serious criminals where?'

'In London. He commutes perhaps twice a week, sometimes three times. I've been told that he drives to Bradford on Avon and leaves his car in the station car park.'

I said, 'You've just intimated that Patrick will get orders. Why have you come down to interview us first?'

'To warn you.'

'Warn us?' Patrick said.

'Convicted and jailed for attempted murder or not, he has several friends in positions of power.'

Patrick was probably thinking 'not another one' but said, 'I can only thank you for that then and say that I shall await developments.'

'I'm sure you'll be given more details. And be very careful.'

'Tell me,' Patrick said very quietly, 'is this visit of yours official?'

Dixon gazed out of the window for several moments. 'Er . . . no.'

We thanked him for the coffee and left but, thinking we might need to get in touch with him again, I went back and asked him for his contact details. He gave me his card.

'A little worrying,' I commented a few minutes later when we were walking through Queen's Square, chilly January drizzle in our faces.

'Yes, I take warnings from MI5 very seriously. I'm also surprised that he admitted he acted unofficially.'

'But someone must have asked him to come. I mean, you don't know him, do you?'

'Never even met the guy before. But don't imagine for one moment that it's his real name.'

'Such a funny little man, though.'

'The perfect spy.' This was followed by what I can only call an ironic snort.

Nicholas Haldane was dead but simply wouldn't lie down.

This episode was largely forgotten, by me anyway, and we continued to help and support Elspeth. There are always a lot

of formalities to deal with after a bereavement – the funeral
had taken place a week earlier – and Patrick spent a lot of
time with his mother going through the extensive paperwork
and personal effects of a man who had never had a computer
nor thrown anything away if he thought that, one day, it might
come in useful. Nor, it soon became obvious, had poor John
had any inkling of his death even though taking medication
for heart problems, as his engagements diary, that is the one
for church and parish matters, was fairly full for the immediate
future and it was only the second week of the year. Sorting
all that out entailed making quite a lot of phone calls to those
who hadn't heard of his demise, a job which I undertook
myself.

'He did rather ignore how he was feeling,' Elspeth said
when we got home to the old rectory and I had called in to
the annexe with some flowers for her. 'I'm sure he thought
that he could mentally tell his body how to behave. Mind
over matter doesn't work when you get older, though, does
it?' Tears threatened but she fought them away, proving that it
did. 'A couple called while you were out. The man said his
name was Simon Graves and he introduced his wife, Natasha.
Apparently he's a churchman and soon to be helping with
the services here for a while. He was asking about accommodation. Naturally, I told them the church would arrange
that for them.'

There was something about her manner that made me ask,
'I get the impression you didn't like these people very much.'

'No, they made me feel uneasy – but that's probably me
being out of touch, old fashioned and a fogey.' She thanked
me for the flowers and went off to find a vase for them.

Elspeth is none of those things. I called after her, 'Are you
having lunch with us? I've enough smoked salmon and freshly
baked bread rolls for all of us.'

'Thank you, lovely, but I do seem to be living with you at
the moment. I have to get over this on my own, you know.'

'Your company helps Patrick,' I said simply. I also wanted
him to talk to her about her visitors as the way she had spoken
about them had left me feeling uneasy too.

We sat in the conservatory to have lunch, a deliberate ploy

of mine as through the courtyard archway Elspeth could see into the garden she had created all those years ago from what had been little more than a rough paddock and cabbage patch. I still regard it as hers and, although I plant up the various pots and other containers around the outside of the house, I always consult her if I think any particular tree or shrub needs attention or to be replaced. Patrick involves himself with pruning the fruit trees and growing vegetables when he has the time and a man is employed to cut the grass and hedges and do the heavy digging. This system works very well and on one weekend during early summer the garden, together with others in the village, is open to the public in aid of local charities.

'Ingrid said something about your having visitors,' Patrick said lightly to his mother after lunch and some general conversation.

'The Graveses,' Elspeth said gloomily. 'They didn't seem to understand that this place is now a private house, including my home in the annexe, and not the official rectory. The woman asked, not rudely though, when I thought I could move out so they could live here.'

'Bloody hell!' Patrick exclaimed, immediately apologizing. 'I think that's damned rude. Look, if they come back do please refer them to me – or Ingrid, if I'm not here.'

'Oh, I will,' she promised. 'And this evening I've planned dinner for Matthew and Katie just as we used to on Fridays before . . . John . . . died. As you know, I love having them.'

She went off to have what she called her 'zizz'.

Patrick caught my eye and said, 'I shall research the Graveses as I have one of your funny feelings about them.'

There was no sign of either of them with regard to the following Sunday services however, morning Communion being taken by a retired vicar now living in Norton St Philip. The pair assumed even less importance when on Monday morning, early and just as he was setting off for work, Patrick got a phone call from Detective Chief Inspector James Carrick of Bath CID, a friend of ours.

'He needs to talk to me in his office at nine thirty,' Patrick reported. 'He didn't go into details but if it's about this

Mannering character – *if* – it's probably a good idea for you to come along as well.'

As already stated, I worked with Patrick in his MI5 days and also do for the NCA now, although my role, officially that of 'consultant', is not on the scale it used to be. This is mostly because we have five children, three of our own – Justin, Vicky and baby Mark – and we adopted Matthew and Katie, who are older, a few years ago after Patrick's brother Laurence was killed. Their mother, always 'recovering' from alcohol and drug addiction, wants nothing more to do with them which is, frankly, a relief to everyone.

In between all these demands on my time I endeavour to write and have had several crime novels published, one of which was made into a film – a rather bad one. Right now I was roughly halfway through my current effort but couldn't see myself tackling it again any time soon.

Elspeth had been adamant that the family celebration of Christmas must not be curtailed in any way on account of John's death, saying that such a move would have horrified him as it was about something far more important than he himself. Nevertheless, the three eldest children were downhearted because of his absence and Vicky had been asking where 'Gan-Gan' was for days. John had not been the sort of man to romp with his grandchildren and, always heavily involved with church matters, can best be described as having been a benevolent presence in our lives and, if necessary, a harbour in any storms. Later, on Christmas Day, I had found Katie in tears in her bedroom saying that she couldn't bear the thought of him in a 'fridge' in a mortuary while they were enjoying themselves. I had felt a bit out of my depth but tried to explain that it was only Grandad's body that was in the fridge, not the lovely man he had been. He was somewhere much better and one could only call it heaven.

Carrick offered us his condolences again – he and his wife Joanna had attended the funeral – and then, glaring through the window at the murky morning as though taking the gloomy state of affairs personally, said, 'I understand that you've been briefed about a man calling himself Julian Mannering.'

'It was hardly a briefing,' Patrick replied. 'More a warning that something potentially nasty is going to land in my in-tray. I'm thinking of emigrating to New Zealand.'

The DCI, a boiled-in-the-tartan Scot, blue-eyed and blond, very good at his job, once described by a friend of mine as wall-to-wall crumpet, nodded sagely. 'I feel like that most mornings.'

'Do you know anything about this character?' Patrick asked.

'No, but it appears I'll soon have the job of finding out as much about him as possible, which I resent rather as no crime appears to have been committed. All I've had so far is a short email from a chief super at HQ who hinted that you would be the one in dark-blue long johns snooping on him from a tree.'

'To hell with that!' Patrick retorted. 'I said as much to Dixon, the MI5 bloke I told you about. I'm not going to knock on this character's door and try to sell him double glazing either.'

'I'm only joking.'

Patrick smiled reflectively. 'Ingrid once flattened a guy I was working undercover with by galloping all over us when she'd hired a horse while endeavouring to be part of the scenery.'

Carrick chuckled and said to me, 'You've seen quite a lot of action on horseback in connection with cases since, haven't you?'

Monday morning? The distaff side of the family diverted from jobs that needed doing at home despite the employment of a nanny and two home helps? Was I a bit impatient with this blokeish repartee and failure to get on with the job?

Too right.

Ignoring the remark, I said, 'According to the website of a business calling itself Mannering Luxury Cars, based in Great Mossley, which as we all know is a small market town not all that far from here, Julian Mannering is the managing director. Dixon told us that he lives at Upper Mossley, which I discovered is around two miles away almost on the border with Wiltshire, which would explain why he gets a train from Bradford on Avon when he goes to London. It seems to be a comparatively new company and sells high-performance cars as well as hiring out the more sedate varieties for weddings and so forth. Who knows what really goes on?'

'Er . . .' Carrick began as both men looked at me.

'Not only that,' I continued. 'When I rang on Saturday morning – from my untraceable work phone obviously – pretending that I was pricing wedding cars, a girl answered and was telling me that she was new to the job when the phone was snatched from her – at least, that was the impression I got. A man came on the line and I'm convinced it was him.'

'And?' Carrick asked.

'He very curtly told me to ring back this morning as no one was there who could help me.'

'Magnificent way to run a business,' Patrick commented. Then added, 'You didn't tell me about this.'

The slight criticism had been more than negated by a smile of congratulation for my one-upwomanship. Even though Carrick is a friend, Patrick enjoys being one step ahead of what he refers to as 'normal cops'.

'You were helping your mother with paperwork and my call didn't achieve much,' I replied.

'Are you really sure it was him?'

'He had the same deep voice with the supercilious affected drawl that I remember.'

'I think you achieved rather a lot actually,' Carrick said thoughtfully. 'You established that he runs a business and confirmed what the MI5 man told you with regards to the area where he lives. All we have to do now is find someone to watch him who he hasn't clapped eyes on before.'

'Which lets off everyone in this room but you,' Patrick said with a grin.

'And you know damned well that DCIs don't do things like that,' Carrick pointed out. 'Leave it with me.'

'There's no choice until we get some definite orders.'

When we got home – Patrick to have a quick coffee before heading off to interview someone in connection with a case – Elspeth came out to meet the car looking anxious.

'Those people came back,' she told us. 'Just after you left. Mr Graves said he'd been doing some research into local history and despite my originally telling him that you'd bought the freehold, he's discovered that there's some kind of old deed which forbids the church authorities from selling the rectory and it is to remain for the use of clergy. He said he realizes that times have changed and there simply aren't the numbers of clerics but feels the least I can do is move out of the annexe and rent it to them for a while. His wife added that I could either live with my family or find myself a little flat somewhere. They made me feel so . . . guilty.'

And with that she broke down and cried.

Putting an arm around Elspeth, I looked at Patrick and found myself wondering what the correct term was for killing someone who had been ordained. *If* the man *was* ordained, was the thought that then crossed my mind.

'Please don't worry,' Patrick said to his mother, kissing her cheek. 'And we mustn't forget that it was the church authorities who originally put the place on the market. If they don't know what's what, no one does.' Muttering that he would phone our solicitor, he went indoors.

I asked Elspeth but the Graveses had not given her any hint as to where they lived at the moment, nor had they left a phone number so they could be contacted. Needless to say, she had no intention of doing anything of the sort and was very worried as she thought, probably rightly, that that meant they would return. My first reaction to this was that it would be necessary for someone to be with her temporarily during the times Patrick and I were not at home, as to have these appalling people pestering her again was simply intolerable. Having anyone to stay though was difficult as the annexe has only one bedroom and we have no spare rooms in the main house.

The problem was unresolved even though our solicitor told Patrick that he had done all due research at the time of the sale. A deed had indeed existed and initially referred to a much earlier church house on the site – possibly first erected to house the men who had built the church – that had then been reserved for clergy but burned down in 1730. Another building, or perhaps more than one over the years, had been erected – the records were vague – but disaster had again struck in 1810 when a hay barn adjacent to the house of the time had caught fire, the flames had spread and both buildings had been burned to the ground. Some years elapsed before a replacement rectory was built, the present one in 1836, by which time the deed's timescale conditions had lapsed.

All Patrick could do for the time being was to arrange to have a 'spyhole' fitted into the front door of the annexe so his mother could see who was outside before she opened it. This would take place the following afternoon.

Joanna, James Carrick's wife, had at one time in her unmarried days been his CID sergeant but had left the police and now, a few years, a wedding and a baby daughter later, had successfully rejoined. At the end of November we had attended her passing out parade at HQ and she was at present stationed, as a probationer, in Frome. For several very understandable reasons her husband was hoping to get her posted to Bath and, by all accounts, they had made a very good team. This was not to say that he didn't share his cases with her now, which was proved a little later in the week when the four of us met for one of our regular evening 'briefing sessions' at the Ring o' Bells public house in our village, the Carricks living just a few miles away.

'This Julian Mannering . . .' Joanna began after taking a sip of her wine. 'Can whatever he's doing be traced through his contacts in London? I mean, the MI5 man said he's been seen in the company of an ex-MP and serious criminals. *Which* ex-MP and serious criminals? Did he say?'

Patrick shook his head. 'No, and presumably that info is to follow. But I haven't received any orders from either Mike or anyone in this neck of the woods. Meanwhile, I shall carry on with the cases I'm working on already.'

Commander Michael Greenway is Patrick's boss at the NCA HQ in London.

'One could take a trip and have lunch in Great Mossley or the village where this man lives followed by a little snooping,' Joanna suggested.

'Patrick and I can't,' I said. 'He knows us by sight.'

'James and I could.'

'No, we couldn't,' her husband said heavily. 'I haven't

received any official orders yet concerning this man and you're not even part of the set-up here.'

'Rats!' Joanna scorned. 'Can't we have lunch together some-where on a day off and then go for a walk without contravening some bloody police procedurals manual?'

'Yes, you can,' Patrick whispered.

Carrick glared at him.

'Or I could wear a false beard and go with Joanna,' Patrick went on to propose, not terribly helpfully.

Carrick said he would think about it, but nothing was decided just then.

Justin was going through a 'nature study' craze, which meant that, a week previously, I had found a large toad in his bedroom, which he shares with Matthew. It was not the first time he had brought one indoors, and this was soon followed by a very dead mouse, green with rot, and some slimy fungi like decom-posing fingers he had found growing on a tree trunk. Praying that he'd washed his hands with regards to the mouse, I had dealt with this as tactfully as possible as I did not want to put him off learning, but when Elspeth found a snake in her living room I hit the roof.

Although not having a horror of them, she had kept right away from it. It was not very big, just over a foot long, and obviously not a native of the British Isles being brightly coloured in shades of orange and yellow. After having sent Justin to his room, despite his tearful denials, with a promise of fatherly justice pending, I rang the RSPCA, who sent an inspector round quite quickly. We learned that it was a corn snake, which are kept as pets and are non-poisonous. Thankfully, our little visitor, which had remained where it was under a radiator, departed to be handed over to a reptile specialist.

'I know he's naughty but please don't be too hard on him,' Elspeth entreated. 'Patrick got up to some dreadful pranks when he was young.'

Plus quite a few much worse ones since, I thought.

I said that I had told Justin he must know that you don't just let creatures like that loose in the house, never mind where

Grandma lives, and they have to be kept under suitable conditions. My son was left to think about this and because of another couple of minor domestic emergencies – Vicky tripping and rolling halfway down the stairs, one of the kittens falling down behind a chest of drawers during one of their mad chases round the house and getting jammed, necessitating this heavy piece of furniture being pulled out – I forgot all about him until dinnertime, the younger children's dinnertime, that is.

Patrick arrived home early from work, just as I was serving up surrounded by steaming pots and pans.

'Oh, God,' I keened, 'Justin's still in his room.'

'What's he done this time?' was the immediate query.

'A snake in your mother's living room.'

'But aren't they hibernating at this time of the year?'

'*It was a foreign snake!*' I bawled, having burned a finger on one of the Rayburn's hotplates.

'OK, keep your hair on,' my husband murmured and left the room.

The two youngest were having their meal, baby Mark with assistance from me after I'd run my finger under the cold tap, when Patrick returned, bringing Justin with him.

'He didn't do it,' Patrick said to me quietly when Justin had been persuaded that everyone still loved him hugely and was eating his dinner.

'But . . .' I began, then stopped speaking, not wishing just then to question the verdict.

Patrick said, still whispering, 'No, look, he loves his grandma too much to do anything like that. And he doesn't like snakes – Voldemort and all that. It could have escaped from a house nearby and came in out of the cold.'

'Or someone put it through the letter box,' I said, also whispering and mentally promising Justin a few chocolates from a large expensive box I had been given for Christmas that the children were banned from hoovering up when I wasn't looking.

'Who, though?'

'How about the Graveses?'

'Are you serious?'

'Have you checked up on him yet?'

'No, I haven't had time.'

'I think you ought to.'

I suddenly became aware of Mark resembling a baby bird with its beak wide open and gave him another spoonful of food.

Katie, who had just come into the room, no doubt hungry and to check on any recent developments in the situation, said, 'Dad, did you do anything really naughty when you were young?'

'I *didn't* do it!' Justin yelled.

'I once stole a pair of very large knickers off someone's washing line and flew them from a church flagpole,' Patrick recalled happily.

Small jaws dropped.

A week and a half went by and there were still no official notifications regarding the man now calling himself Julian Mannering. All Patrick could do was research and write up everything that was known about him before and after his arrest in connection with the plan to kill Richard Daws together with his friends and acquaintances, adding his own knowledge and memories of events. Meanwhile, James and Joanna Carrick had driven to Great Mossley one Saturday and lunched at the Red Lion, a pub near the market. They had 'strolled' as Joanna put it, past the car dealership in question, which was housed in what appeared to be a converted engineering works of some kind on the edge of the town. Her husband, refusing to be seen any nearer to the place, had carried on walking and she had gone in and, as had I, made enquiries about wedding cars. There had been just a young woman in charge. The boss, she said was, 'out on business'. Only he apparently could arrange things like that while she was under training but if madam would care to leave a contact number . . .

Madam had politely declined.

After consulting Crockford's, the directory of Anglican clergy, and finding no record of Simon Graves, which could merely mean that he was newly ordained, Patrick had called the offices of the Bath and Wells diocese enquiring about him. But it appeared that kind of information could not be provided over the phone and, despite saying that he was a police officer, the woman he spoke to was adamant. He would have to attend personally, bringing proof of identity. Of the Graveses themselves there had been no sign, retired and visiting priests still taking the services.

This presented Patrick, who was very busy, with a problem because, as James Carrick had said, no crime had been committed. Therefore to request someone at Bath police station to ask questions in connection with what was, in effect, a private matter, was a misuse of his authority. I volunteered to make the enquiries but Patrick said that he had a better idea and phoned the vicar of Midsomer Norton, who had been a close personal friend of his father's. This gentleman professed himself puzzled by the situation – Patrick mentioned the couple's wanting to live in the annexe – and promised to make enquiries.

'In the days when he was known as Sir Julian he lived in a large house, a mansion, near Maidenhead,' Patrick said that same evening, looking up from his Mannering research on his iPad. 'And as you're probably aware he'd made his money in what's described as financial services and ended up as the boss of a small bank in London where all the best people deposit their money and valuables. According to this secure police website I was also looking at earlier today, one of the NCA's actually, he had dodgy friends even then. There was a suspicion that one or two of them were responsible for a heist in the Knightsbridge branch of another bank around ten years ago that netted around two million pounds in cash and jewellery.'

'Hence the mansion in Maidenhead?'

'It does make you wonder. Especially as he came from what used to be referred to as humble stock. His father was a bookmaker and his mother worked in a nightclub but died young after being knocked down by a car. At the time there was a question mark over whether it had been an accident or not. Neither the driver of the car nor the vehicle involved were ever traced.'

'Was the house sold while he was in prison?'

'It doesn't say here – there's very little detail about it.'

'What about women in his life?'

'His wife Gloria sued him for divorce shortly before he was arrested, citing another woman, and he didn't contest it. Perhaps she got the Maidenhead pad.'

One of the kittens – the female, a tortoiseshell and called after her predecessor Pirate – woke up suddenly, her ears pricked. She had been asleep on their blanket on a sofa with her brother Fred, a less exotic-looking black and white moggy. He also woke, jumped up and growled, staring in the direction of the window.

'A dog in the garden?' I hazarded.

'Or a badger?' Patrick said, still reading.

Curious and fully trusting in the efficiency of feline early-warning systems, I got up and went to the window to peep cautiously between a gap in the curtains. I could see nothing so went into the conservatory without putting on any lights. Still unable to make out anything unusual, mainly because of the illumination behind me, I unlocked the exterior door and stepped outside, crossing the courtyard to look round one pillar of the archway. There was no moon and it was very dark as well as cold. I stood quite still, listening, but could hear nothing unusual, just light traffic on the village road and a distant owl. I moved until I was standing roughly in the centre of the archway. Still nothing could be seen. Perhaps it was a deer.

Then, right in front of me, a shape materialized in the darkness – two shapes. Nightmare shapes. One of them gave me a violent shove and I went over backwards. And despite being ex-MI5, ex-SOCA, now working for the NCA, I yelled for the man in my life.

Yanked peremptorily to my feet several long moments later, I clung to Patrick, shaking but making a huge effort to pull myself together. I was then steered indoors, plonked into one of the conservatory chairs and, after a making a quick enquiry into my still being in one piece, he disappeared into the night.

'Someone – but possibly two of them – ran off down the drive,' he reported when he returned.

'Or *something*,' I said, still tending to shiver and feeling a bit ashamed. I don't normally scare this easily. And the bottom of my back hurt from where I had landed heavily.

'No, Ingrid. Blokes. They had heavy footfalls.'

'They had horrible heads with bulging eyes – like aliens. Just to frighten people perhaps.'

'Night vision goggles?'

OK, night vision goggles.

'Is everything all right?' Elspeth said, flustered and coming quickly into the conservatory through her side door into the annexe. 'I thought I heard someone scream.'

'Ingrid was spooked by some kind of animal in the garden,' her son told her.

Which was quite true when you thought about it.

TWO

When it was light the next morning, Patrick had a look round the garden. He discovered several foot-prints in the soil of the vegetable bed made by youths or men – two, he thought – wearing heavy boots. It was only when he came back past the annexe that he saw the mud smeared on his mother's living-room window. This formed the readable scrawl *Old Bitch*. After taking a couple of photographs he washed it off with the garden hose then came into the kitchen, where I was making tea, to relate what had happened.

'I simply can't see anyone in the village doing that,' I said, horrified. 'Your father was much respected and so is Elspeth.'

'What next, though?' Patrick said furiously.

Fortunately, Elspeth was still in bed and hadn't heard anything.

What came next was a return visit the following night, at just after two a.m., when someone walked around the outside of the annexe banging on all the windows with either both fists or something like a wooden mallet. We heard the racket and I leaped out of bed and ran down the stairs in my pyjamas.

It might be necessary to explain here that my husband, having suffered serious injuries when serving with Special Forces, has a below the knee man-made right leg. This, although state of the art, cannot be brought into use like throwing on a hat but takes a little time, which meant that by the time I had reached the kitchen and grabbed the first weapon that came to hand – a chunky carving knife – he was still in our bedroom. By the sound of it he was then invaded by a small herd of suddenly woken and alarmed children.

Burning with revenge after my gibbering terror of the previous night, I tore into the conservatory, which is the quickest route to outside, wrenched open the exterior door having, this time, switched on the exterior lights, and cautiously went out.

No one was in sight, but I could hear the crunch of feet on the gravel of the drive. Retreating a little and wishing I had had the foresight to acquire John's shotgun from its locked cabinet before I came out, I stood still for a quarter of a minute or so, listening, shivering, and then decided to wait for reinforcements. Taking a step back, I reversed into someone wearing not much at all.

'Please go and calm down the kids,' Patrick urgently whispered in my ear.

This became even more important when, shortly afterwards, Patrick fired both barrels of the aforementioned shotgun. Expecting the children to be in tears, having hysterics even, and collecting Elspeth, who had predictably come rushing out of the annexe in her dressing gown, I discovered a quorum of young people and our nanny, Carrie, on the landing, all – except for Vicky, who looked upset – bright-eyed and bouncing with excitement.

'Was it a burglar?' Justin shouted. 'Did Daddy shoot him? Is he dead?'

'No and no and no,' I said as sternly as I could. 'Just a silly prankster banging on the windows. Please go back to bed.' I spoke to them for a little longer and then picked up Vicky and carried her downstairs.

'Can we have some hot chocolate?' Katie called after me.

'Just warm milk,' I told her. 'I'll bring it in a minute.'

'Very wise,' Elspeth said quietly. 'Excitement and chocolate add up to being sick. Ingrid, what on *earth* was that all about?'

Before I could think of anything to say we encountered Patrick in the kitchen, shivering slightly as he was clad only in pyjama shorts. Elspeth tutted and went away, returning with what must have been his father's dressing gown. While she was out of the room Patrick locked away the shotgun.

'I sincerely hope you didn't hit anyone,' Elspeth said to him.

'I fired into the air so just bagged a couple of bats for dinner tonight,' he told her with a grin, endeavouring, I'm sure, to lighten the mood. He didn't fool us; he was fuming.

'Were they just silly local yobs, do you think?'

'It could have been. I'll mention it to James Carrick in case anyone else locally has had similar bother.'

When it got light it was found that one of the windows was cracked, which, as it was a double-glazed unit, would have to be replaced, necessitating a claim on the house insurance. Patrick said that he would make it official and open a case of criminal damage, and, with the previous night's incident also in mind, another of assault, perpetrators unknown. He also decided to have two exterior lights fitted, those that come on automatically when movement is detected. We had been reluctant to do this up until now as with wildlife roaming around the garden at night, even deer, they can be more nuisance than they're worth.

The following Tuesday morning, at around ten – I didn't actually look at my watch – Patrick called me with the news that Julian Mannering had been found dead at his home and had been identified by his cleaner. The cause of death was not known at present but as the man had had a chancy heart operation since being released from prison, the early assumption was that he had died from natural causes.

'Do you want to come over?' Patrick finished by saying. 'I'm at the crime scene.'

'I take it you're at Upper Mossley?' I said.

'Yes, the house is around two hundred yards from the White Stag, which is right in the middle of the village. Just keep going past the pub and you'll come to it.'

Suspicions as to the cause of death apart, there were enough police and crime-scene vehicles parked, untidily, in the road outside the property to convince me that I had arrived at the right place. I had borrowed Carrie's car – not hers personally, it came with her job – and found a space to park directly behind our Range Rover. Quick impressions were of a tall, somewhat slab-like three-storey end-of-terrace house built of dark-grey stone that fronted directly on to the road. The general dreariness was only relieved by variegated ivy growing up the wall to the left of the main entrance door. This was reached by going up a fairly steep path and was at the side of the house – it appeared to have been built on a hill – and actually on the first floor. A uniformed constable stood guard. When I had walked closer, zipping up my quilted jacket against the intense cold, I saw that the main stem of the ivy had been recently severed, the leaves of the plant drooping.

From where I stood I could see that the area at the rear was far larger than might have been expected, with a few mature trees and, nearest to the house where the ground had been levelled, there was a tiny knot garden. This comprised low clipped box hedges that had been planted to outline swirling patterns, the spaces between filled with several kinds of tiny perennials with variegated foliage. The effect was of an elaborate embroidery. I have to confess that I became so entranced with this, despite the fact that it needed weeding, that I failed for a moment to notice Patrick now trying to attract my attention from just outside the entrance.

'I'm going to have a knot garden,' I informed him breezily.

I went in, and we walked along a somewhat dim hallway into a large beamed living room, also gloomy. There, I was introduced to a DI from Radstock, fair, tubby and forty-ish, who was chummy and said, 'Just call me Steve.' I immediately got the impression that he thought the presence of the NCA quite unnecessary, in my experience quite a common reaction from 'normal' cops.

'I'd been keeping this one on my radar,' he said importantly, gesturing to where scenes-of-crime personnel were grouped around something on the floor, presumably the corpse. 'Not actually having people on watch, you understand, you don't get funds for that, more a kind of getting members of my team who live locally to keep their eyes and ears open in the pubs.'

'He was a regular at the White Stag then?' I said.

Steve gave me a tolerant I'm-sure-you'd-much-rather-be-watching-a-TV-soap smile. 'No, that was probably a bit too low-brow for him. Matey didn't do darts, sausages and mash. He was often seen in the Wheatsheaf at the other end of the village where I understand the food's quite good.'

'Why had you been keeping him on your radar?' Patrick wanted to know.

'There have been rumours about him being what I'll call a sex pest. No evidence, you understand, just whispers.'

'Who found him?' I went on to ask.

'His cleaner, Mrs Linda Smythe. She reckons he was a paedophile. There was no sign of him indoors when she arrived, which was unusual, and then she noticed that the back door, the one from the kitchen, was open and the house at that end very cold. As you probably know, it was bloody freezing last night. She then went on a more careful hunt for him and eventually found his body virtually behind that sofa, which, as I'm sure you've seen, we've had to pull out. She's still here if you want to talk to her. She came round to get her wages, I gather.'

'She's aware no doubt that his health wasn't too good.'

'Quite likely.' He turned to Patrick. 'Be in no doubt, Gillard, this man died from natural causes.'

'But you won't know for sure until the PM,' Patrick said. And to me, 'Have a look – tell me what you think.'

I had an idea from his expression that Steve had been about to say, 'What does she know?' But he swiftly substituted it for, 'Er, that's if Ingrid doesn't, er, mind dead bodies.'

I just gave him a look. I could hardly tell him that the deceased had once had my little son kidnapped and gone quite a long way to killing my husband. Viewing his corpse was not going to upset me one bit.

The body was lying flat on its back and the people surrounding it taking measurements or photographs made room for me. The man I remembered as fat-cat conceit had gone; a change that must have taken place in life, the remains merely that of a grey-faced individual with flabby features. The eyes were open, staring.

'People who have died from heart attacks often lie hunched over because of suffering severe chest pains,' I pointed out.

'Well, it must have hit him like a bolt from the blue. *Kerrpow!*' Steve cried, gesticulating wildly in a fashion that reminded me of Justin battling imaginary aliens.

'I still don't think it was that,' I said. 'If he'd had a heart attack he'd have been much more likely to have collapsed on to the sofa, surely not into a space behind it that, judging from the indentations made by the castors in the carpet, was around a yard wide. It looks to me as though he was shot.'

'What does the pathologist say?' Patrick enquired.

'Hasn't arrived yet – car on the blink or something. By the way, how did you get to hear about this?'

'I work partly out of Bath nick, or rather the place that's being used as the nick right now. DCI Carrick told me.'

'Any reason why?'

'Several. This morning, but before the news of the death broke, he had official notification to investigate this man. My connection with Mannering, who quite recently changed his name to that, is that MI5 has shown an interest due to a case I worked on during my time there. Eventually, he was tried and found guilty of creating a complicated plan to murder a very senior official in MI5. All I have to do now is get my NCA boss involved.'

'I see,' Steve said faintly. Then, 'But I can't think that it's necessary now he's no longer in the land of the living.'

Patrick took a deep breath. 'As Ingrid has just said, this man has every appearance of having been shot. In my view, he was hit at least twice in the chest. But until the pathologist arrives and the PM's done . . .' Patrick broke off with a shrug, smiling like the non-imaginary alien he pretends to be that sends said little son running, shrieking with ecstatic dread.

'The cleaner's in the kitchen if you want to have a word with her,' Steve said, taking a step backwards.

'Where the hell did they get him from?' Patrick whispered in my ear as we went towards the rear of the house.

'He came out of a box marked Instant DI – just add water,' I replied.

We entered a dark, cold and dated kitchen – it didn't look as though much had happened to it, or in it for that matter, since the death of Queen Victoria – and quickly established that Mrs Smythe did not come from the West Country.

'Well, 'e was 'orrible, wasn't 'e?' she exclaimed in a strong East End of London accent when asked about her employer. 'Dirty old man 'e was. Not that one should speak ill of the dead,' she added with arrestingly false piety.

'Would you care to tell us why you came to that conclusion?' Patrick said.

Mrs Smythe was seated at an old wooden kitchen table

that was so scratched and knocked about it was probably host to the National Collection of Salmonella and *Clostridium difficile* bacteria. She had a mug of tea in front of her, was in her seventies or even early eighties, and her hands spoke of years of unrelenting hard work. She gave me an anxious glance and said, 'Well, you know . . . porn. On his computer. Kiddies. I went in the room where 'e was once and there 'e was . . . you know . . . looking at the screen and doin' what dirty old men do.' Slightly stooped with age, she drew herself up. 'I'm saying no more about *that*. My son-in-law said 'e oughta be strung up.'

'No, and we completely understand why you don't want to talk about it,' I said sympathetically, feeling even more cheerful that the bastard was dead. Did we really have to find out who had killed him?

'And 'e'd get out of payin' me if 'e could,' the woman went on. 'Say 'e'd forgotten to go to the bank or summink like that – as 'e did this week. Skin a cat for the price of a fag, that one. We 'ad words yesterday – I told 'im I was leavin'.'

'Any particular reason?' Patrick asked.

'Yus. I told 'im I was an 'ome 'elp, not a doormat and wasn't goin' to do the job any longer. 'E left the bathroom like a pigsty but don't ask me to tell you *exactly* how 'e left it; it'd fair turn your stummicks. Drunk, most likely.'

'How long have you been working for him?'

'Since 'e bought the place around six months ago. I worked for the previous owner before that, and a lovely lady she woz. But after 'er 'usband passed away she went to bits, poor soul, and 'ad to go and live with 'er daughter and be looked after. That was another thing that made me mad – 'e cut through the ivy by the door that she planted in memory of 'im. Said it made 'er feel a bit better, as though 'e was still around and protectin' 'er. I cried when I saw what 'e'd done. It 'ad a real posh name too.'

'*Gloire de Marengo*,' I said.

'That's it. Can see why you're a cop,' said Mrs Smythe with a big smile that revealed stained dentures.

Patrick said, 'I understand that when you arrived this morning . . . What time was that?'

'At just before ten – but only to get my pay that 'e didn't give me yesterday. I always do this place on Mondays.'

'Mannering wasn't around so you looked for him outside as this door was open and everywhere was cold.'

'Well, it wasn't like 'im to do things like that as 'e was mean with the 'eatin' too. I shut the door and 'ad a look round the 'ouse in case 'e'd just forgotten like. But there was no sign of 'im so I 'ad another look. And there 'e was, practically behind the settee in the livin' room. Stone cold, stone dead. 'Is 'eart most likely – 'e said 'e'd 'ad a big op.'

'Are you sure the body was quite cold?' Patrick enquired quietly.

'Quite sure. I put my 'and on 'is 'ead, didn't I? Cold like 'e'd been in a fridge all night.'

'Was anything disturbed in the house? Have you checked to see if anything's been stolen?'

She shook her head. 'Didn't notice anyfink and the cops arrived before I'd 'ad a chance to look.'

'Were any interior lights on?'

'No, not one.'

'What about in here? Had he prepared a meal?'

'Yes, there was a right old mess. It was the first thing wot I did – cleared it up before the cops came.'

'You might have destroyed valuable evidence.'

'Go on! A greasy frying pan, a plate, knife and fork.'

'You said there was a mess.'

'Yes, grease everywhere, splashes of it on the cooker, up the tiles behind. Greasy smears everywhere. Looked as though he'd dropped it on the floor before he ate it – wouldn't be surprised either. As I've just said, he left rooms like a pigsty.'

There was no point in getting angry with her.

'Thank you, you've been most helpful,' Patrick said.

As we were going outside – the rest of house was cordoned off so we couldn't yet have a look round – and as she had seemed upset about it, I told her that the ivy would grow again.

On an afterthought, Patrick went back and asked her for the name and address of her son-in-law. To eliminate him from enquiries, of course.

*   *   *

'I think this man was killed yesterday,' Patrick said as we entered the White Stag with a view to having a bite of lunch. 'Probably before it got dark as Mrs Smythe said there were no lights on.'

I said, 'But was the meal he'd cooked lunch or dinner? No, on second thoughts, it must have been lunch as it gets dark really early at this time of the year, so he would have had to put some lights on later. He might have planned to go to a pub for his evening meal.'

'In which case, there would have been no useful evidence in the kitchen unless his killer touched anything.' Patrick added, gloomily, 'And of course it's not my brief to get involved with this right now so I'm not going to tread on anyone's toes until it is.'

'Yet this morning James was asked to investigate,' I reminded him.

'I was half expecting him to turn up. He's the senior DCI in the area. Oh, by the way, someone phoned the police and reported a shotgun being fired in Hinton Littlemoor the other night. I believe it's going to be looked into but official thinking is that it was probably someone letting off fireworks.'

Regrettably, we both giggled.

While we were waiting for our sandwiches Patrick tried to contact Commander Greenway but he was in a meeting.

Something rather disturbing occurred to me.

'What's on your mind?' Patrick asked.

'It's one of my off-the-wall things,' I told him.

'Which *have* proved to be very useful in the past,' he cajoled with a smile.

Before I could speak, his phone rang and it was Greenway, who said tersely before ringing off, 'I've just found out that something's going on in Somerset and I'll get back to you when I know more,' before Patrick had a chance to tell him that something was indeed going on.

I had gathered my thoughts and said, 'Charles Dixon from MI5 requested that you meet him and then sort of briefed you about Julian Mannering and told you that you would be asked to investigate him. Dixon then went on to warn us in a vague

kind of way. At about the same time James Carrick had an
email from someone senior at the Avon and Somerset HQ
saying that he would be ordered to do roughly the same thing.
Nothing official happened until this morning when Carrick
got his orders and it was discovered that the man had been
murdered. *Now* it looks as though Mike's on board. That's all
a bit odd.'

'Are you saying it's a conspiracy of some kind?'

'I don't quite know what I'm saying. It just stinks. But,
come to think of it, Carrick, or Steve, whoever, won't be able
to delve into the MI5 side of it because you're the only one
who knows all the circumstances of Mannering's arrest when
he was Sir Julian as it's all still covered by the Official Secrets
Act because of the connection with Daws. You'll also be told
to investigate it locally – Mrs Smythe's son-in-law, Uncle Tom
Cobley and all – because of now working for the NCA and
Carrick's always up to his ears in work.'

'And work with that idiot DI. Great.'

'I might be quite wrong.'

'What's a knot garden?'

'I'll show you when we go back.'

The pathologist and her assistant had arrived while we were
having lunch and as we returned to the scene the body was
being moved. It transpired that they had been involved in a
minor traffic accident, and although they were quite unhurt it
had nevertheless resulted in her car being rendered temporarily
unroadworthy.

'I'll do my best to get my initial findings to you tomorrow
but I'm very busy at the moment – people seem to be dying
all over the place from no obvious causes for the past week,'
she was saying to Steve, her gruff tone suggesting that she
was rather cross with them for being so inconsiderate.

Patrick introduced us and the doughty lady, five feet nothing,
large steel-rimmed tinted glasses, somewhat swamped by her
anti-contamination suit, fixed him with a severe gaze.

'National Crime Agency?' she queried. 'What, for a death
in the sticks?'

'The deceased was a one-time knighted banker who tried

to murder a senior man in MI5,' Patrick informed her sweetly. 'What was the cause of death?'

'I can't confirm that until I've done the PM.'

'There seems to be quite a lot of blood on the floor beneath the corpse.'

I wasn't looking at Patrick but reckoned he would beat her efforts to stare him down, owl-like specs or no, easily.

'He was shot three times in the chest,' the woman said at last.

'Thank you.'

After a subtler browbeating on Patrick's part, of the DI this time, we were permitted to don protective suits and boots and set off to have a look at the garden to see if there was any evidence of an intruder or intruders. I hung back to allow the ex-army sniper to use his expertise while I eyed the glorious creamy-white bark of a group of *jacquemontii* birches. Would Elspeth want a knot garden *and* some of these at home?

But all the while I was back in that castle room, the armory, where the man whose body now lay a short distance from where I stood had, with Nicholas Haldane, gathered together Richard Daws, Pamela Westwood (who was his lady friend, soon to be his wife), Patrick and me, Terry Meadows, a colleague of Patrick's, and Dawn, his fiancée. Also there were Mike Abelard, a young army officer who had become involved with the case, and my son Justin, kidnapped from where he was being looked after by friends of Patrick's parents on Sark. All gathered together to be murdered. Not only that—

'You're daydreaming,' Patrick observed gently from around ten yards away, breaking into my thoughts.

'I'm letting you do your own thing,' I countered. 'As you know perfectly well I have absolutely nothing to offer when it comes to people lurking around with firearms.'

He gave me a smile and walked away to the other side of the trees in the direction of what must be the nearby boundary wall, but immediately turned to the left and went from my sight around one end of a yew hedge.

We – that is Patrick, Mike Abelard and I – had gone to Hartwood castle as there was a suspicion that Daws, who we knew had been abducted by Nicholas Haldane, had been taken back to his country home. It was nevertheless a shock to discover that indeed he had, and Haldane had reinforcements in the shape of several hired thugs. And Terry, who had convinced Haldane that he hated Patrick after the way he had been treated when he worked for him. We were overwhelmed by the sheer weight of numbers. Mike and I were locked up, separately – I had no idea what had happened to him at the time – and Patrick had been tied to an ancient granite cross in the castle's circular courtyard. They had left him there. In the morning I had been fetched to cook breakfast for those inside the castle and was appalled to see that Patrick was still tied to the cross, the stone setts around him glittering with frost.

'Someone climbed over the wall in a utility area in a corner that's screened off by the hedge – compost heaps, a bonfire site, that kind of thing,' Patrick now said, a matter of feet away, startling me. 'The leaves of ages are piled high against the wall and you can see where someone landed on the heap – there are two quite deep indentations made by someone wearing boots, almost certainly a man as they're so large.'

'There's something I think you ought to know,' I said. 'I didn't bother you with it before and only heard about it last week. It's that Dawn, Terry's wife, has recently had some kind of breakdown. She's been having panic attacks and flashbacks to that incident in the castle. She too, I'm sure you remember, was abducted by Haldane when he was working for the one-time Sir Julian.'

'How bad is she?'

'A bit better now apparently, responding to treatment. Terry rang to tell me and it was obvious that he was still angry about what had happened to her, but was also feeling guilty that she'd become involved.'

'By pretending to side with Haldane he did help sort it out but went rather over the top.'

'More than *rather*, he actually beat you up to prove to Haldane that he hated you. Dawn threw her engagement ring back at him.'

'Ingrid, it *looked* as though he beat me up. When you work

undercover with people you do practise things like that in case you end up on opposite sides. You must be aware of that.'

Perhaps I was, but that hadn't made it any easier to have to watch.

Patrick went on, 'And then he took out the pump-action shotgun he'd previously concealed in the barrel of a small cannon down the far end of the armory and gunned down Haldane's gang, bar one who'd done a runner. It was actually a priceless piece of theatre.'

I should have expected that he would have a different viewpoint to me on what had occurred and said, 'That kind of situation can affect people forever.'

He gave me a penetrating look. 'Has it affected you?'

'I was just thinking about it. This murder has brought it all back to me, but to answer your question properly, no. But . . .' I broke off, for some reason tears ready and waiting.

Patrick came to put his hands on my shoulders. 'What?'

'Yes,' I gulped.

'I'm sorry.'

I swallowed hard. 'I don't want you to apologize because it wasn't your doing. I don't even want to think about it, but Terry could have easily killed this man if he suddenly saw red because it all came back to him when Dawn was taken ill.'

'A possibility that I think we keep to ourselves until strong evidence suggests otherwise, eh?'

'Of course.'

He gave me a big hug.

Having duly told just-call-me-Steve of our intention to question those in neighbouring houses, we left. It proved to be a waste of time as most in the immediate area were large, detached properties with correspondingly extensive gardens. Of those in the terrace itself, some five others, two were seemingly in the process of being knocked into one, scaffolding everywhere but no one around, and the remaining three were lived in by people who could tell us nothing. This suggested that although the murder victim had had people living around him they had never been aware of his presence while he was at home. Having seen him in the local post office-cum-village stores, one woman remarked that she only knew it was him because she'd overheard him give his name and address to the person behind the counter. It appeared that this individual, of forbidding mien someone said, had not entertained nor been the sort of person to be invited to pre-dinner drinks, or 'drinkies' as another woman put it. We persevered, visiting other houses in the village, and got roughly the same answers to our questions. No one had heard anything strange or unto-ward the previous day nor during the night. That suggested a silenced weapon might have been used.

Mrs Smythe's son-in-law lived in the village but, we discov-ered, worked in a garage in Great Mossley, a couple of miles away, only a short detour on our return journey to Bath. The garage proved to be in a side street quite close to where Mannering's car dealership was situated, and I wondered if those who worked there knew of the owner's demise.

'It'll be interesting to find out – we'll go there next,' Patrick muttered after I had voiced my thoughts as we entered the workshop.

'Reception's next door – you've walked right passed it,' a burly, dark-haired man bellowed over the din of various power tools being wielded by various other blokes.

'Police,' Patrick shouted back. 'I need to talk to Brian Cowley.'

The man emerged fully from under the bonnet of an old Land Rover. 'That's me.'

The three of us went outside into the comparative quiet, crossing the small parking area. I was trying to work out whether the black on Cowley's face was rather a lot of oil smeared on it or because he hadn't shaved for a couple of days. He walked with his shoulders hunched like a slowly charging bull and I found him a bit intimidating.

'Julian Mannering,' Patrick said, having produced his warrant card. 'Know him?'

'Not personally, no. Why d'you want to know?'

'When did you last see him?'

'I don't normally see him, not unless he drives past here in his Jag.'

'Do you own a firearm of any kind?'

'Yes, a shotgun. It's quite legal. I belong to a group – in

the winter we pot mostly rabbits and pigeons and sell them to the butcher here.'

'Mannering's dead.'

'I see.'

'You don't seem surprised.'

'I don't feel anything – I didn't know the bloke.'

'I gather that you knew he was likely to be a paedophile, though.'

'Oh, you've been talking to Ma-in-law. She told me what he was getting up to and I said that people like him shouldn't be allowed to live.'

'I didn't say that he'd been murdered.'

'Well, surely you wouldn't be here if he'd died in his sleep!' said Cowley, rattled.

'Where were you yesterday?'

'Here. The Land Rover's mine and the boss said I could use the workshop to service it. Then I discovered that the cylinder head gasket had blown so couldn't finish it until today.'

'And last night?'

'I worked here until around seven doing the rest of the service and then went home. One of the blokes gave me a lift. The wife's away visiting her sister so I popped out again after I got cleaned up and had something to eat at my local – a pie and a pint – then went home at around nine thirtyish.'

'The White Stag?'

'That's right.'

'Are you a regular there?'

'I am. The other place is a bit too fancy for my taste. Little bits of this and that. That's no good to me.'

The one questioning him doesn't go in for what he calls 'piddling artworks on a plate' either.

'People saw you there then?'

'Must have done. And I chatted with a couple of blokes – as you do.'

'Did Mannering bring his car in here for servicing?'

'God, no, he took it to the dealership in Bath.'

'How do you know?'

'Ma-in-law told me. Did she tell you she was chucking in the job?'

'Yes, she did.'

'Filthy in his personal habits as well by all accounts.' Cowley grinned. 'She probably wanted to knock his block off too.'

After Patrick told him that the police might need to speak to him again, we left.

'So where's the Jag?' Patrick said in an undertone. 'Is there a garage of sorts on the lower floor of that house that fronts on to the road?'

'I don't think it has doors wide enough to get a car in,' I replied.

Mike Greenway rang again when we were on our way back to the car and I stood close to Patrick to enable me to overhear.

'Where are you?' was the commander's opening question.

'Somerset,' said my husband.

'In connection with some character who was found dead and appears to be another of your MI5 leftovers?'

'That's the one.'

'Well, it would seem that they've nudged the elbow of the director of the NCA, who now wants us to get involved in the investigation.'

'I probably can now the bastard's dead but you might need to check.'

'How did he die?'

'He was murdered – shot three times in the chest. And in case that was your next question, I didn't do it.'

There was a little silence, and then Greenway said, 'I got your emailed memo about being asked to meet that MI5 bloke Dixon who said something was in the wind. Did they pull the trigger?'

'I don't work for MI5 now,' Patrick said, not for the first time lately. 'So I'm not in a position to know and can't think of any reason why they'd want to.'

'He couldn't have been threatening to expose one of their bods who's undercover in somewhere like Russia, I suppose?'

'Mike, you need to talk to Ingrid about off-the-wall plotlines, not me.'

Obviously unabashed even though probably realizing that he'd been thinking of MI6, Greenway went on, 'Nevertheless,

I'd like you to look into what the hell this man was up to that may or may not have been the reason behind his death.'

'You'll have to do a little rank-pulling for me and get rid of DI-just-call-me-Steve. We need a DCI on this – James Carrick.'

'I'm not sure I can do that. We're supposed to work *with* the local force, you know.' Then, when Patrick offered just silence, he added, 'OK, I'll give it a try.'

It says a lot about the character of these two – one a commander, the other a one-time lieutenant colonel but now with only the nominal rank of constable to enable him to arrest people – that things run so smoothly. Normally, that is.

THREE

T he employees of Mannering's car hire business had already been visited and questioned by the police so we returned home. When we got back to the rectory – Patrick reckoning that he could work from home for the rest of the day – a car, a small red saloon of some kind, was parked near the entrance to our drive. Patrick asked me to stop the Range Rover, got out, made a note of the registration, had a quick look through the windows and then came back. I parked our vehicle in its usual place near the front door, and he got out again and went around the side of the building and out of my sight. By the time I caught up with him, having gone in the front door and through the house, he had accosted a couple who were walking in the garden.

'Simon Graves,' a thin, fair, almost white-haired man was saying, holding out a hand. 'This is my wife, Natasha. I hope to be helping in taking some of the services here soon and came to see Mrs Gillard about renting the annexe. But she appears to be out.'

Patrick ignored the hand and said, 'Patrick Gillard, this is my wife and we're both connected with the police. My mother will not be letting the annexe to you for the simple reason that it belongs to me and is her permanent home.'

'I think you'll find that—'

Patrick carved him up. 'Also, I'm investigating some recent incidents of criminal damage and threatening behaviour at this property and have to add that I've made enquiries and no one knows anything about you. Nor are you listed in Crockford's directory.'

'I'm a newly registered reader, not an ordained priest,' the man rejoined smoothly. 'And you must know by now that a deed exists that forbids the sale of this house to lay people; it is to be kept for the use of the Church.'

'Which, according to my solicitor, applied to a series of

structures on this site, the last of which burned down in the eighteenth century, after which the deed became invalid and any future building merely became church property. They sold it. Go, and leave my mother in peace.'

'I'm a man of God, Mr Gillard. No pressure will be applied – I shall merely appeal to the lady's better nature.'

'If you're a man of God, Graves, I'm a pole dancer,' Patrick said through his teeth after a little eternity had elapsed and during which I actually thought he was about to kill the man with his bare hands. He added, when the pair just remained standing there, 'If I even catch a glimpse of you here again I'll arrest you for aggravated trespass – and that applies to you both.'

After a few more tense seconds they swept out, the woman, whose expression had an uncanny resemblance to that of a disgruntled hamster, turning to give me a look that promised trouble.

'He's mad,' I whispered as we followed them to make sure they really were leaving. 'Bananas.'

'Either that or there's a very good reason why he wants to live here.'

Elspeth was at home and cautiously opened her door that leads into the conservatory as I entered it, Patrick having said he would make sure that the car we had seen was theirs. 'Have they gone?'

I told her that they had.

'I looked through the spyhole when the doorbell rang and then hid in the bathroom in case they peered through the windows,' she said. After a short pause, she went on, 'You don't think I ought to let them have the annexe for a little while, do you? I mean, if he's going to help with the services it seems so selfish of me to stay here and do nothing useful to . . .' She petered out unhappily.

I said that in no circumstances should she feel like that and the couple's behaviour was outrageous.

Patrick returned shortly afterwards and she repeated what she had said for his benefit. For a moment I thought he was going to burst into tears.

'No,' he said, sounding a bit choked. 'After all the years

and years of hard work you and Dad have put into this village, no slimy-tongued upstart is going to appropriate your home.'

Abruptly, he left us.

'Oh dear, I've made him really angry,' Elspeth whispered.

'You're absolutely the last person on Earth he'd ever be angry with,' I said.

It occurred to me that it was a very efficient way to get to a man: attack his mother.

Patrick checked up on the registration number of the car we had seen. He discovered that the vehicle was indeed registered to one Simon Graves, the address in Wood Green, north London. A search through police files yielded nothing; no one who had the same or a similar name had a criminal record, although one had to factor in the possibility of one or more aliases. I suggested he check up on the woman and that drew a blank too.

'He's creepy,' I said to him. 'Like something that's been cloned.'

'You watch far too many repeats of *Star Trek: Deep Space Nine*,' was the comment.

We decided, for everyone's peace of mind, to act immediately on the idea that someone ought to stay with Elspeth for a week or so. This was suggested to her as tactfully as possible because it would mean that John's study would have to be rearranged and a few pieces of furniture disposed of. She agreed to this but insisted that she wanted to keep his antique desk and bookcase. As far as the desk was concerned I offered to move out the modern one I had been using to write – which was actually made of sections that could be stored – to enable John's to return temporarily to what had been his study in the main house before he had very generously said I could have it as a writing room. The bookcase, with its contents, could stay right where it was. Elspeth gladly agreed to this, a double bed was ordered and she said she would invite a couple to stay whom she and John had known for years and who now lived in Kent.

'The bloke's not an invalid or anything like that, is he?' Patrick asked her the next day as we left the refurbished room

having helped to hang new curtains, the previous ones deemed
to be 'tired'.

'Barry? Heavens, no. He still runs half-marathons.'

'Good.'

But there was immediate disappointment: they were about
to go on a cruise. Patrick was at work, in Bath with James
Carrick, so I took the matter into my own hands and rang
Terry Meadows.

Obviously I first asked after his wife, Dawn, who had been
our nanny at the time of the Haldane and Sir Julian episode
some years previously.

'She's quite a lot better and has gone off, taking the sprog,
to see an old school friend,' he reported. 'I think she was
glad to see the back of me for a while.'

'Surely not,' I protested.

'Well, it's having me around that seems to trigger it all off
– nightmares, crying fits, flashbacks. I was part of it, wasn't
I? Acted as though I'd sided with that bastard Haldane and
the knighted scumbag. She keeps having horrible dreams that
your Justin was killed in front of her and that it was her fault.'

For a brief moment I thought of offering to send him to her
next-day delivery but realized that was too flippant by half. My
big failings: flippancy and getting the giggles in solemn moments.

I said, 'You're free for a few days then?'

'She said she'd stay for at least a week and only went
yesterday.'

'You run your business mostly from home, don't you?'

'Yes. What's on your mind?'

'Would you like to be Elspeth's minder for a little while?'
He laughed. 'Really?'

I explained and after the merest hesitation he agreed, saying
he would travel down the following afternoon.

All I had to do now was trot it past Elspeth.

'Well, I do know him quite well, from the days he worked
with you,' she said. 'It'll be nice to have him around.'

I went on to assure her that he would only be sleeping there,
would use our downstairs cloakroom or the upstairs bathroom
and no one was expecting her to cook for him.

'Ingrid, we can hardly expect the poor man to traipse all

the way into the main house should he have to get up in the night. And I'd love it if he had a few meals with me.'

Patrick's only reservation was that Terry was still recovering from a serious shoulder wound when he had been shot during the final showdown with Haldane. As I was a bit frazzled after more minor domestic upsets – was I losing the plot in more ways than one? – I'm afraid I retorted that surely the situation wouldn't descend into open warfare.

Silly of me.

Neither of us had actually voiced having the opportunity to now question Terry about any role he might have played in the death of the man latterly known as Julian Mannering but it had certainly gone through my mind. However, to quiz him as soon as he arrived was out of the question. Outwardly, he appeared much the same, a fit and still-youthful figure, the wavy brown hair longer than when we had last seen him, the same twinkle in his eyes. He dropped his sports bag on the floor, gave me a hug and shook hands with Patrick, who had only just got home.

'Good to see you again, Chief,' he said.

'How's the shoulder?' Patrick asked.

'Almost like new. But don't ask me to get into any fights.'

'Heaven forfend,' Patrick murmured and took him through to see Elspeth.

Patrick himself had been quite seriously hurt recently when his Glock 17, in its shoulder holster – which he carries officially – took the full force of a bullet intended to kill him, fired by a man in the pay of a London mobster. He had suffered three broken ribs, one of which had punctured his left lung. The bullet had then skimmed across his chest causing a wound that, although not serious, had meant that he had lost quite a lot of blood. I was hoping he wasn't going to get in any fights either, nor for that matter have to undertake hazardous assignments where he would again be at risk. Ever.

Right now I was cooking dinner, Katie helping me. As Terry was with us I had invited Elspeth to eat with us tonight – plus Carrie on an afterthought as it seemed downright mean to leave her out. This arrangement entailed roasting a large joint

of beef that had only just fitted into the main oven of the
Rayburn. All the children love roasts, even Mark who has only
recently started eating solid food. I had crossed the kitchen to
finish preparing vegetables when I saw someone walk past the
window. The new courtyard security lights came on. I immediately ran into the conservatory and went to lock the outside
door but was too slow to prevent this person wearing a grin-
ning skull mask from violently pushing their way in, sending
me staggering backwards. Whoever it was then came towards
me making obscene gestures, forcing me, yet again, to shout
for reinforcements.

Several things occurred very quickly. Patrick came rocketing
out of the annexe, closely followed by Terry, the former grabbing the intruder by the back of his jacket collar as he turned
to flee. The mask was torn off. When the visitor had been
identified as male the three went outside and away from sight
and I had a good idea what would happen next. I was wrong,
however: Patrick merely arrested him and phoned to have him
taken into custody.

'A boy in my class brought one of those to school yesterday,'
Katie said from behind me. 'He frightened all the little children
in the reception class with it when they were in the playground.'

'Are you all right?' I asked, putting an arm around her, not
realizing that she had seen what had happened.

'Yes, now Dad's dealing with him.'

'Was the mask exactly like that one?'

'I *think* so.'

'Did the boy get into trouble?'

'No, Miss Green didn't see.'

'That's a shame.'

'Justin punched him though and when he pulled the mask
off his nose was bloody. We all laughed.'

Ye gods.

'Is everything all right?' Elspeth wanted to know, appearing
with a large bowl containing a trifle she had made for dessert.
'D'you think it was it the same stupid person who banged on
my windows?'

'Probably,' I said. 'I don't think he'll do it again.'

'Someone to be questioned tomorrow,' Patrick enthused,

rubbing his hands together when he and Terry returned some fifteen minutes later. 'We might even get to the bottom of this crazy situation.'

'At the risk of bringing back more unpleasant memories,' Patrick said, having given Terry a tot of single malt whisky and detailed our reasons for having requested his presence, 'I have to tell you that the knight of the realm who caused – and as far as you're concerned is still causing – such personal trauma, has been murdered.'

'So whoever did it gets a medal when?' was Terry's reaction. Then, 'Was it you?'

'No. And I'm going to ask you the same question.'

'Not me. Not with one sprog and another on the way.'

'Congratulations,' I said, thinking that was a good enough reason for Dawn's present problems. The woman's hormones were all to hell.

It was quite a while later that same evening and the three of us were seated in the conservatory. Matthew and Katie were in the process of getting ready for bed; the younger ones had been asleep for some time. I still felt shaken by what had happened, my glass of white wine having an interesting wave effect on it unless I set it down, and was trying to hide the fact that I was jumping at the slightest sound. Shocks like that, that happen at home with your children present, are quite different from those which occur on a work basis. I hadn't felt like this for a long time – vulnerable.

'Discounting that rather splendid affair of the cannon not so long ago and having no choice but to make a stand against that bunch of armed thugs at Daws' castle, I think I've only ever killed one other person,' Terry said reflectively.

'For which I seem to remember getting into rather a lot of trouble over as you were working for me at the time,' Patrick said with a grin. 'Where were you last Monday?'

'Yes, of course, you're a cop now,' Terry muttered. 'I was at home and then at work.'

'Alone?'

'Yes. Dawn had gone that morning, early. I drove them to the station.'

'Where does her friend live?'

'In Dorset, Lyme Regis.'

'Dawn would have known if you'd gone out overnight then.'

'No, she might not have done as lately she's taken herself off into the room where Emma has her cot. Look, Patrick—'

'I have to be absolutely clear in my mind that you weren't involved,' Patrick interrupted. 'It must be at least a three-and-a-half-hour drive from where you live in Sussex to the area where he was killed. What time was it when you went to bed the previous night, the Sunday?'

'I didn't look at the clock, but it must have been shortly before ten.'

'If you'd stayed in bed until it was all quiet, say until ten thirty, and then driven to Somerset you'd have got there by about two a.m. Finding the house and—'

Terry interrupted. 'Assuming I knew where the bastard lived.'

Patrick blithely carried on, 'Finding the house and undertaking a reconnaissance prior to breaking in and shooting him wherever he happened to be would have taken another good hour. And then the three-and-a-half-hour drive home. What time did you get home?'

'You're a bastard too,' Terry said good-naturedly. 'I didn't.'

'Well, it wouldn't have been much before six-thirty and Dawn would have been up by then. How far is the station from where you live?'

'Pulborough. Eight miles.'

'What about for the rest of that day? What was your programme?'

'I was at work. I have an office in Pulborough over the branch of a building society. I got there before I usually do as I'd got up earlier than usual, at around eight, and dealt with the usual things – emails, phone messages.'

'No staff?'

Terry sighed. 'Yes, but she's on sick leave – got some kind of bug.'

'So no one can vouch for you.'

'Not then. After dealing with the routine stuff I had an early meeting at a large house, an estate really, on the outskirts of the town with a guy who wants me to set up security for an upmarket wedding there in three months' time. The groom's a pop star. Never heard of him, actually.'

'And after that?'

'I had a bite of lunch in a pub, no booze, and then went back to the office. Left there early, about four thirty.'

Patrick made no further comment on that and continued, 'I have a theory that Mannering was killed either after lunch on the day before he was found or during the night – probably the former. I haven't yet had sight of the PM report, but his cleaner said the body was stone cold so that's why my money's on during the middle of the day or early afternoon. And we must bear in mind that there's every chance the motive for this murder had absolutely nothing to do with Richard Daws, nor what happened at Hartwood. I'm sure he was the kind of man who would have made many enemies.'

I said, 'Do either of you think it's possible there could be a connection between Mannering's death and what's been happening right here?'

There was a short silence and then Patrick said, 'The only thing I can think of is that someone is trying to divert the attention of an investigating officer by creating a nasty situation at his home.'

'But who would have had the first idea that you'd be the investigating officer in this particular case?' Terry asked.

'MI5,' I said. 'They not only sent someone to talk to us before he was even dead but it would appear they nudged the NCA into looking into it when he was.'

'But the fact that I'm the embedded NCA officer where this man lived is such a coincidence,' Patrick argued. 'And who would be giving MI5 that kind of information?'

'It could be a very happy coincidence for someone,' I said, really concerned now that Terry appeared to have no alibi at all. He would have had time to drive to Somerset and back after his early meeting.

The next morning our intruder, who finally confessed to having consumed six pints of beer and half a bottle of whisky since noon the previous day, turned out to be the father of the boy who had taken the skull mask to school. His son had a bruised

nose and a black eye, he growled, and had told him that he
had been 'beaten up by a big lout called Justin' who lived at
the rectory. Lynn Outhwaite, the acting DI who was sitting in
on the interview out of sheer curiosity and rang me afterwards,
pointed out to him that to her certain knowledge – she has
met all the family – the accused was a pupil at the same
primary school and around three feet tall in his socks. Also,
this child had to be several years younger than the injured
party. Lynn then confirmed that the arrested man was to be
charged with being drunk and disorderly, forced entry and lewd
behaviour. Plus, perhaps, anything else she could think of.

Patrick had said not a word to Justin about it but told me
when he came home that evening that he would keep an eye
on him.

While this was taking place, we returned to Upper Mossley.
Scenes-of-crime personnel were in the garden and, outside, a
police dog handler was waiting in a van with his canine assistant. The house was free of incident tape and, having shown
our warrant cards to the uniformed constable trying to keep
warm by the entrance and putting on nitrile gloves, we went
in. As before, the place was freezing cold, to my mind colder
than it was outside, not helped by a chilly breeze in the hallway
presumably coming in through the open back door.

'No signs of a struggle,' Patrick mused to himself when we
were in the living room. 'Nothing at all looks as though it's
been disturbed. I wonder if he knew his killer.'

I had noticed small details in the room on our first visit but
now looked more closely. On a small table was a half-full
bottle of whisky, Glenmorangie, a tumbler with just a little
drop in the bottom, a packet of cigarettes, a silver lighter and
a copy of a free local newspaper. The table had sticky-looking
rings on it which gave every appearance of having been there
for some time, and I wondered how much cleaning Mrs Smythe
had actually done here. Even though I knew everything would
have been examined for fingerprints, I didn't touch anything.
I didn't actually want to be in contact with any of this man's
possessions.

In passing, we glanced into the kitchen where, courtesy of
Mrs Smythe, we already knew there was nothing in the way

of potential evidence. To one side of this was a small utility room – the one-time scullery? – containing a washing machine and a tumble dryer. A plastic basket of dirty clothing was in one corner. Opposite the door to the living room where the body had been found was what I could only describe as a study, perhaps at one time used as a dining room. Obviously the police had been through everything as all that could be seen from the doorway was a huge jumble of belongings on the floor. Paperwork, files, holiday brochures, letters, books, pamphlets were all piled up where they had been pulled out of a filing cabinet and off shelves on the wall. A cheaply made desk was on one side of the room with a rectangle of dust on it, perhaps where a computer had been, and if so it almost certainly had been removed by the police.

We continued and went upstairs. I gazed out of a landing window and waited while Patrick wandered round, as even just a quick peep though the open doorways of both dingy bedrooms and the bathroom confirmed everything that Mrs Smythe had said. They were all in a mess. Clothes and towels, the latter wet by the look of them, were on the floor everywhere and there was a smell that suggested that there was vomit some-where. Again, I felt slightly sick. Also utterly pathetic.

'Do you want to go back into the fresh air?' Patrick asked when he caught sight of me for a moment. 'You look a bit pale.'

Yes, I did, and went right outside and down into the road. The lower floor – the one that faced it and where Patrick had thought Mannering's car might be – appeared to be some kind of basement or store room, definitely not a garage. Perhaps at one time a shop, it had an ancient wooden door – covered in dirt from traffic but just discernible as having once been painted green – that fronted the road and there were no door-knobs or handles remaining, the holes where they had been crudely blocked up with some kind of wood filler. A large window to one side of it, one pane of which was cracked, was similarly filthy, the dirt and an ancient and torn blind preventing anyone from seeing in.

I returned to the kitchen and investigated the other four doors that led off it. One provided access to a small outside yard and was open so I shut it – to hell with forensics.

Another was locked; the remaining two led into a walk-in
larder and coal hole respectively. For some reason the locked
door was more substantial than the others, a hefty construc-
tion of oak that, judging by wear and various knocks, had
been painted in at least four different colours since new,
mostly grim old-railway-station shades of brown and green.
There was no key in the old-fashioned lock and I went on a
protracted hunt for it in the kitchen cupboards and drawers.
I found a couple but they were far too small. As I stepped
back with a whispered expletive, having slammed the last
drawer and sending the cutlery it contained hammering into
the back of it, I realized that Patrick was standing by the
doorway from the hall, smiling.

'You're smirking at me,' I snapped.

'I'm not,' he protested.

'OK, perhaps you don't realize what your face is getting
up to.'

He blew me a kiss. 'What are you looking for?'

I pointed. 'The key to that door. The ground floor, cellar,
whatever, has to be down there somewhere.'

Patrick had a look. 'I can open this.'

When on the job he always carries a set of what I think of
as 'burglar's' keys and it took no more than twenty seconds
of deft work with a strong wrist to unlock it. The door had
obviously not been used very often, groaning open on its
rusting hinges as Patrick applied leverage with a shoulder. A
blackness yawned inside and he clicked on his little torch –
another useful tool – and shone it within. It is not really meant
for illuminating large areas though, and the tiny beam got lost
in the space beyond.

'Stone steps – going down of course – what looks like the
junk of ages, enough cobwebs to knit yourself a hat,' Patrick
said, lack of space in the doorway necessitating his giving me
a running commentary. 'Interesting . . . there's lot of dust at
the sides of the steps but less in the middle so he must have
come down here sometimes. There doesn't appear to be any
lighting though.'

He disappeared below and Utterly Pathetic took one look
at the cobwebs, black and waving around in the draught in

utterly nasty fashion, and stayed right where she was. This case, I told myself, wasn't for me at all.

'Nothing seems to have been touched in here for years,' Patrick said from somewhere down in the gloom, his voice dead-sounding, the light from the torch flicking this way and that. 'Just a load of old bikes, home gym equipment and God knows what else. Plus another door that would appear to allow access to, or from, the next house. On the other hand . . .'

'What?' I asked when he stopped speaking.

'There are boxes under the stairs that don't look as though they've been here all that long . . .'

There followed scuffling noises, grunts, a sneeze and then protracted sounds of rending cardboard. I was about to point out that they might belong to someone next door but then thought, hey, we were cops, weren't we?

'What's in them?' I simply had to ask after ages had gone by.

'One had already been opened – someone checking the contents perhaps. There are toilet rolls on the top couple of layers of all of them, old 9mm Browning pistols and Webley revolvers underneath. These must be destined for criminal gangs, which, as you must know, are finding it increasingly difficult to get hold of guns.'

My knowledge of firearms is basic but I said, 'Aren't the Webleys sort of antiques?'

'Oh, yes, Brownings originally dated from 1935 and versions were used by the British army until quite recently. The Webley goes back to the First World War.'

'But they can be fired.'

'Too right. Criminals get the ammo from underworld armourers.'

'They can't have come into this country like that surely, just in cardboard boxes.'

Patrick came up. 'No, this is almost certainly only one in a series of ports of call for them. Is that idiot Steve around, d'you know?'

I had no idea and went outside. Steve was nowhere to be seen but James Carrick was coming down the garden having obviously been talking to those still working out there.

'Saw your wagon at the front,' he called. 'Does this case really need me?'

'It does now,' I said.

'I can't see how those weapons in the basement can have had anything to do with Mannering's death, due to the fact that they're still here and bearing in mind that you had to pick the lock as you couldn't find the key,' Carrick mused a little later, having had a look for himself. 'But one thing's certain, they must be removed immediately.'

I said, 'There's no sign of a disturbance either, other than that presumably made by the police in the room used as an office, to indicate that anyone, including the murderer, looked for them.'

'It'll be interesting to know if the body had any marks on it that might suggest he was tortured to reveal where they were,' Patrick said.

Carrick found his mobile and paused, looking him square in the eye. 'I want you to tell me if you think there's any connection with this death and what went on that day at Hartwood castle when Sir Julian, as he was then, tried to kill the lot of you.'

'Ingrid and I have already worked through this and I'll give you a written account of exactly what went on by tomorrow. But, in a nutshell, the injured parties were Pamela, who was Daws' lady friend at the time and now his widow, Terry Meadows, whose fiancée, Dawn, then our nanny, now his wife, was kidnapped, and a young army captain, Mike Abelard, who was helping Ingrid and me at the time. Meadows was pretending to have joined the enemy.'

'Any thoughts on this Abelard?'

'He's a major now and working at a Ministry of Defence establishment in London. I know for a fact that although he found himself in a tight spot he regarded it as part of the job and enhancing his experience. The man was never really emotionally involved and I think expected the senior officers present, Daws – who was still in the army then – and me, to sort out the situation. Which, with Meadows' help, we did, of course.'

'And you have no theories?'

'No, not right now.'

'What about Meadows? Was his wife-to-be hurt?'

'Not physically but I understand she can't forget what happened. I don't think he's stupid enough to have killed Mannering – there's a second child on the way.'

The weapons were removed but we had gone by then, leaving Carrick to conduct the investigation.

Not for the first time lately there was a strange car parked in the rectory drive. But the visitor was of a benign nature, the vicar friend of John's who Patrick had contacted to make enquiries about Simon Graves. Over coffee, Elspeth was chatting with him. As her living room is not large I invited them into the main house and discovered Terry amusing Mark and Vicky, he having tactfully removed himself when the visitor arrived.

The Reverend Paul Broadley was middle-aged, dark-haired and jolly and, according to my late father-in-law, 'had a screw or two very slightly loose'. I had taken this to mean that he was unconventional and so it would prove to be.

'No, please stay,' Patrick urged as Terry rose to take himself off again. 'This meeting might be in connection with why you were asked to come here.'

Broadley beamed upon us all. 'Patrick, you wished to know about a man by the name of Simon Graves. I can tell you categorically that he's not a clergyman, in that he's never been ordained, but appears to be some kind of casual reader at a set-up that's calling itself a mission in London. It's not recognized either by the Church of England or the Catholic Church. You'll immediately say that there are other religions, other faiths and indeed other branches of all the recognized main faiths in this country. Whatever the truth, the fact is that he cannot conduct services, or even assist with them at your church here as the Diocese of Bath and Wells has no record of him.'

'If you don't mind my asking,' Patrick said. 'How does the C of E know that he's some kind of reader?'

'There are several grapevines,' the man answered with

an enigmatic smile. 'We're talking about written and verbal evidence.'

'Could he have been ordained abroad?' Elspeth wanted to know, taking Vicky on her knee.

'Indeed he could, dear lady, but records still have to be kept. No, I think you'll find that Mr Graves is something of an enigma.'

'Why hasn't the mission been recognized?' Patrick enquired.

'It's called Saint Edwina's. Although their website says that she was an early thirteenth-century Christian martyr there appears, if one does a little digging in irrefutable sources of knowledge, to have been no such person. The building they're using, a rather nice old house in the north of London, was indeed a mission that was founded donkeys' ages ago by a local benefactor and I'm sure it did a lot of good. It wasn't called Saint Edwina's in those days. However, due to recent lack of support – and let's face it there are thousands of charities that folk are expected to give money to these days – and the fact that the committee of the time were all in their dotage, ill, or had actually died, the organization foundered and the property was sold off just over six months ago.'

'So what do they actually do, sir?' Terry asked when Broadley paused to drink some coffee.

'You may well ask. It would seem that what exists now is run mainly as a hotel but they offer conference and meeting facilities. I haven't been able to find out if they still enjoy charitable status but their website also mentions retreats and the support of local action to help the homeless and other unfortunates living rough. I have to confess that I went on a retreat once and found myself trapped with a bunch of complete nutcases, almost literally. It was not much to do with God, more of a rolling in the dew, eating dubious mushrooms and seeds and other stuff that belonged in a horse's breakfast. It played havoc with my insides.'

'You said "it would seem",' Patrick observed.

The man chuckled. 'You can blame my nasty suspicious mind for that and also my distaste for anything that has a smell of the phoney about it. The fella in charge of it all, referred to as the principal – he's wearing a dog collar in the photo of him on the website – has a look about him that reminds me of an old reprobate I used to know when I worked in London years ago, who ran a stall in Berwick Street market. Everything on the stall itself was probably OK; the stuff that had been pinched from heaven knows where was on the ground beneath it.'

'This place might be a front for criminal activities then,' Terry said to himself.

'D'you want me to go and have a nose round?' Broadley offered eagerly. 'This business is really fascinating and I'm being nagged into having some time off.'

John had told us that Broadley had thrown himself into his duties following the sudden death of his wife.

Unable with his mother present to go into the full details of what had occurred at the rectory which we, rightly or wrongly, had laid at Graves's door, Patrick was unsure what to say for a moment.

'The people who came here weren't very nice,' Elspeth said. 'I wouldn't like to think of you getting involved with them in any way.'

'I used to be a good prop forward,' Broadley told her. 'Wouldn't stand for any nonsense.'

Thoughtfully, Patrick said, 'A priest could go there and make enquiries about the place's suitability for a retreat that he could give the impression was being planned. Someone like that could ask to be shown round, see the rooms people would be staying in, sample the catering arrangements, investigate the transport links, ask a few questions.'

'I'm up for that. I'll do it next week if they have any vacancies.'

'Do you have the full address?'

'Yes, the grapevine knew that too.' He consulted a small pocket diary and wrote it down for us.

'Please be careful, sir,' Patrick said.

FOUR

James Carrick was in overall charge of the investigation into the murder of Julian Mannering but due to pressure of work and an ongoing and seemingly never-ending shortage of personnel in Bath he had no choice but to use reinforcements. This came in the shape of just-call-me-Steve from Radstock or, more correctly, Detective Inspector Stephen Potts, who, everyone had to admit, teeth gritted, had already done a lot of work on the case.

The initial search of the house had found no passport or driving licence in the name of Julian Mannering although utility bills and a council tax notification were addressed to that name. It was only when some enterprising soul went through the bookcase that she found a dummy book, the kind that are used as hidden document boxes. This contained Mannering's army records – in his own name, Hardy, in those days – and sundry other papers, including an invalid old paper driving licence also in the name of Hardy. But still no passport. Towards the top of the pile was a receipted invoice dated two months before Mannering's death for two hundred and fifty pounds from the garage where Mannering's cleaner's son-in-law, Brian Cowley, worked, signed by him.

Three days later Potts' investigations culminated in his arrest of Cowley, the mechanic promptly protesting that he had already been interviewed by the National Crime Agency and 'cleared'. Potts then sent a cocky email to Carrick with this information, also setting out his views on the inefficiencies of certain newfangled crime detection agencies. The DCI, Scots not being noted peace-makers, forwarded it to Patrick for his comments.

Patrick, to his credit, replied as he might have done in his service days if criticized by a brother officer. In short, he related his side of the story, the truth, that he had merely told Cowley he might be interviewed again. No one had said anything about 'clearing'. As far as Potts was concerned I could only think that the oil to be boiled was on a very slow back burner.

So far there had been no more 'events' at the rectory. Terry worked from 'home' and went for short walks in the surrounding country lanes if Elspeth was out, or read in our conservatory in between strolling in the garden when she was around. I didn't like to enquire about any ongoing problems he might be having in his relationship with Dawn, thinking that he would tell us if and when he wanted to. And of course this quiet time was aiding his recovery from the shoulder wound.

In receipt of a report from DI Potts with regard to his arrest of Cowley, James Carrick had expressed dissatisfaction and ordered the suspect to be brought to Bath for further questioning, more time to do so having been applied for and permitted. I did not yet know on what evidence Potts had based his decision, partly because I was trying to get involved with my latest novel. Patrick was working long hours, mostly on other cases until local police preliminary investigations into the Mannering case had been completed and when he came home, tired, I reckoned work was the last thing he wanted to talk about. And yes, I had to confess that I still didn't care at all that Mannering was dead. This did not mean though that I was ignoring the possibility that the wrong man had been accused of his murder.

'Potts' team received a tip-off,' Patrick announced when he came home the following day. 'You remember Cowley said he was working on his old Land Rover at the garage? Someone saw it parked close to Mannering's place late the afternoon it would appear he was killed. He's saying that's impossible as the vehicle couldn't be driven then. But there can't be many other red Series 3s in the area, if any.'

'Is that good grounds for arresting him?' I asked. 'And I understood it was thought Mannering was killed around midday.'

'Well, I don't think it's good grounds at all. And I can't imagine that the receipted invoice has any bearing on the case even though Cowley said Mannering had his car serviced at the main dealership. You would if it was still under guarantee, wouldn't you?'

'Have they searched Cowley's house?'

'Yes, and found nothing incriminating. His shotgun was in a locked cabinet, as the law states they have to be, but as we know, Mannering wasn't killed with a shotgun.'

'Have you spoken to Cowley again?'

'No, Lynn's been doing the questioning and her gut feelings tell her that the man does have something to hide but it might not necessarily involve murder.'

I'm a firm believer in gut feelings but evidence is the watchword: evidence.

'Suppose I talk to him,' I suggested. 'That's if I'm allowed to.'

'You work part-time for the NCA in conjunction with me so I can't see why not, but it'll have to be before ten tomorrow morning as he'll have to be released then. Phone Carrick now – he was still at work when I left.' Patrick yawned. 'In between other jobs I've been trawling through police files and learned absolutely nothing about Mannering that I didn't know already.'

'Have you thought about this murder from the angle of the death of the young officer whose car brakes were tampered with? The one of which the one-time Sir Julian was suspected of being responsible and, as we know, years later admitted his guilt.'

'That was an awfully long time ago, Ingrid.'

'That's a no then.'

'OK – no.'

'So why not revert to his real name of Hardy instead of changing it to Mannering?'

'He must have had other things he wanted to hide too. Is it OK if I go and have a shower?'

I kissed his cheek. 'Sorry.'

Brian Cowley had refused the services of a solicitor right from the start and had the expression of a man who knew he could legally walk out of the door in an hour's time – that is, smug. I had an idea he was not sufficiently intelligent to realize that this might not be wise on his part and decided to play along with him, seating myself wearing a sunny smile and with the manner of one who was merely going through the necessary formalities. A uniformed constable, whose name I knew was Keith, stood by the door.

'You were at the workshop,' Cowley said to me. 'With that tall bloke.'

'Yes, he's working on other angles of the case,' I told him. 'Witnesses and things like that.'

'The poncey character who arrested me said someone saw the Betsy parked near Mannering's house during the afternoon. Never. I hadn't done the gasket job then.'

'Is that what you call your Land Rover?'

'Yeah. Dad had all the Saint books and I read them as a kid. Great stuff. He had a sidekick called Hoppy someone or the other who called his shooter The Betsy. Old-fashioned stuff now, I know, but at the time I thought it was really cool.'

'There can't be too many red ones in your area though.'

'No, she's the only one – she'd been hand-painted that colour when I bought her.'

'So how d'you reckon someone saw it? They made a mistake?'

'No. They're lying. And I think I know who it was.'

'Who then?'

'A bloke called Nathan Briggs. He keeps telling everyone that I buggered up his car. I didn't. It was a wreck and I refused to fix a problem and service it as I knew it would be a test failure and he might take a chance and drive it anyway. Or someone in his family would and get killed. The chassis was rusted to hell.'

I made a note of the name and pretended to make a few more notes, actually writing down a few things I needed in Sainsbury's on the way home. Then I said, 'Were you the last to leave the workshop that afternoon?'

'Yes, I'm the senior bloke when the boss isn't there and I set the alarms and lock up. He's still in Austria, skiing. We finished quite early that day although Mondays are usually busy.'

'A receipted invoice from the garage with your signature on it was found at Mannering's house and yet you said you didn't service his car.'

'I didn't, no one there did.'

'So what was the bill for then?'

'God knows . . . Wait, I remember now. He came in – this was a while back – said he was going away for a week or so, would be doing a lot of driving and would we check the oil, tyres, brake fluid and things like that.'

'And you charged him two hundred and fifty pounds!'

'Let me think . . . yeah, that's right, he said he'd only just managed to start it that morning. It needed a new battery.' Seeing that I was still surprised by the amount, he added, 'Lady, it's a diesel car and the battery itself was over two hundred. Not only that, he spoke to the lads as though they were dirt so I was damned if we were going to do the checks for free.'

'This gasket job on your Land Rover . . .' I continued after a few moments had elapsed while I noted that down too.

'Yes, it was leaking slowly at the front two cylinders. And you get a nasty emulsion of oil and water in the sump.'

'Did you have any idea of the problem when you took it into the workshop?'

'I thought she'd got really sluggish since the previous day but with Series 3s they go on with you until they drop dead. Land Rovers aren't cars, they're a legend,' he added proudly.

Having had personal experience of this I fully agreed with him. However . . .

'So it was just about drivable then,' I persevered.

'Yes, limping like.'

I put both elbows on the table, rested my head on my fists and regarded him steadily.

'That is . . .' the man began and then broke off, gaze somewhere on the wall behind me.

I said, 'Briggs grassed on you because he hates your guts but your Land Rover *was* parked near Mannering's house?'

He shrugged.

'Why was it parked there?'

The man shook his head and said nothing.

'You wouldn't necessarily have had to drive there as it's less than a ten-minute walk from where you work.'

'I didn't go there at all. I've been saying that until I'm blue in the face.'

'You said that one of the other mechanics gave you a lift. How did you *really* get home that evening?'

Cowley opened his mouth and then shut it again.

'Look, you've been arrested on suspicion of murder!' I shouted at him. 'Tell the truth!'

After a long pause he said, 'OK, I drove home. Nursed it like. The bus service is next to useless.'

'And you called in on Mannering on the way.'

'Why the bloody hell would I do that?' he protested. 'The old fart was nothing to me. No, I called in on a customer – with her invoice.'

'And that's near where Mannering lived?'

'Yes, just along the road.'

'So why not say so in the first place?'

He blurted out, 'Because you damned cops always add two and two together and make fifty. That's why.'

'We do appear to have done that,' I pointed out soberly.

More silence.

'Your wife was away, you said,' I added with what I hoped was one of Patrick's crafty smiles.

'Are you suggesting . . .?' he said angrily.

'Yes, I am.'

'Doesn't it infringe my human rights or something for a cop to make that kind of indecent accusation?'

Hardly able to believe my ears, I said, 'I'm inviting you to tell the truth and admit that you called in to see a woman with whom you're having an affair and the pair of you bonked away the rest of the afternoon knowing full well that you didn't have to hurry home to your wife. This Briggs character probably knows all about it and thought he'd really drop you in the brown stuff.'

I have quite wide vision and saw that Keith over by the door had a big dirty smile on his face.

'Well?' I said to Cowley.

He sighed deeply. 'OK. Yes.'

'And afterwards you went to the pub.'

'When I'd got cleaned up. Yes.'

'I want the name of this woman and her address,' I told him, thinking that whoever it was didn't appear to be particularly fussy.

'Does it have to be like this? The wife'll find out.'

'Yes, I'm afraid it does.'

He told me, and I noted down the details.

'Did you happen to notice anyone hanging around Mannering's house when you left?'

'No, it was dark by then and there are no street lights in that road.'

'Will you now make a correct statement to Acting DI Outhwaite?' When he hesitated, I said, 'Unless we discover further incriminating evidence against you it'll probably get you off the hook.'

He nodded. 'OK.'

On the way out I whispered to Keith, 'Be careful with your grins in future.' All of a sudden for some reason I was intensely irritated by male smirks.

Carrick phoned later to thank me and added, 'Lynn suggested I ask you to question him but you beat me to it. We'll check on the info he gave you.'

Patrick spent part of the day checking back through the records of the regiment involved when the young officer's sports car had gone off the road, killing him. He discovered that there had been a thorough police investigation which had culminated in the arrest of a local man who was employed at the barracks as a cleaner. He had admitted to having had a grudge against the dead soldier because one day he had shouted at him that he wasn't doing a good enough job. He confessed to having scratched the car with his own car keys about a week before the car had gone off the road – the police had assumed the damage had occurred when the vehicle plunged into a small ravine – but denied having touched the brake pipes. There had been no evidence whatsoever against him and the police had been inclined to believe him as he was planning to visit his married daughter in Australia, this with a view to living out there when he retired. In the circumstances there had seemed little point in prosecuting the man for criminal damage.

Although I thought this conclusion a trifle fragile I made no comment when Patrick shared this with me after he'd done a little more work on his iPad. I was cooking and not the kind of woman, I hoped, to remind her husband that he had taken her advice. It was merely a line of enquiry that had been explored.

'There's no evidence against anyone,' Patrick concluded.

'I can't imagine a worse place to look for it than in a barracks,' I said. 'All brothers together and so forth. Although Daws had his suspicions.'

'He did mention the episode to me once and I got the impression evidence was of the circumstantial variety. Money was missing from the mess funds and Julian Hardy – as Mannering was then – was the treasurer. A junior officer aired certain views. He then died in suspicious circumstances. Hardy went on to have an illustrious career and was knighted. Mostly, though, I think Daws hated everything about him.'

'And if he didn't have any evidence and the police didn't find any, it was unlikely anyone else could have done either.'

'No, and the dead man just had his widowed mother, no other family to demand more investigations be carried out.'

I voiced what had been on my mind for days. 'Patrick, I don't want to find out who killed that disgusting man.'

'Nor do I really, but I'm very interested in trying to discover which mobsters he'd been in contact with, if any. Those weapons in the cellar are a link to criminals and were being stored, or in the process of being sold to someone. That's what I shall concentrate on now.'

'A criminal he was doing business with might have arranged his death.'

'Yes, but why? They didn't take the weapons with them, did they? If they even knew they were there. It's all supposition. The NCA knows the identities of several illegal armourers who usually, for obvious reasons, hang out in cities so the next job might be to track down some of them.' He gazed out of the window. 'Where are the kids?'

'Mark's asleep and Matthew and Katie are with your mum. She's sorting through John's books, making up her mind what to do with them all. Justin's kicking a football on the village green with Terry and he took Vicky along for some fresh air

before she went to bed. It was actually past her bedtime but
I didn't have the heart to refuse.'

'I hope he doesn't mind being lumbered with them like that.'

'It was his idea. I think he's missing his little daughter. You
do realize that he'll have to go home soon.'

After discussing it with Terry later it was decided that he
would leave after lunch the following Sunday. We understood
that Dawn had been in touch with him and told him she would
stay with her friend for a little longer as a birthday party had
been planned for one of the children in three days' time.

On that Sunday morning Simon and Natasha Graves were
among the congregation at the morning service.

There was nothing anyone could do about it – of course,
you can't stop people attending church. But, watching them
smiling and shaking hands with everyone during the Peace
with all the panache of those who consider themselves 'upper
class' or who have lived in the village for years was simply
too much to be borne and I'm afraid, in the middle of the
service, those Gillards present quietly left.

'Let them gossip – I don't care,' Elspeth said furiously as
we approached the rectory. Then, starting to cry, she hurried
indoors.

'This can't go on,' I said to Patrick. 'Your mother can't take
much more of it.'

'But *why* is it happening?' Patrick asked helplessly. 'What
the hell's their motive?'

'I still think you might be the real target. Have you heard
from the Reverend Broadley?'

'No, I'll phone him.'

Which he did, and discovered that Broadley had done as
he said he would and had had no trouble booking for a two-day
stay at Saint Edwina's, returning the previous evening. He had
met the man referred to as the principal and discussed arranging
a retreat for a dozen or so of his parishioners. The man had
asked why people living in rural Somerset had wanted to come
to London when they had the quietness of beautiful countryside
all around them. This question would have stumped me a bit
but Broadley had replied that people living in large towns and

cities always had an erroneous belief that rural areas were a haven of peace and tranquility. They weren't and it was usually townspeople, he had said, who complained about farm machinery and livestock, church bells and the movements of heavy lorries around places like quarries, of which Somerset had quite a few. No, his flock were interested in tracing historic sites in London, especially missions that had alleviated poverty and suffering during Victorian times and subsequently during both World Wars. Quiet times for them could take place in the evenings.

Someone else had shown Broadley around and in his opinion the accommodation, at least the two rooms of which he had seen the interiors, left quite a lot to be desired. This had nothing to do with the fact that there were no televisions in them, which he already knew was quite usual in such a venue, but a general air of neglect that made him think that the furniture and bedding had all been bought second-hand. His own room was little better although the towels in the en-suite looked new. The staff were unfriendly, avoiding conversation, which made him feel that he was in a monastery with people under a vow of silence. More doors than might have been expected had *Private* notices on them. Also, he had felt it strange that the place was surrounded by high brick walls that had obviously been made even higher at some stage and there was barbed wire on the top.

'Did he mention the food?' I asked.

'Yes, it was sparse. Breakfast was a continental-style buffet and they weren't providing an evening meal but he understood that it was available when groups were staying, although it had to be booked and paid for in advance. Lunch was sandwiches which also cost extra and had to be ordered at breakfast. He ate out on both nights and visited an old friend in fairly nearby Enfield, which I got the impression made up for what would otherwise have been a miserable weekend. The few other people staying there didn't look too cheerful either. He finished by saying that nothing would persuade him to take anyone there even if they were desperate for sackcloth and ashes. Which is damning to say the least.'

'I want to know what's behind those doors with *Private* notices on them.'

'So do I.'

The Graveses had made no attempt to approach us but they had, it emerged, made contact with the chairman of the Parochial Church Council after the service. This position is filled by a woman, Wendy Dando, who always makes it plain she has no time for political correctness and doesn't want to be known as a 'chair' or 'chairperson' as she thinks they sound utterly ridiculous. Simon Graves had told her that they would soon be living in the village and would like to be involved in local activities. Wendy, I gathered afterwards from a concerned friend who was present and had seen us leave, had gushed delightedly, welcoming them – to be fair, this kind of enthusiasm from newcomers is rare – and introduced them to several people who hold positions on the committees of various clubs and societies.

My late dear father used to refer to a certain intuition of mine as my 'cat's whiskers', a trait that has come in handy while working with Patrick, causing him sometimes to refer to me as his 'oracle'. It is not always accurate but has paid off most of the time. Right now, in receipt of the latest news, they were bristling. This development meant trouble.

I did not expect, though, that Wendy would arrive at the rectory that same afternoon not long after Terry had set off for home.

'Is Elspeth all right?' she asked anxiously. 'When I saw you leave I thought something must be amiss with her but I haven't been able to pop round and ask as I had to cook Sunday lunch for all the family and then they simply went on talking and this is the first chance I've had to—' She broke off with a wide enquiring smile.

'Everything's fine,' I told her, and left it at that as I didn't think I owed anyone explanations and didn't like her anyway. Too bossy and interfering.

'Oh. I see. And such *nice* people were in church, Simon and Natasha someone-or-the-other – I've forgotten their surname. Apparently he's a reader, loves Somerset and has done quite a lot of research into our local history. Did you know that there's some kind of old document that says the rectory mustn't be sold into private hands? I know it's too late

now and you can hardly be asked to leave but they do seem
to have a bee in their bonnet about it and I got the impression
they were hoping to live here as he's going to help with the
services.'

'I can assure you that he isn't,' I said when she paused
for breath. 'There was a document, but the conditions lapsed
well over a hundred years ago. Do go and tell your gossipy
friends that and also that they're trying to get Elspeth out of
her home here.'

'Oh.'

'Sorry, I'm busy,' I said, and shut the door in her face,
seething.

Divide and rule, eh?

'I suppose I could go and have a little break somewhere not
too far away,' Elspeth said later, having come into the kitchen
with a lemon meringue pie she had made as, tonight, we were
all eating together.

'Is that what you want to do?' I enquired. Where on earth
would she go in January?

'I don't know but this business is really getting me down.
Patrick'll probably say I'm running away, giving in.'

'Hardly,' I said.

'And I'd still have to come back, wouldn't I?'

I turned off the tap and turned to face her from where I had
been preparing vegetables. 'Elspeth, these people are *not* going
to be allowed to make your life a misery.'

'No, and I do appreciate that you're both doing all you can
but I have been thinking about perhaps moving away since
John died – before these wretched people turned up. I could
go and have a look round places, couldn't I? I've always
wanted to go back and live by the sea. I was brought up in
Cornwall, as you know, in Falmouth. But while John felt
obliged to carry on here there was no question of it. The
really sad thing about it all is that he never retired. I never
dreamed it would come to this – that we'd have no more
holidays together.'

She left the kitchen abruptly, perhaps because she didn't
want me to see her shed more tears.

Dispassionately, I made myself think about it. The children would miss her terribly. Was it really fair of her to go just after they had lost their grandfather? But on the other hand, I reasoned, they had all their lives in front of them; she did not and more than deserved her remaining years by the sea if that's what she really wanted. One problem was that although I was not aware of the exact amount, I knew they had put funds into the new roof needed for the house and to create the annexe where she and John would live. Would we be able to afford to repay that money? Or was she planning to rent somewhere – and in a popular holiday town where housing costs would be sky-high?

When Patrick came home, he said, 'Mannering had what would have been terminal liver cancer that would have finished him off inside twelve months. I saw the PM report just before I left work.'

'I wonder if he knew,' I said.

'Just-call-me-Steve is going to get someone to ask his doctor. I have to confess that this news gives me even less of an incentive to find out who killed him.'

Quite late that evening, when we had a chance to have a private conversation, I told him what Elspeth had said.

'It's understandable, I suppose,' Patrick muttered. 'But I really hope we can get rid of the Graveses before she makes any decisions about it so there's no pressure on her at all.'

'Patrick, I'm *sure* now that this is a deliberate ploy on someone's part to either seriously distract you from something you're working on now, or is in revenge for a past case. Thinking about Mannering for a moment, he used to be Sir Julian – wealthy, respected and in the public eye. Because of his criminal activities and your efforts together with that of others he was sent to prison. We've already coped with revenge from Haldane, whom he hired to wreck Daws' department in MI5. More of the same then?'

'Yet Mannering's been murdered. Who killed him? And why?'

'I think we have to work to see if there's a connection between his death and the Graveses turning up here.'

'I agree it would be neat if there was, and something one

would hope for to simplify everything. But I'm not sure about it.'

'We'd never get Mike Greenway to agree to carrying out surveillance on Saint Edwina's, would we?'

'No, there's no evidence to justify it, not one scrap.'

'There's nothing to stop us from having a weekend in London.'

Patrick knew exactly what I meant. 'That's risky. And if Graves is there he'll recognize us.'

'What is it risking? If there's anything to hide there it might make the pair of them stay away from here for good.'

'I'll think about it,' Patrick said and picked up the book he had been reading.

He was distracted already; someone was winning. But because of Simon Graves my responsibility right now was to Elspeth.

FIVE

P atrick did think about it but said nothing to me until another couple of days had gone by. During that time DI Potts had interviewed the woman Brian Cowley had said he had spent time with and she had corroborated his story. But Potts was not satisfied, the grapevine buzzing with news of his resentment at what he regarded as his failure to make a case against Cowley. His anger might have been partly due to the Land Rover enthusiast having called him something that James Carrick – the source of this information – told me was not suitable for a lady's ears. When I approached my husband about this he also refused to say what it was – this from someone whose repertoire of blistering obscenities is one of the weapons in his armoury, sometimes having to be shouted at what my father would have referred to as 'gallows fodder' in difficult situations when I'm within earshot.

'I never use language like that when I'm at home,' Patrick explained with a little smile. 'Oh, by the way, I think your idea of having a snoop at this so-called mission is a good idea, but we ought not to do it *yet*. It will have to be done very carefully and, as we discussed before, we must bear in mind that it's not official until a connection's been made between Mannering and the place. Otherwise I'd be using police time to look into what is, so far, a private matter.'

'Concentrate on the weapons then.'

'Yes, the weapons.'

I was in a lull of cooking dinner and fetched a glass of white wine from the kitchen – it helps me to think – seated myself and said, 'Tell me how the murder investigation is going first. Has Potts now given up trying to pin the murder on Cowley?'

'Apparently he's not saying much at all. His team discovered what I did – the place where someone, presumably the killer, but we mustn't bank on it, got over the wall at the far end of the garden. Forensics found some fibres from what appears to be a sweater, strands of wool caught on several sharp edges of the stonework. They've actually narrowed it down, believe it or not, to the dyes used for Pringle sweaters.'

'That might point to a middle- or upper-class murderer.'

'Or someone who bought it at a charity shop or jumble sale. Or it was given to them by a grandfather, father, uncle or golf-mad cousin.' This with a big jolly you-hadn't-thought-of-that-had-you grin.

'Point taken,' I said. 'Where's his car – the Jag Cowley said he had?'

'I'd forgotten about that,' Patrick muttered.

'And does anyone yet know if Julian Mannering had a stolen or false identity or was just using that name because he felt like it? And why is there a door between that cellar room at Mannering's house that may or may not connect with the neighbouring property?'

'You've done this before,' Patrick said, glaring at me. 'Sinking me without trace when I get a bit too big for my boots.'

'Perhaps because I'm fed up with being stuck at home and not being able to get involved with the case.'

We both glared for a few more seconds and then Patrick got up to fetch himself a tot of single malt – to help him to think perhaps – sat down again and said, 'You're quite right, I haven't really been applying myself to this. I should have chased up Potts about those points.'

I said, 'The reasons you haven't being the awful shock of losing your father, worrying about Elspeth, and the situation the Graveses have created and also, like me, inwardly being quite glad that the murder victim got what he deserved.'

'It's still horribly unprofessional.'

'Perhaps, but in the circumstances perfectly understandable.'

We silently toasted one another and then Patrick said, 'We'll have to arrange for someone to watch over Elspeth all the time until this business is over.'

'Good idea,' I said, and went away to finish cooking dinner.

A morning's work on Patrick's part the following day resulted in discovering that Mannering was unlikely to have had a stolen identity – at least, there were no records of anyone by that name dying within the past six months or so in the UK other than a baby of six weeks of age and a businessman who had been living in Nigeria suddenly dying when he had returned home to Portsmouth. No passports, credit or debit cards or any other personal papers of the latter had gone missing and there was nothing in recent police records that would indicate such things having been stolen except from a woman by the name of Juliana Mannering who lived in Grimsby. Ms Mannering was contacted and admitted that she had left her handbag with the items in a friend's car after a party but had been too embarrassed to inform the police that they had been found.

Patrick also learned, from DI Potts, that the door in the cellar had been investigated and found to be sealed up. Enquiries with the neighbour had provided the information that it dated back to late Victorian times when both properties had belonged to the same family who had opened shops, one a grocer's, the other a butcher's. The door had been for ease of access.

Which just left the car.

I was not blaming Patrick for any oversight at all, for the routine enquiries into this case simply weren't his responsibility, but I was nevertheless staggered that no one had thought of it before. My hope of some kind of breakthrough, that the killer had stolen it for example, was soon dashed when it was quickly discovered that the vehicle was with the main Jaguar dealership in Bath for its annual service and had been taken in four days before Mannering was murdered. He had declined a courtesy car, saying he would get a taxi home and collect it when the work had been done. Obviously, he hadn't and it was still there. The police had appropriated it for forensic testing and where, the garage manager was asking, was their money?

That same afternoon Henry Dando, the husband of Wendy, the Chairman of the PCC, called on Elspeth. Luckily, I was in the conservatory at the time watering the plants, 'helped' by Vicky with her new acquisition from Grandma, a tiny pink plastic watering can. Quite a lot of the water was going on the floor but this didn't matter as it's tiled. I heard Elspeth's doorbell ring and quickly went outside to walk round the corner of the house to see who it was.

'Ah, Mrs Gillard,' said Dando. 'Chilly afternoon, isn't it?'

I agreed that it was and invited him in.

'Oh, sorry, it was the senior Mrs Gillard I came to see.'

'Does she know you're coming?'

'Er, no.'

'Elspeth's having her rest,' I told him. 'And at the moment Patrick and I are dealing with cold callers.'

I didn't care if he was offended by this.

Dando, a short, balding figure who strutted self-importantly and for some reason annoyed me even more than his wife, followed me through into the living room and seated himself. I positioned myself on the sofa opposite so I could keep an eye on Vicky who, although her watering can appeared to be empty, was giving one of her teddy bears a 'drink'.

'The PCC's been approached by a man by the name of Simon Graves,' Dando began. 'I believe Wendy mentioned him to you. I understand that he represents a mission in London and would like, as he's a reader, to assist with the services here for a while and be able to tell the people of Hinton Littlemoor about the work they're doing. I should imagine he's also keen to raise a few funds for it but one can hardly hold that against him.'

'How does this affect my mother-in-law?' I asked. I had suddenly realized that I would have to be very careful. I could hardly share our suspicions about Graves and his wife, if indeed they were married, or hint that they might be connected with the unpleasant occurrences at the rectory, as then I would risk being accused of slander.

Dando cleared his throat and said, 'Ah, well, Mr Graves is in possession of a copy of a document that states that this property should only be for the use of clergy. Obviously no one is expecting you to move out as the deed is of some considerable age but we have agreed that—'

'Who's "we"?' I interrupted.

'The committee. As Mr Graves and Natasha are desperate to find somewhere to live locally we think it would be a nice gesture on Mrs Gillard's part to allow them to use the annexe for the duration of their stay. No doubt she could live with you for a while?'

I gathered my thoughts and said, 'Mr Dando, first, as there are three adults and five children living in the main house, it's already slightly overcrowded. Second, as I explained to your wife, the deed refers to a building that was on this site but burned down hundreds of years ago. The document is now of no legal consequence whatsoever. Third, it was the church authorities themselves who decided to sell the freehold of this property and when we bought it our solicitor went into the whole business very thoroughly. Fourth, the Graveses have been trespassing here and behaving in an unpleasant manner towards Elspeth in order to get what they want. And, finally, this man is not a reader registered with the Church of England and his mission is dedicated to a saint who doesn't appear to exist.'

'I see,' Dando murmured. 'But don't you think we ought to give him the benefit of the doubt?'

'There's no doubt at all in our minds. Patrick and I are of the opinion that he's not genuine.'

He began to get annoyed. 'But Christian charity has a bearing, surely.'

'Of course. You can invite them to stay at *your* house.'

'That's not possible,' he retorted stiffly.

'Then do arrange accommodation for these people if you feel it's the church's responsibility. I shall ask our solicitor to write to the PCC laying out the legal facts so they're clear in everyone's mind. And while you're waiting for the letter to arrive I suggest that you and the committee mull over the Christian ethics of trying to evict a recently widowed elderly lady from her home. Good afternoon.'

He rose and marched out.

'Oh, and has he offered to make any kind of donation to the church – or to anyone?' I called after him.

'How dare you!' Dando snorted and left, slamming the door.

Had I accused him of anything?

There seemed little point in telling Elspeth of this encounter but I was nevertheless concerned that the ploy now seemed to be an attempt to drive a wedge between us and the village.

My first reaction to this thought was that it wouldn't be a catastrophe if they succeeded, perhaps temporarily, but then I recalled Patrick's words about the contribution his parents had made to the place and realized that indeed it would. And none of the Graveses' current actions were, of course, illegal.

'You said yourself that we must be careful,' I reminded Patrick after I'd told him what had happened and got the impression that he was about to detonate.

'But you know what it's like here,' he fumed. 'For all their supposed confidentiality at PCC meetings word will get round, there will be gossip, troublemakers will make comments to Elspeth's face until she feels compelled to leave.'

'All we have to do is expose the Graveses as criminals.'

'We're meeting the Carricks for a drink at the pub later. They might have some ideas.'

'You should have mentioned this to me before,' James Carrick said.

'It's a private matter,' Patrick replied. 'I can't expect police resources to be used for something like that.'

'As a *friend*,' the DCI emphasized, giving him a look. 'And the arrival of these people does seem to be a strange coincidence seeing that you've had the incidents of trespass and criminal damage you reported.'

Patrick went on to tell him what we knew about the London mission and the saint who never was. I'm not psychic but, the four of us sitting there, the Ring o' Bells uncharacteristically quiet but for hail beating on the windows, a blazing log fire in the huge grate, it was as though a collective shiver went through us.

'So where are these weirdos staying?' Joanna wanted to know.

'Pass,' Patrick said.

'Is your mother on her own right now except for Carrie?'

'No, she's gone to a WI meeting. The parish hall is quite close by but because of the weather a friend offered to pick her up and bring her home. She'll stay with her if we're not back by then.'

Carrick said, 'The Reverend Broadley thought this mission strange and I ken from what you said he knows what he's talking about. I'll get on to the Met and see if they know anything about the place. So does the coincidence of the Graveses turning up and your episodes at home also stretch to the Mannering case? There's already the connection *you* have with the murder victim. Are they endeavouring to distract you or, worse, planning to do something else in an effort to get you off the case?'

'Ingrid thinks so.'

'Ingrid thinks it stinks to high heaven,' I said. 'And because of the weapons that were found at Mannering's house I'm asking myself if the mission is a front for something illegal. That might just be my overactive imagination, though.'

'But how did these characters get to know where you live?'

'Dad's obituary was in the local and county newspapers and also on the Somerset BBC radio and internet news,' Patrick replied. 'He was decorated when he saved someone's life during his service in the Royal Naval Reserve. It did mention a family of two sons, whom they named, one of whom was deceased.'

'But if they are trying to get you off the case what does it achieve? Another person would be given the job.'

The DCI had just uttered those words when the Graveses walked in, shedding a few hailstones.

They were formally dressed, he in a dark suit and tie, she in a red dress and jacket, and had come in through the door from the other bar so Patrick – who never sits with his back to access doorways if he can help it – and I were the only ones in our group who initially saw them. We were sitting shoulder to shoulder on a window bench seat and although he made no move I felt him tense. The pair looked around and, practically simultaneously, their gaze fell upon us.

'Good evening,' said Graves to Patrick as he came over, an oily smile on his face. 'We called in at the rectory to see your mother but she didn't appear to be in. Won't you introduce us to your friends?'

'Certainly,' Patrick said. 'This is Detective Chief Inspector James Carrick of Bath CID. The lady with him is also a police officer. James, this is the couple I was telling you about who think they have the right to live in my house and I have already warned off.'

Carrick, who had turned in his chair in order to observe the arrivals, got to his feet. 'Haven't I seen you somewhere before?' he asked Graves, his Scottish accent very crisp.

'Probably not,' the man answered. 'We're quite new to the district and hoping to—'

'I'm sure I have,' Carrick interrupted. 'I've an extremely good memory for faces and although it was quite a while ago I have an idea it was when I served in the Met's Vice Squad. Yes, I know – I've seen you somewhere in mugshots and case notes.'

'Mugshots!' Natasha Graves cried, causing the heads of the few people present in the bar to turn. 'I'll have you know that my husband was—'

Again Carrick butted in. 'Forcing female illegal immigrants into prostitution and dealing in drugs on the side. Three years, wasn't it, chum?'

Graves grabbed the woman's hand and towed her out, causing her to almost trip over her own feet.

'James, thank you, that was quite, quite perfect,' my husband sighed after a brief shocked silence.

'And thanks to you too for not mentioning my name,' Joanna said to Patrick.

Still surprised by the DCI's uncharacteristic creativity and also their sudden departure, I said, 'With a bit of luck that's the last we'll see of them.'

I then realized that he was smiling gently at us.

'What?' Joanna asked.

Carrick took a mouthful of beer and then said, 'I didn't make it up.'

What I can only describe as a golden glow went through me.

'Oh, brother,' Patrick said. 'I did some checking on the name and those similar but simply didn't have the time for an exhaustive search.'

'He's *odious*,' Joanna whispered.

We returned home very shortly afterwards.

Carrick promised us that he would make time to go through police records and also try to remember more about the case, or cases, involved. It was possible that the man had changed his name but, as the DCI had said himself, it had happened 'quite a while ago'. I think he was as keen as we were to find a connection between these people and the Mannering case, partly because there was a chronic lack of leads. Why the hell else, we were all asking, had the pair of them turned up *now*?

Although this latest development was useful, and gratifying, we could hardly relax. Carrie and I arranged between us that someone would always be present in the main house, this hopefully a temporary measure. As it was the arrangement was hardly required as Patrick dealt with routine work, the Mannering case investigation having exhausted house-to-house enquiries, completed interviewing the murder victim's car hire staff and trawling through forensic evidence, of which there was very little. So, not required to assist him, I stayed at home. Then, late the following day, Patrick rang me to say that the ballistics report had come in, with apologies for the 'slight' delay, giving the information that the man had been killed by a handgun using 9mm bullets and it was likely to have been a Browning pistol of a similar vintage to the ones found in the victim's house.

Was that a link? If so, to what?

This writer's imagination trotted out various scenarios. It was possible that someone, a go-between working for a city mobster perhaps, had called at the house with orders to pay for and collect the weapons that Mannering had procured. Mannering had upped the price or refused to hand them over after receiving the money. His visitor had lost his temper and shot him, failed to locate what he had come for after a quick search and, having been careful and worn gloves, had left no fingerprints or discernable forensic evidence. He, or she, had taken any money handed over to Mannering away with them. If that had any truth in it then why had whoever it was gone to the trouble of climbing over the wall at the end of the garden when all they'd had to do was drive a car up to the front of the property? And the boxes would have been quite heavy. On the other hand, perhaps the person climbing over the wall had merely been taking a shortcut through the garden. Historic villages often have ancient byways going through them that have been built over or incorporated into private property, probably illegally, and, no doubt, resented by hard-headed old pedants who insist on exercising their 'rights'.

Or, the boxes of weapons had absolutely nothing to do with the murder and Mannering had had a serious falling out with a criminal who had finished him off with appropriate stealth. Or, Brian Cowley had drunk far too much beer, obtained an old pistol from somewhere and killed him after hearing accounts of his behaviour from his mother-in-law.

Reluctant to factor in Saint Edwina's and the ghastly Graveses as it was just too, too handy, I nevertheless made myself think about it. As we all thought, their arrival was too much of a coincidence, almost ridiculously so. We now suspected that he had a criminal record although James Carrick was apparently having difficulty in pinning him down in Records and in view of this was going to contact an ex-colleague in London. I was really hoping that he hadn't made a mistake.

The only other thing I could think of was that Simon Graves' behaviour stemmed from a past case that Patrick had worked on that was nothing to do with Mannering's death either. Perhaps, on the other hand, Graves was suffering from delusions as well as being odious.

In the middle of these fairly hopeless deliberations, having actually sat down at John's desk to work on my novel, I inwardly groaned when the doorbell rang. The book had ground to a standstill and writing was becoming a thing of the past.

It was Wendy Dando, again.

'I came to see Elspeth but she appears to be out,' she began.

'She's gone into Bath with a friend,' I told her.

'Do you know what time she'll be back?'

'No, I think they're planning to have lunch out.' When she remained standing there I added, 'If it's about those people who want to live in the annexe I'm afraid she doesn't want to discuss it. You're wasting your time.'

'We think you're all being very unreasonable and selfish about this,' she retorted. 'It would only be for a little while.'

'How do you know that?'

'Mr Graves has assured us it that would be.'

Not wishing to interrogate her on the doorstep, I invited her in. This appeared to embolden the woman for as soon as she had sat herself down on one of the sofas she said, 'They've been *most* generous and offered to make a handsome donation to the restoration of the village war memorial fund. We do think now that—'

I interrupted. 'So is this the whole committee you're referring to or just you and your husband?'

'Why, the whole committee of course!'

'And you've had a vote on this?'

'Er, no.'

'Look, you can't tell me that the whole committee has decided that Elspeth ought to make way for these people if it's not true.'

'Er, no, perhaps not . . . but we've talked about it and most seem to be in favour. And Simon did come to our meeting the other evening to tell us about the mission. It's called Saint Edwina's. There could be reciprocal donations to the mission after the war memorial's been restored. I think that's a wonderful idea.'

Glad that we now had confirmation of the name of the mission involved, I said, 'I wasn't aware that the war memorial needed restoring. John never mentioned it.'

'Yes, it does, but not extensively.'

'Also, I'm fairly sure that you can apply for a grant from the War Memorials Trust.'

'Oh.'

'Has Graves actually made any donations so far?'

'I think that's confidential, don't you?'

Somehow I remained outwardly calm and said, 'I rather thought that PCC meetings were also confidential until the minutes were approved. But you invited a complete stranger to one without so much as checking his credentials. We have checked, and preliminary investigations would suggest that he's suspect. Do you want it to go down on the minutes of the next meeting that you were all taken in by a confidence trickster?'

'I don't believe a word of that!' the woman exclaimed.

'It's your choice,' I said. 'Your husband became very angry

when I suggested that Graves might have already given a sum of money that I'll call a donation. Why was that?'

'Because he thought you were accusing him of taking a bribe, that's why.' She jumped to her feet. 'I'm leaving. I'll tell them how rude and horrible you are.'

'I didn't accuse him of anything. But since you've turned up again and insisted on banging on about it, I think I am. How much did Graves offer you both on the quiet to get my mother-in-law out of the annexe?'

'Really!' She headed for the door.

'You're forgetting something,' I said to her back.

'What?' she spat.

'I work for the National Crime Agency. Please don't get into a situation that ends up with your arrest.'

'I'll tell everyone you threatened me too,' was her yelled remark as she went from sight.

Heaven help me, she immediately came back, still shouting. 'It was really lovely with just the rector and his wife living here. And then you lot turned up with your out-of-control kids – attacked a boy at school recently, your Justin, didn't he? We have to put up with guns being fired in the night, shootings at the pub – that was you, shot a poor man for some reason that no one was told about. And your husband behaves as though he's lord someone or the other, driving round in his big car with his nose in the air. It would be a good thing if you did leave.'

Patrick had spent a large part of the previous weekend tidying the graveyard and cleaning the brass in the church, the latter a job that his father had always undertaken. On the Sunday morning, as usual, he had sung in the choir. Ray Collins, the man I had shot and wounded a few months ago, after due warnings had been given, had been on the Met's Most Wanted list and had come to Hinton Littlemoor to kill Patrick, hired by a London mobster. There was no point in telling the woman this, the latter event having been carefully explained at the time, by John from the pulpit before the following day's service. Of course she knew all this, she was lying and I had a good idea that she and her husband had sold out to Graves. But had I any proof? Of course not.

I sat there saying not a word more and, after glowering at me for a few more moments, she left.

Carrie came in, carrying Mark. 'Are you all right, Ingrid?' she asked anxiously. 'I heard shouting.'

I assured her that I was and added, 'You might keep your ears open when you go to the post office and village shop. I think Patrick and I could do with some good gossip right now – the identities of the people who broke the window and were in the garden wearing night vision goggles for a start.'

'I heard what she said. How did she get to hear about what was little more than a playground tiff? They don't have any kids at the school, do they?'

'Good point,' I replied. 'But village gossip does spread at amazing speed.'

'What do you know about the Dandos?' I asked Elspeth later, finding her in the garden.

'Are they making trouble?'

I had to smile. 'As usual, you get right to the point,' I observed. 'It would appear that they might be.'

'I've never liked either of them much as they seem to enjoy stirring things up. They came here about two years ago and do work hard for the village. I shouldn't say it but they're the kind of people who move somewhere and jump in with both feet with the attitude that they can do far better in organizing local affairs than anyone else. They regard themselves as modern, experts with computers and so forth. Locals – people I actually heard Henry refer to as yokels – are, according to them, old-fashioned and ignorant. It does cause offence especially as some of the folk here are retired professionals – medics, teachers and people like that.'

'Another question,' I said. 'Does the war memorial need restoration?'

'Not so far as I know. Oh, occasionally we have to arrange for someone to restore some of the letters as they fade on the sunny side, but that's all. Once a year, usually just before Remembrance Sunday, several people turn up to give the granite a good clean. Why do you ask?'

'Well, apparently the Graveses have offered to give a generous donation towards the cost.'

'Have they now?' Elspeth bent down to look at something on the ground. 'It's lovely when you see the first snowdrops coming up, isn't it?'

'I've been thinking of asking if you fancied having a knot garden and a few *jacquemontii* birches.'

She straightened. 'A knot garden . . . yes, lovely, perhaps where the bed this side of the archway is. The roses there are very old. *Jacquemontii* birches are those that have white bark and are grown in groups, aren't they?' Without waiting for me to reply, she went on, 'Why not? They'd look beautiful as a focal point where the rowan seems to have died.'

'Please don't leave us,' I said.

Elspeth shrugged sadly. 'I've always enjoyed watching *Midsomer Murders* but it's horrible being in an episode of your very own.'

Oddly, gossip – or more correctly, information – came my way. At home more than I might be normally I started taking Mark, in his pram, and Vicky for walks in the afternoons, weather permitting, to give Carrie a break. And let's admit it, to really get to know my two youngest children. This usually involved little more than a circuit of the village green on the narrow lanes that bounded it and then a pause while I sat on a seat on the green while Vicky played with a ball or sat at my side talking to a favourite doll. It was too cold to stay out any longer. I have to keep an eye out for dogs as since a terrier snatched and shredded one of her teddy bears she has been terrified of them. I was keen to address this at some stage, perhaps if I knew someone who had a new puppy, but not yet.

I had previously seen the woman who now approached me in the village, but didn't know her name and had an idea she cleaned or helped in some way at the Ring o' Bells. Nervous-looking and not strong in appearance, she was nevertheless clearly determined to speak to me and I braced myself for another tongue-lashing.

'You're the rector's widow's daughter-in-law, Ingrid, aren't you?' she began in a low voice.

I told her that I was and slid along the seat a bit to make room for her.

'I don't really know what to say,' she resumed when she'd sat down. 'Only that there seems to be some kind of nastiness going on round here that's even affected my own family. I feel ashamed and very, very angry.'

'Please explain,' I urged.

She looked me straight in the eye. 'I don't s'pose you know my name, but it's Dorothy Hedges. I was called after my grandma and frankly, I've always wished I wasn't as everyone calls me Dot, as she was, which I hate. Such a small little thing, a dot, and I'm stuck with it. Now I must be a really evil mother as mothers should look after their sons, shouldn't they? But my Nigel has got in with the wrong lot, the village no-goods, the little devils that put fireworks through old ladies' letter boxes. I reckon it was him and another lad on the estate who made a nuisance of themselves and threw mud on the windows of the rectory.'

'What makes you think it was them?' I asked, wondering how news of it had got out.

'I found some funny goggle things in Nigel's bedroom and he got angry with me – not like him at all. I demanded to know what they were, and he told me and said he and Rob Hills had been up in the woods with them, trying to get roosting pigeons with an air rifle. Not public woods you understand but up at the old manor, the place where that man who's supposed to be a millionaire lives but no one knows who he is. I said I'd heard there was security up there and they'd end up getting arrested for trespassing carrying a weapon. But I didn't actually believe him.'

'No?' I queried.

'No. What would a lad do with dead pigeons when all he ever wants to eat is burgers and chips? A butcher wouldn't touch things like that in case they'd been poisoned or something. It's not his idea of fun either as he's like his dad, only interested in football. No, someone put them up to it.'

I said, 'Whoever it was – and it might not have been the same people on the two occasions – didn't just make a nuisance of themselves. They wrote the words "old bitch" in mud on a window of Elspeth's annexe the first time and broke one of the double-glazed units on the second when they banged on them.'

Her hands flew to her mouth. 'Oh, God,' she whispered through her fingers.

'How old are they?' I asked.

'Nigel's seventeen and Rob must be around the same.'

'Quite big for their age?'

'I suppose so. Rob's fat actually.' Expression hardening, she added, 'Piggy eyes, come to think of it – yes, piggy.'

'I will have to tell the police about this.'

'It would do them good to get a talking-to. That's why I've told you. But they'll know it was me. That's what scares me – that and the person who I'm sure is behind it will get back at me.'

'Don't worry, the information will be kept anonymous to protect you.'

'Oh, thank you.' She gazed at Mark and Vicky and sighed. 'You are lucky – such lovely kiddies.'

SIX

'Telling the police' involved a phone call to James Carrick, who had asked to be kept in the picture. He knew, of course, that because of police protocols we could do little ourselves as we were personally involved. Initially telling me that he would arrange for a community support officer to speak to the boys, he then changed his mind when, having checked, he discovered that Rob had been in trouble previously for vandalism and shoplifting. He had received an official warning. Nigel Hedges, on the other hand, was not known to the police at all. Feeling that he couldn't rightfully pull his overstretched staff off cases which, right now, were far more serious, and Hinton Littlemoor being close to home, Carrick decided to talk to Rob Hills personally. I found out about this when he called me the following morning.

'I still can't track down Graves in Records,' he began by saying. 'But there's such a familiarity between him and someone I've come across before that I'm convinced I've interviewed him personally.'

'Surely then he would have recognized *you*. Perhaps that's why they bolted.'

'He might not have done. I had a bit of a beard then.'

'Really?'

'Aye, I was with the Vice Squad, remember, and in those days when we worked partly undercover the thinking was that if you didn't shave very often it was an easy way of looking scruffy.'

I could relate to this. If Patrick sports 'designer stubble' and a suitable scowl he looks downright unsavoury.

'I called in to talk to that Hills lad,' Carrick continued. 'It turns out that he's the elder brother of the boy who Justin punched and whose father got drunk and turned up at the rectory to make a nuisance of himself.'

'It must run the family,' I observed, hearing the sour tone in my voice.

'His mother said he wasn't at home but as I was leaving I heard a noise in the garage – or rather in a dilapidated big shed – and when I looked in I saw this youth trying to hide behind an old car. He'd dropped a large spanner. He bent to pick it up, at which point I told him to leave it right where he was. He did pick it up, so I showed him my warrant card and he put it down again. We had a little chat, in the garage. I got out of him that the night vision goggles belong to him and his father had given them to him as a present. Rob didn't know where he'd got them from, hadn't asked. Nigel Hedges was "looking after" them for him, he went on to say. When I asked him if they'd done any night-time activities with them he clammed up.'

I said, 'I have a feeling that his father might have given them money to engage in a bit of vandalism.'

'This Rob's a tall lump of a youth too; he'd have shoved you over, easily.'

'There's no evidence, though.'

'No, but I intend to ask someone to talk to his father. It's a pity I can't get Patrick to do it.'

'I'm interested in why he was trying to hide.'

'Perhaps he was supposed to be somewhere else.'

I thanked him for his trouble, adding that there didn't seem to be any progress being made on the Mannering case. For obvious reasons I didn't mention it to Carrick, but thought we might have to use one of Patrick's ploys and make something happen. This proved unnecessary, in the short term anyway, when, that same day, Matthew, Katie and Justin were harassed, shouted and sworn at by a group of four youths they didn't recognize as they crossed the village green having just got off the two school buses which, unusually, had arrived together. They then went for Justin, punching and shoving him with a couple of spits for luck but probably hadn't reckoned on Matthew, who although shooting up in height is slender and outwardly quiet and retiring. He waded in, Katie provided back-up, and before anyone else who might have been nearby could immediately stop it a full-blooded fight was in progress.

Fortunately, I was strolling down the drive, as I do some-times to meet them when I know they're due to come home, and heard children shouting, including voices I recognized, not happy ones. I ran, arriving at the battle scene shortly after a stout village matron famed for her foghorn voice. Obviously realizing exactly what was happening she hauled on the attackers' collars, clipped a couple of their heads and otherwise bawled them out. They ran off.

Having thanked the woman profusely and after we had expressed the view that we had no idea who the youths were, I turned my attention to my family, expecting frightened tears from two of them. Justin was muddy from being knocked down and his bottom lip was bleeding, Matthew's blazer had been hauled off him, trampled underfoot and ripped, Katie's ponytail had been yanked undone and she had a large scratch on her cheek, inflicted, we realized later, by being hit by a hand wearing a ring. They were all breathless and fizzing with excitement.

'You got in a really good one there, Katie!' Matthew panted. 'Right in the guts!'

'I didn't know you could twist someone's arm up their back like that!' she told him admiringly.

'Dad's been showing how me to defend myself in case I'm mugged.'

'I got one too!' Justin yelled. 'Kicked him in the willy!'

Gillard genes having played a part as well obviously.

This was serious, though – perhaps part of a plan not only to drive a further wedge between us and the village but depict us as rough undesirables. If anything, Patrick took it even more seriously than I and after dinner there was a debriefing. The children had quietened down by now, a few red marks and bruises appearing, and I knew as well as Patrick, who had also quietened down from his initial outrage, that the episode had to be 'talked out' and the promise of measures put into place to protect them or they would quite likely have a sleep-less night.

'First of all,' Patrick began quietly, 'I want to congratulate you all for sticking up for yourselves in a difficult situation and not resorting to the bad language that they did.'

This was fact, Patrick having spoken to their rescuer whom he smilingly referred to as 'Wodan's daughter', apparently his late father's nickname for this Nordic lady, Mrs Greta Svensen. She had been in the front garden of her cottage on the green putting food on the bird table and had seen and heard everything. At least we had an independent witness.

'But,' Patrick went on, 'we must find out who they were because it might, *might*, be part of the pattern of things that's been happening here. Do you have any ideas? Were they from your school, Matthew?'

He shook his head. 'No. At least, I don't think so. Some older boys did join last term but they weren't on the bus.'

'Were any of the ones who attacked you in school uniform?'

'No. Just jeans and football shirts.'

'Any particular team?'

'No, all sorts.'

'The one I hit had sort of crossed eyes,' Katie said reflectively.

'Was that before or after you hit him?' her brother enquired and all three fell about laughing. Patrick and I couldn't help but exchange broad smiles, and then he asked each of them to give an account of exactly what had happened to them personally and what they had done. I noted down the fairly good descriptions they then gave us of the four, and Patrick went on to tell the children that while it was considered necessary I would meet them off the buses – this would mean two trips for me on most days but it was only a few hundred yards – and finally impressed on them the importance of not talking about it – nay, bragging about it – at school. I felt we could trust the older two with this but Justin? Perhaps not.

Afterwards, when the young ones had gone their various ways, their father having told them that he would investigate what had happened as a matter of priority, I said, 'You know, this is working out as a brilliant way of keeping me at home, as though it might be deliberate.'

Patrick looked up from doing the crossword in the morning's paper. 'Someone who knows we work together? Now, that *is* an interesting idea. I will mention this affair to Carrick, by the way.'

'Someone local,' I said, mostly to myself, a theory having

just neatly knitted itself together in my mind. 'Someone who's behind what's been going on here. Someone who's directing the Graveses, someone connected to both Mannering's murder and Saint Edwina's mission.'

'Ingrid, that's really ambitious.'

'I was only thinking aloud,' I hastened to say.

'But if you're right . . .' He stopped speaking for a moment, looking grim. His greatest fear has always been that his family will get dragged into something following a case he has worked on. Which, if I was right, had already occurred. Then he said, 'Shall I fetch you a glass of wine to really fuel the oracle?'

'No, it's all right, thank you. I have another thought for you. Do you know this man Mrs Hedges mentioned to me who lives at the old manor? In her words, "who's supposed to be a millionaire but no one knows who he is".'

'I know nothing about him either.'

'Mrs Hedges said she'd heard there was "security" there, whatever that means.'

'Which is probably sensible. Ask Elspeth if she knows anything about him.'

This was a good idea as she is a fount of local knowledge. But she had heard no reliable information about the man, only the inevitable gossip. According to various sources he was reckoned to be a lottery winner or someone with a 'past', or a fugitive from justice, a disgraced politician, or, heaven help us, Lord Lucan. That he might just be an ordinary, albeit wealthy, bloke who wanted a little peace and quiet seemed to have eluded everybody.

The next day Elspeth wasn't very well. I called the doctor – the surgery is always concerned about those who have recently been bereaved – and as she was elderly a young locum visited, said that she was suffering from exhaustion and stress and prescribed rest. Although given a prescription for something to help her to sleep, the patient was adamant that she didn't want to take pills.

According to Somerset county records, on the internet, the house referred to locally as the old manor and now apparently called The Spinney had been extensively altered over the years.

It wasn't a listed property and it was now difficult to tell from
the exterior, the account continued a trifle tetchily, the period
of history in which it originated. Having discovered that I
delved a little deeper and, among other maps on another
website came across a sixteenth-century reproduction of one
on which the place was merely marked as a 'ruin'. A ruined
what? But it didn't actually matter – we were far more interested in who lived there now. Finding out more still couldn't
be official police business though – Patrick said he would
think of a reason for visiting the place and suggested going
the next morning, a Saturday.

We didn't have far to go as the house was situated down
an unmade lane off the road that led to the village of Stanton
Cary, a couple of miles from Hinton Littlemoor. Elspeth had
heard that the drive was long and rough. ''E don't want anyone
to go up there, do 'e?' as one local worthy had put it to her.
This appeared to be quite correct as having passed one large
No Trespassing sign and another smaller one with *Private*
written on it, we bounced over ruts in the Range Rover,
splashing through the deep puddles between them, causing
Patrick to remark with a wry smile that a little off-roading
wouldn't do the vehicle any harm at all. On either side was
neglected woodland, dead trees leaning at angles against the
living, the whole area choked with ivy and brambles which
were colonizing a rusting burnt-out car and rather a lot of
fly-tipped rubbish. A little farther on we emerged into comparatively open ground bounded by broken-down post and rail
fencing – pasture at one time perhaps but now carpeted with
dead weeds and sedges. Still the track continued.

We reached a place where it forked, the right hand one
seemingly heading towards where the chimneys and part of
the roof of a house could be glimpsed above a clump of pines.
The left fork was overgrown, little more than a footpath, disap-
pearing into woodland gloom.

Patrick stopped the vehicle and then turned it, reversing a
short distance into the narrow track's opening before parking
facing the way we had come.

'I fancy going the rest of the way on foot,' he told me. 'D'you
want to stay here?'

I took this to mean that if I went with him I would have to refrain from the giggles, a bad trait of mine when undertaking surveillance. It can strike without warning. Nevertheless, I got out of the vehicle, gave the man in my life a bright smile in lieu of a reply and, having changed into walking boots, we set off into the bitingly cold morning.

We had scarcely gone fifty yards when Patrick whispered, 'Someone else is here,' and a man, stocky, unkempt, grizzled beard, stepped from behind the trunk of a large tree. He was carrying a shotgun.

'Can't you read? It's private!' he said in a gravelly voice. 'Clear out.'

'Are you the owner of this property?' Patrick asked.

'None of your business. Clear out!'

'Do you have a licence for that weapon?'

It was levelled in our direction.

'Obviously not,' Patrick drawled. 'Do I need to add that threatening behaviour is also a criminal offence?'

'What the hell d'you want anyway?' asked the man after a few moments during which he obviously thought about it. He lowered the weapon.

'To speak to whoever lives here. I live in the village and I'm trying to find out who roughed up my children.'

'That's nothing to do with anyone *here*!' The tone had been incredulous.

'Possibly not. But it appears that the yobs responsible might have either personally trespassed in these grounds carrying an air rifle or have friends who have.'

'Nah,' was the reply with a shake of his head. 'Nah. Nothin' like that. Folk read the signs.'

'Where is the owner of this place?'

'Away.'

'Away?'

'Yes. Sod off. Both of yer.'

We left but I had an idea we would be returning, tonight probably. It would remain nothing to do with the police.

Night. Still very cold. Windless. A few flakes of snow falling. An occasional glimpse of the moon in gaps between the clouds.

Just after midnight. No traffic. Right now, I was taking in my surroundings like that, in short bursts, as despite the fact that we had driven part of the way and then walked the rest, quickly, I was frozen to the marrow. The sound of the car would have announced our presence. Now that we had entered the long, rutted lane – I refused to call it a drive – lights had to be rationed so Patrick just had his tiny torch – mine was in my pocket – and I was holding on to his arm. For added security we weren't talking either and, although I had volunteered to come, under absolutely no husbandly pressure, I was regretting it already.

Fifty or so yards farther on, the snow coming down more quickly now, I had a megaton nasty thought.

Patrick felt me tense and slow down and stopped walking. 'What?' he hissed in my ear.

'No photos, no passport, no formal ID,' I whispered, my teeth chattering as I spoke. 'Is the body really Mannering's? He doesn't look like the man with Haldane that I remember.'

He gave it thought. He remained uninvolved with the day-to-day investigations into the murder, relying on DI Potts to keep him, and therefore the NCA, updated. And Carrick, of course.

'No DNA testing?' I went on to query. 'No close relative went to the mortuary?'

'Oh, God, that would change everything,' Patrick muttered.

'Yes, it might mean that the corpse was someone else and he's still alive.'

After another short period of reflection Patrick said, 'Ingrid, in view of what you've just said I really, really want you to go home. Use your torch again when you reach the road. I'll phone you if there's a problem.'

'I'd much rather watch your back.'

'I know. But my conscience won't let me take you anywhere that might be really iffy – not now.'

No, I thought . . . not now.

'OK,' I said, and he kissed my forehead and escorted me back to the road where he gave me the car keys.

When he had gone, I stood for a few moments in the silent darkness, not even able to hear his footsteps. But the man can move as silently as a cat and I had to recognize that he was probably safer without my presence. Then I heard a car coming and swiftly hid myself behind a tree trunk. The vehicle went by, the headlights sweeping through the trees as it rounded a slight curve, large feathery snowflakes glistening in the brightness. I was about to move off when another vehicle approached from the opposite direction. This one slowed right down and, thinking that it might be turning into the track, I moved and pressed myself against the trunk of the next tree, a bigger one, convinced that I would be spotted. It swung into the track and drove off accelerating to a speed that suggested the driver didn't care about his vehicle's suspension. It appeared to have a slight clatter already.

I had no worries that anyone would spot Patrick – ex-Special Forces soldiers can make themselves invisible, especially to members of the public. And criminals. I was mulling this over when I realized that I was absent-mindedly, and stupidly, walking back up the track hardly able to see where I was going. The moon, almost full, came out for a few moments and transformed the drab scene of our first visit into sparkling whiteness and making visible the low branch I was just about to hit my head on as I was walking right on the edge of the track. The rear lights of the car gleamed red and then went from sight, and I prayed that I hadn't been seen in the driver's rear mirror. Then, presumably up by the house, a blaze of exterior lights came on. Whoever lived there was security conscious.

While snow floated down around me I stood stock-still for a while in an agony of indecision, but finally turned and went back towards the village road. I absolutely hate it when Patrick goes off alone. Then another vehicle's lights appeared but it went straight by and on towards Stanton Cary. Resolute but not at all happy, I crossed the road so as to be facing any traffic and went in the direction of where we had left the car. Through the trees, I could see that the lights by the house were still on. Seconds later there was a crash like breaking glass followed by several burglar alarms going off, bells and a siren.

It then occurred to me that if my partner was responsible for any of this cacophony he would be unlikely to come back this way but would strike across country. I walked quickly, only having to conceal myself when I heard a vehicle approach, half expecting it to be police who had been in the vicinity and heard the alarms. To be stopped and questioned would be embarrassing. But it was a private car and I climbed out of the ditch I had jumped into, extricating my boots from the icy mud with difficulty while muttering that perhaps, after all, I ought to try to concentrate on writing books as that was just about the only thing I was good for.

Having got home and parked I could see my way easily without using my torch because of the light layer of snow. Patrick had covered the new security lights to the rear by the conservatory with a cloth when we left as there was no point in waking and/or frightening those indoors. That's if the car's arrival hadn't already woken them.

Courtesy of a small fan heater that keeps the winter cold from killing my tender plants, the conservatory was dark and warm with the scent of greenery. Having automatically just walked in, I then realized that the door had been unlocked. Had we forgotten to lock up? Surely not. I groped for the light switch to the left of the double doors and had just found it when a powerful light was shone directly in my face, blinding me.

'I hope we didn't scare you,' said Simon Graves with what can only be described as sickening *faux* concern when I had succeeded in clicking down the switch.

Natasha, smirking, was seated at his side on one of the cane sofas.

I'm not sure what the man expected me to do but, temporarily unable to see clearly as the powerful beam was still aimed directly into my face, I nevertheless lunged forward and kicked it out of his hand. It clattered along the floor.

'Now you've probably woken your mother-in-law,' he chided.

'You broke in!' I exclaimed, hoping that the door into the house was still locked.

'I have one of those little gadgets that locksmiths use to remove the barrels of locks,' he sighed. 'So useful sometimes.'

'What the *hell* are you doing here?' I demanded to know, furiously aware that I was sounding like the third-rate dialogue in the third-rate movies that are shown on American TV at this time of night.

'We want to talk,' said Natasha.

I sat down as far away as possible from them. 'Then talk.'

'Where's your husband?'

'No idea.'

'That's not an answer,' Graves snapped.

'I don't have to answer your questions. Leave, or I shall call the police.'

He tutted. 'And with your house full of little children too . . .'

'I've come to the conclusion that the pair of you are raving mad,' I said furiously. 'And harassing people is a crime. You're behind all the unpleasant things that have been happening here, criminal damage, people lurking in the garden, insults smeared in mud on windows. Aren't you?' I ended by saying furiously.

'No evidence, though,' the man simpered.

My real worry was that Elspeth had indeed woken and would appear at any moment, wondering what was going on. The actions of these people would end up killing her. Right now though I wanted to grab hold of them and rend them limb from limb.

There was then a soft click and the interior doors slowly swung open. No lights were switched on in there and the three of us froze. The twin barrels of a shotgun appeared.

'Now you put that bloody thing down before you hurt someone!' Natasha Graves shrieked.

Matthew came into open view. 'Get out of my dad's house,' he said.

'Kids don't have guns!' the woman went on to yell at me.

'This one does,' said my adopted son. 'Grandad showed me how to use it – sort of.' He followed this with an off-the-wall smile that was straight out of Patrick's repertoire.

Natasha jumped to her feet, wrenched open the outside door and disappeared. There was a crash and a scream as she tripped over something in the dark. As Graves looked in that direction, I signalled to Matthew to give me the shotgun and when the man's attention returned to us the end of the barrels were around a foot from his head.

'Out,' I said quietly.

He went, saying over his shoulder, 'I'm sure you love your family.'

I shut the outside door but couldn't really secure it as part of the lock had been removed. 'Well, at least it's not put away loaded,' I said to Matthew. 'I wasn't aware that you knew where the key's kept.'

I then realized that I was being very grumpy when he had come to the rescue.

'Grandad showed me that too. He told me that when I was fourteen, soon, I could get a licence and he'd take me clay pigeon shooting. He said he'd be my official mentor.'

He was shaking a little, from cold mostly as he was in his pyjamas, so I grabbed a tartan blanket, one of Elspeth's, from a chair and wrapped it round him, giving him a hug at the same time. I then picked up the gun from where I had leaned it, broke it and saw that it was indeed loaded.

'It seemed a bit silly to carry it with no ammo in,' said Matthew simply.

The next morning, we discovered that Elspeth had decided after all to take one of her sleeping tablets and hadn't heard a thing. Patrick had come home about twenty minutes later and slept for the rest of that night on a sofa in the conservatory, his Glock beneath his pillow, and I had an idea that Graves would have signed his own death warrant if he'd returned. I had been in a bit of a quandary regarding Matthew. Should I pack him off to bed with some warm milk as though he was a child? He was no longer a child, but a young man. So I'd asked him if he wanted a hot drink and he'd opted for warm milk. Perhaps I wasn't such a lousy mother after all. Obviously, though, after what had just occurred Patrick would have to take on the clay pigeon shooting 'official mentoring'.

'I'm staggered,' Patrick said over an earlier than usual morning cup of tea when I had returned from giving Elspeth one, actually to check that she was all right.

'About Matthew?' I queried.

'It was an incredibly brave thing to do. Had he heard them arrive, do you know?'

'Not their car but, as you know, his and Justin's bedroom is right above the conservatory. Matthew heard a noise. Graves must have dropped something in the dark and switched on his torch to see what he was doing. Seeing the light, Matthew got out of bed and opened the window a little. Then, shortly afterwards, he heard someone else arrive, me, and opened it wider so he could hear more clearly and eventually heard raised voices and me saying I was going to call the police. I think the thought uppermost in his mind though was that he'd look a real fool if he'd read the situation wrongly.'

'I'm going to get on to Carrick first thing on Monday morning and get his support for putting out a warrant for their arrest. Unfortunately I don't have the authority to do that myself. *And* I'll go into this business of the formal identification of the murder victim. We have to be absolutely sure the corpse is who we think it is – was.'

'You do realize that we have two boys in the family who are giving every indication of growing up to be just like you?'

I don't think he'd slept much and rubbed his hands over a bristly face with a grimace. 'Yes, and now they've lost their grandfather they need me around more to advise and guide them away from the more revolting and violent side of my character. It had occurred to me.'

I asked him what had happened at the house.

'Oh, the car's arrival – I'm sure you saw it – made a whole lot of security lights come on. Several blokes got out of it – no idea who they were – and went indoors. While the lights were still on I sneaked across and lobbed a rock through a downstairs window. That set off God knows how many alarms.'

'You threw a rock through a window!'

'Those blokes looked a real bunch of louts.'

'Did anyone come out?'

'Yes, the louts, at the double. I came back across country.'

'But they could have followed your footsteps.'

'Probably not. They'd have been buried almost instantly by the snow. Haven't you looked outside this morning? There's around six inches of the stuff.'

Well, no, it was still pitch-dark.

Patrick yawned. 'I'd better go and have a shave.'

I stared at the closing door as he left the room. Had this sally been the smallest bit strategic along the *verboten* lines of making things happen, or the action of a man utterly hacked off with sundry people attacking his home and family?

That many alarms, though?

SEVEN

There was no point in letting the rest of the family know what had happened, least of all Elspeth, and we impressed on Matthew that this was important. But I did whisper to him that it was OK to tell his sister as although they have occasional noisy differences the pair are very close and I didn't want there to be any secrets between them. At one time they set themselves up as a local detective agency and turned up so many goings-on and intrigues, actually discovering a money-laundering scheme at the pub that resulted in arrests and the place being closed down for a while, that it was necessary to ask them to rein in their activities. Right now, they were having breakfast with their grandmother – her suggestion – and Vicky had wandered in as well. This had never happened when John was alive as he had preferred to read his newspaper without the clamour of young voices.

'Did Graves give you the remotest idea of what's eating him?' Patrick said, loading marmalade on to a slice of toast.

'No. Perhaps he's a relation of the one-time Sir Julian.'

'He looks nothing like him, though.'

'OK, Haldane then. He looks a bit like *him*.'

Patrick shook his head dismissively. 'It might have been better if Matthew hadn't come in just then. You might have discovered something.'

'Thank you, but I was rather glad he did.'

'Yes, of course, sorry, you're right.'

Having fed Mark most of his boiled egg and eaten the bit he didn't want I rose to make more toast. 'Perhaps this mission place is actually a cult.'

'No, Ingrid, it's an HQ for a bunch of crooks.' He went back to brooding over his toast and coffee.

'Then let's go and find out,' I said.

I was given a humourless smile. 'You know that I'm

completely tied down with strict protocols now I'm a cop. No actual crimes have been committed except here and we have no evidence of criminal connections with this so-called mission *or* with the murder inquiry. Right now those facts are engraved on the inside of my skull.'

Justin had said that he didn't want any breakfast, not surprising as he had eaten far too many grapes he had 'come across' in the kitchen the previous day and they had upset his stomach. I made him some milky coffee and he sat at the table, subdued. Perhaps he wouldn't do it again.

Patrick couldn't wait to phone James Carrick until the following day and instead contacted him mid-morning. In all fairness the DCI had made us promise that we'd keep him informed. Before doing that Patrick checked to find out if anyone had reported the matter of a rock being thrown through a window of a house near Stanton Cary. No one had.

'He's doing all he can to track down Graves in Records,' Patrick said when he came into the kitchen where I was clearing up. 'He's happy about the arrest warrant too – thinks we might get somewhere.'

'And the formal identification of Mannering?'

'He agreed that it's iffy and is going to look into whether there were any DNA samples taken when he was sent to prison.'

I try to give Carrie as much of Sunday off as possible, plus another day, or even two, in the week – Mark is her only real responsibility when everyone's at home on other days – and this morning I took Vicky and the baby into my writing room, the former with her usual retinue of dolls and teddies. An emergency locksmith had promised to come at nine thirty to change all the exterior locks for others that could not so easily be tampered with. Until then my husband was staying very close to home, building a snowman in the garden with the other children. Vicky had gone outside with them at first but Justin, no longer subdued, had initiated a snowball fight, thrown one at her, she had slipped over and that had been that. Patrick doesn't normally shout at him – none of the others ever need shouting at – but he had then.

The thought that the Graveses had been in our house, so close to the family, was actually making me feel sick. My thoughts drifted back to the days when we had worked for MI5. Dangerous days but just the two of us. No added responsibilities. We were older now and nothing was the same. For some reason this depressed me utterly and I was feeling very guilty about it.

MI5 might be able to tell me something . . .

Charles Dixon, the man we had met in Bath, had given me his business card. There was an email address and also a mobile phone number. It was almost certainly his work number but I dialled it anyway. Surprisingly, he answered.

'I was waiting for you to contact me,' he said.

'Why's that?' I had to ask.

'Hardy, Sir Julian, Mannering's dead, isn't he? Murdered. And your husband's involved with finding his killer. Circumstantial evidence points to young Meadows having had every reason to kill him as his wife is still suffering repercussions from her ordeal, and someone trained by MI5 would have the know-how and leave no evidence, so he has to be a suspect. Come to think of it, Patrick would have had even more incentive to remove him from the face of the Earth as no man who has laid hands on you has ever lived to tell the tale.'

'Is that what you were hoping for by telling him where the man was to be found?' I demanded to know, thoroughly unsettled by what he had just said. How did he know all this? I continued: 'And by telling Patrick where he was, Mannering would thereby be silenced for ever from revealing anything incriminating he knew about certain people in positions of power?'

'No, I was not hoping he would do that,' Dixon replied but not, to my mind, very convincingly. 'And, I'd like to remind you, our organization is designed to protect the country from those we regard as enemies.'

'Which you do, but only sometimes,' I retorted. 'Tell me if you know anything about a man calling himself Simon Graves.'

'Ah,' said Dixon and then there was silence on his end of the line.

'Well?' I prompted.

'I think I've heard the name but not sure in which context.'

'He and a woman he refers to as Natasha, possibly his wife, are pestering us, and that's putting it mildly. Our local DCI reckons he has a criminal record and I'm wondering if he's on your radar.'

'How interesting. Give me a short while and I'll get back to you.'

Mark had been progressing around the floor like a demented beetle while I was talking and occasionally deliberately colliding with Vicky's big blue teddy bear, knocking it over, setting the pair of them chortling delightfully as only little children can.

'I'm sure you love your family,' Graves had said.

Had I imagined the cold sneer? A threat?

My mobile rang a couple of minutes later, startling me from a miserable reverie.

'Dixon,' the man said in his whispery voice. 'Your request for information about this man comes under the heading of what some of my colleagues might call the "Can of Worms category" and I have to confess that previous to your enquiry I knew nothing at all about him – there was just a vague memory. I've discovered that, years ago – I understand that he's older than he looks – Graves worked for the Metropolitan Police in what used to be referred to as the Vice Squad. Apparently, in our more enlightened times, that was thought to sound too critical of sex workers as they ought to be regarded as victims so, a few years ago, the department was absorbed into the Specialist Crime Directorate. Graves, one of the names he used when he was working undercover, became aware that he could earn a lot more by getting involved in crime rather than fighting it and, although still in the police, secretly went into business with a couple of career criminals, who shortly afterwards were killed in a private plane crash in South Africa while they were on a safari holiday. After that happened the illegal undertaking was investigated by the police, there were arrests and trials and Graves served several years in prison.'

'How did this have anything to do with MI5?' I asked.

'The upmarket prostitution set-up Graves bought into had

a select clientele, including members of parliament and also the late Sir Julian, as he was then. There's a recently dated note on the file that I've just located and I'm still reading – which for some reason wasn't cross-referenced – saying that, although there was no formal evidence, Graves and the esteemed knight were in another scheme thought to involve a fake religious centre as a front. But it wasn't known whether they were the big fish or not and no doubt it's now down to the police to investigate – if they aren't doing so already.'

I said, 'It might explain why Graves is harassing us – because he doesn't want Patrick to investigate Mannering's death as he was involved with him. It's already been established that he's posing as some kind of reader at a so-called mission in north London, no doubt the same one.'

'That would be logical, and presumably Mannering told him all about your husband some time ago and how he and others had put him behind bars. If I was Patrick, I'd ask to be taken off the case. I believe I did warn him.'

Part of me agreed with him but I said, 'That's giving up, though, isn't it? He wouldn't do that.'

'No, but he has a family to think of. I assure you that if I'd known this Mannering character would end up dead I wouldn't have contacted you in the first place.'

Still cautious, I said, 'There's a warrant out for Graves and the woman's arrest.'

'I'm not sure that's a good idea at this stage. The main players might never be caught.'

'Mr Dixon, these people broke into our house last night!'

After a pause, Dixon said, 'I'm sorry but I really don't think I can help you any more.'

Realizing that he had given me a lot of valuable information, I thanked him and we ended the call.

I wrote down the details of what Dixon had told me and picked up my phone again. It seemed to be time to get a main player of our own involved. But before that I would have to give the news to James Carrick.

'It's probably why you couldn't track him down in Records,' I said when I had related what Dixon had told me. 'Is there a special website or file for bent Met cops?'

'Yes, and there's also a wall in a defunct Tube station on the District Line that has their mugshots and details on it and once a year all the Met – blokes, that is – go down there and pee on them,' he answered.

I rather felt I ought not pursue that subject further.

The new locks were fitted and Patrick contacted Commander Greenway, who asked us to report to him at the NCA HQ the following morning, Monday – late-ish morning, I hoped – to enable the matter to be discussed. This left us with the problem of finding someone to 'hold the fort' at home as Patrick refused to countenance leaving his mother and Carrie without some kind of protection, if only from certain members of the PCC. After a little brainstorming, I suggested that part of the problem could be solved if we drove to London, taking Elspeth with us to stay with my sister, Sally, and her husband, who have a house by the Thames at Sunbury. I rang them and Sally said they had the decorators in so, if we didn't mind, they would prefer to come and have a break at our house for a short time to get away from nearly everything being covered in dust sheets. They would set off after breakfast and try to arrive mid-afternoon. Obviously this was an even better arrangement. That organized, Patrick asked for, and got, the services of a community support officer, a CSO, to walk round the village and cover the few hours after we had left and Sally and Derek arrived. Carrick thought this a good idea anyway as there had been thefts of horse tack from several local private homes and a riding school recently and the presence of the law, even temporarily, never did any harm.

'This can't go on,' Patrick muttered. 'I'm damned if I'm living my life under siege.'

Michael Greenway shook hands with us both, offered his condolences, asked us to be seated and dropped into the leather revolving chair behind his desk which, as usual, creaked alarmingly. He is a big, fair-haired man, slightly taller than Patrick who is six foot two, and strongly built. His deceptively good-natured features are slightly battered as a result of playing contact sports in his youth, and the reason I use the word 'deceptively' is that he definitely doesn't suffer fools gladly. His formality at the beginning of this meeting was probably because we hadn't seen him for a while, during which time he had been involved in cases which had nothing to do with us.

'Well?' the commander said.

'You want the story, the whole story and nothing but the story?' Patrick asked.

'I do, as even though you only gave me the bare details over the phone it sounded a real pig's breakfast.'

Army officers have to be very good at giving briefings and Patrick is no exception. Critical by nature, I could find no points missed in what he now said.

'Ingrid?' Greenway queried when Patrick had finished.

'That's all the facts,' I said. 'But I have a couple of intuition and gut feeling bits to add if you're interested.'

'I'm always interested in what Patrick's oracle has to say,' he replied with a smile.

I hadn't been aware that he knew Patrick sometimes referred to me as that and was a bit annoyed about it but said, 'I've a horrible feeling that the body isn't Mannering's. DCI Carrick's checking if there are any DNA records. There hasn't been a formal identification and no passport was found in the house, only an old paper driving licence, which, as you must know, didn't have photographs on them. His cleaner identified him as the man she worked for who called himself Julian Mannering but no next of kin have been traced who could confirm identity.'

'Does he look like the man you remember as Sir Julian?'

'No, not really. But we're aware that he'd been ill and had a major heart operation. And when the PM was done it was found that he had cancer of the liver.'

'Do we know where the heart operation took place?'

'Possibly somewhere in London,' Patrick answered. 'He had a big house in Maidenhead before he went to prison and that was his last known address. His wife divorced him and someone else owns it now. I checked.'

The commander said, 'It might be worth asking a few questions there, though. And to contact all the hospitals in Berkshire. No, leave that, someone else can do it. This Saint Edwina's set-up . . . after what your friend the Reverend Broadley said it sounds as though it could be iffy. Go there using whichever method you fancy, covert or otherwise. If these Graves characters are on the premises – he's reputed to have a connection with the place after all – arrest him, and the woman.'

'You know as well as I do that I can't arrest anyone who has committed a crime against me personally,' Patrick commented briskly.

'OK, find him first and then get the Met to do the job.'

I was thinking that this wasn't particularly helpful when Greenway turned to me and asked me if I had anything else to add.

'I've changed my mind about mentioning the other thing,' I told him.

I had been about to tell him of our nocturnal visit to The Spinney but reasoned that we ought to work on it a bit more first as the connection to the case was so vague.

'No one's any nearer to finding Mannering's killer then,' Greenway observed.

Patrick said, 'One theory might be that he was involved with this mission and whatever's really going on there and fell out with whoever's running it. The weapons found in his house weren't something he'd picked up in the street. My money's on Saint Edwina's even though we don't have a scrap of evidence about the place.'

'Then, as I've just said, go there. Get some or eliminate it from the investigation.' He then got to his feet saying that he was due at a meeting.

OK, it was Monday morning even though, at his request, we had gone all that way to speak to him.

'Keep reminding me that we're not the only people working on this case,' Patrick said bitterly a little later when we were having a late light lunch. 'Because, right now, that's what it feels like.'

I reasoned that we could go and throw a rock through a window there too but did not voice the idea as I would be accused of being flippant. Instead, and aware that it was a tame suggestion, I said, 'Suppose we stay overnight in a hotel and go and have a look at the place.'

'OK,' he agreed without a trace of enthusiasm.

But he was still distracted, worried sick about what might happen at home and the children's safety, and really concerned about his mother's health, not to mention he himself now being too old for the job. Graves and Co appeared to have him well under control.

The building's initial function as a private house became obvious when we saw it from a distance as it was on rising ground on the upper edge of a fairly large public park, surely at one time the property's private grounds. That noted, only the top floor and roof with ornate chimneys were visible for, as the Reverend Broadley had told us, the place was protected by high brick walls. We walked across the park towards it, our feet crunching through a thin layer of frozen snow, a biting easterly wind stirring the bare branches of the trees. We rarely drive close to a place under investigation in our own vehicle so had left the Range Rover at a safe distance. I was regretting the need for such security measures as my ears had already gone numb.

Patrick said, 'As I told Dixon, everything's different now. I have no intention of pretending to require entry in order to read meters, check that they're not breaking any health and safety regulations or to investigate a reported gas leak. I'm a cop so I intend to behave like one.'

Not wishing to say anything that might undermine his apparent confidence I made no response, just gave his arm a squeeze.

What would at one time almost certainly have been elegant wrought-iron gates had been replaced with a single – and ugly – steel-barred contraption. On the concrete pillars on either side, again hardly original, were security cameras, one pointing to the left along the roadway we had just crossed, the other at us. As we approached the former swung to point at us too. One was expected to press a button and speak into a small metal grille, which Patrick did, curtly saying, 'National Crime Agency. Let us in, please.'

'Broadley didn't mention this,' I whispered in Patrick's ear.

'If they were expecting him the gate might have been open,' he replied with a shrug.

A woman wearing a navy-blue business suit that was a little too tight for her generous proportions emerged from the main entrance and clickety-clacked towards us across a small car park in her high heels, a huge fixed smile on her face. I reasoned that she was wearing rather a lot of make-up merely to be a receptionist in somewhere that was advertising itself as a religious establishment but perhaps that's how they ran this outfit. It brought to mind when I was working as PA to the elderly managing director of a fairly small family firm in London before I got married. He had told me that it was my decision but he preferred me not to wear high heels as they would either wreck my feet or I would break an ankle wearing them and then where the hell would he be?

'She's dispensable,' I hissed to my husband, and he quickly glanced at me as though I was being flippant.

'May I see your warrant card?' said this female with another flash of perfect teeth.

Patrick produced his and held it up for her to see.

'What about the lady here?' This with a nod in my direction.

'Miss Langley is my assistant,' said Patrick.

'Does she have an ID?'

'And an English tongue in her head,' I snapped, showing mine to her.

'Please wait.'

She clickety-clacked back, went inside the doorway from which she had emerged and, moments later, the gate swung open. We went in and it immediately clanged shut behind us.

'More like an old Soviet embassy than a mission,' Patrick murmured as we set off towards the entrance, beating me by a short head to making a similar comment.

The remark must have been overheard even though she was standing just inside the doorway several yards away, for the woman said, 'We try to help the homeless but some of them are drug addicts or alcoholics and they attempt to break in, in order to steal anything they think they can sell. And we have to ensure the safety of those who live and work here. Surely, as a police officer, you must know that.' That said, she gave Patrick another dazzling and insincere smile.

Fifteen-love, I thought, successfully smothering a giggle. This must have been detected because he gave me another I'm-not-amused look, an indication, I felt, of the dreadful effect that the situation was having on him, and I instantly felt ashamed.

A notice on a room to one side of the entrance indicated that we were entering reception. To my mind, and probably to Patrick's, the only thing about this room that was a little odd was a fairly large plain mirror on an inner wall. There was no frame and it wasn't obviously hanging there, it was more like a window. I had an idea it was a two-way mirror, a window so that those on this side of it could be observed from the next room. Just like a police interview room at one of the larger nicks, in fact.

'I'd like to speak to the principal,' Patrick said.

'I'm afraid he's not here. Perhaps if you make an appointment . . .'

'Who's his deputy?'

'I am.'

Patrick sat himself down in one of the chairs obviously reserved for visitors and I followed suit.

'Then tell me who I'm talking to,' he requested.

'I'm Melanie Hunter. Miss.'

I removed a notebook and pen from my bag and wrote it down, aware that she was frowning at me.

'Miss Hunter, this is a serious matter,' Patrick went on. 'A warrant is out for the arrest of a man whom we believe has connections with this place. He's calling himself Simon Graves, which might not be his real name.'

'I know of absolutely no one with that name,' she responded imperturbably.

'He's masquerading as some kind of reader.'

'We don't have readers here.'

'No services?'

'No, it's a non-denominational organization with the emphasis on peace, harmony and goodwill.'

'The man himself is saying that he has connections here. Furthermore, his involvement also comes from another more reliable source. I'll describe Graves to you. He's around five feet nine inches tall, is in his late forties or early fifties and has straight fair hair cut short. There's a woman with him he refers to as his wife Natasha. She's around the same age, about five feet five inches in height and has dark brown hair worn shoulder-length. There's a small scar on the right side of her neck. She has a shrill voice.'

I hadn't noticed the scar and mentally berated myself for wanting to add 'and she's an absolute bitch'.

Miss Hunter shook her head. 'No, sorry. I don't know them.'

'Despite what you said just now you appear to have rather a lot of security here. There are closed-circuit cameras on each side of the gateway and also microphones to enable conversations to be overheard that are taking place in that area. You heard what I said and I was little more than whispering. And if I'm not mistaken, and I very rarely am in such situations, that mirror is two-way so people in here can be watched from the next room. Feel a bit spied-on, do you?'

'Of course not!' she protested.

'So you're not denying it then.'

'We have to be very careful.'

'Even stoned drop-outs don't tend to be *that* dangerous. Try this then: at a guess whoever it is who refers to himself as the principal is right there now, next door, watching and listening.'

And with that he shot to his feet and out of the door.

'You can't—' cried Miss Hunter and then stopped speaking, looking scared, her slightly prominent pale blue eyes bulging even more.

'He has,' I said and, hearing shouts, followed him. But I went straight back and added, 'You too.' Then yelled, 'Out!' when she just sat there.

She scuttled after me.

In the next room, the one doing the shouting, swearing, was a short, thin man wearing clerical garb. I inwardly congratulated the Reverend Broadley on his summing up of the man, if indeed this was the same individual, when he had said the principal reminded him of an old reprobate he used to know who ran a dodgy market stall.

Leaning on a wall, Patrick waited patiently until the tirade ceased. Then he produced his warrant card again and held it under the man's nose. 'Police. That's fairly fancy language for someone who's supposed to be running a mission.'

'You're trespassing!' the man snapped.

'What's your name?'

'Yellen. Felix Yellen.'

'And you're the one referred to as the principal here?'

'I am.'

'Right, Mr Yellen, I'm minded to get a search warrant,' Patrick drawled, 'as I have a notion that this place is as phoney as you are.'

'We're a registered charity!'

'It wouldn't be the first time that's been used as a front for other activities. As I'm sure you were listening you must know that I came here to try to trace a man calling himself Simon Graves. He's involved, isn't he?'

'No, I've never heard of him. If he's saying he is, he's lying.'

'Why lose your temper? Are you a front as well? Frankly, the last thing you look like is a priest.'

'What would you know about that?' the man almost spat at him.

Patrick bellowed, 'My father was a real man of God and he'd have spotted you for a pile of shit any day!'

I carefully cleared my throat.

The door opened and four men rushed in. One seized me in a tight bear hug from behind. Then the whole lot found themselves looking down the wrong end of a Glock 17, the adrenalin engendered from my partner's previous few seconds encounter still obviously raging through his veins.

'*Armed* police,' Patrick said in the manner of a man just yearning to squeeze the trigger.

My gaze wasn't on him but I was sure that some kind of signal passed between the so-called principal and the incomers. I was released.

'Misunderstanding, guv,' one of the men hastened to say. 'Sorry.'

'Yes, my – my apologies,' Yellen stammered. 'We've had some really undesirable people trying to force their way in here as a rumour went round that there were drugs on the premises.' He rounded on the Hunter woman. 'Did you press the alarm button?'

'Yes, sorry, sir. I must have leaned on it by mistake.'

Yellen waved an impatient hand and she went out.

'You too!' he shouted at the others. And to Patrick, who had lowered but not reholstered the Glock: 'I regret my loss of temper – I've not been very well of late.'

'Why do your security people behave in such aggressive fashion?' Patrick demanded to know.

'Because as I've just mentioned, some of the people round here are quite dangerous.'

I asked myself if that was what might be termed a load of horse feathers. *Four* security staff – were there others? – for a few of society's unfortunates?

Yellen continued, 'I don't know the man you're talking about, never heard of him, in fact. Your source of information must be wrong.'

'I'm also trying to gather information about a man latterly known as Julian Mannering who was recently murdered,' Patrick continued. 'At one time he was known as Sir Julian Hardy but following a spell in prison for attempted murder he changed his name.'

'We have no connection whatsoever with these criminals you mention,' Yellen said stiffly.

'I don't believe you and, as I just said, I intend to get a search warrant. I suggest that you cooperate with further investigations.'

We left, quickly, the gate swinging open as we approached, and I breathed a sigh of relief when we were safely outside on the pavement. My intuition – cat's whiskers, whatever anyone wanted to call it – was screaming blue murder right off the scale.

And, to prove that my intuition was sound, we were not safely outside.

We were walking away quickly, trying not to skid on the icy pavement, hoping to spot a taxi, Patrick in the process of finding his phone to request Commander Greenway to organize a search warrant, when a car roared from somewhere to the rear of where we had just left and came towards us. It mounted the pavement and we jumped out of the way just in time. A shot cracked out and ricocheted off a metal utilities box of some kind. People scattered.

'Across the park!' Patrick said urgently, grabbing my arm and towing me across the road to a blare of car horns, one vehicle forced to swerve to avoid hitting us.

We ran and I was glad I wasn't wearing the same kind of footwear as the Hunter woman. But Patrick can't run very far, and then only slowly, his man-made replacement risking him tripping, it simply isn't designed for it, and after about a hundred yards we concealed ourselves inside a clump of large rhododendrons. It stank like a lavatory because it was used as one.

'When they've turned the car round they'll come on foot,' he said, breathing hard, finally finding his phone. 'If they're stupid enough to drive down here they'll either get bogged down or I'll shoot out the tyres. I hope they do that as it'll make it easier for me to get them as well if necessary.'

I knew he was now calling our emergency number. This is linked to GPS so, in this case, in London, the Met would be able to locate where we were. I hoped they would get on with it as those in the car were almost certainly intending to injure or even kill us. One could only hope that some of the members of the public who had witnessed what had happened would dial 999 or even take photos with their mobiles.

Far too soon for my peace of mind, and although the overcast day was beginning to get dark, I spotted four men on foot who were in the process of fanning out and coming in our direction. They moved in the way that quite a lot of semi-feral hired thugs do, smoothly with tense muscular shoulders. I guessed they might be the same individuals we had already encountered and, if so, were a lot younger than us.

'Look at it from the point of view that I didn't have enough evidence to arrest them when we were there but I do now,' Patrick muttered.

'Two of them have gone from my sight,' I reported, peering

through the leaves and not feeling particularly cheered by the remark. 'They've gone wide.'

'D'you have the Smith and Wesson?'

'It's in my bag.'

'Use it to defend yourself if you have to.'

This shouldn't be happening, I told myself, furious. Greenway had no business to send us into this situation without more preliminary police work being carried out. Since being shot Patrick was supposed to be on 'light duties'. Worse, I had rather got the impression that Greenway hadn't been particularly interested in the death of a man he had already referred to as one of Patrick's 'MI5 leftovers', nor the things that had subsequently happened in Hinton Littlemoor, not that we had yet proved a link between them.

Moments later an admittedly intrepid but also downright stupid someone charged into the bushes with a yell that might have been intended to frighten us. He ended up face down in an extremely insalubrious patch of ground at our feet and lay still, having been clubbed down by the edge of the hand not holding the Glock.

'You're under arrest,' Patrick whispered to him.

The second one came from my side – we were standing back-to-back – saw the Smith and Wesson, performed a nervous jink and had turned to flee when Patrick, whom he hadn't noticed, got him, ditto. Then a shot was fired and some foliage just above my head shattered, showering me with leaves and twigs. I ducked down and turned to locate Patrick but he was no longer there. Then, shouts, his voice ordering them to throw down weapons.

There were three shots and someone started screaming.

I dived out of our hiding place on what I reckoned to be the lee side as far as the confrontation was concerned and then, heart hammering, using the bushes as cover and bending low, slowly went round them until I could see what was happening.

'You're lucky,' Patrick was saying to a man on the ground who was clutching his leg, which was bleeding. He went forward to pick up a handgun from the snow. 'I nearly always shoot to kill people who are firing at me but you're such a bloody awful shot I've decided that you're more useful alive.'

Another one was lying face down on the ground where he appeared to have thrown himself. Understandable really. He appeared to be unarmed and unharmed.

EIGHT

I t took too long, in my view anyway, for back-up to arrive. By the time it did I had provided a tourniquet for the injured man's leg, a rather good silk scarf that had been in my bag, and we had moved him to a nearby patch of grass where there was no covering of snow. I stood guard over him. The two in the bushes had recovered consciousness and were standing, groggy, with the other man who had been permitted to get to his feet before he suffered from hypothermia, all four shivering. No one appeared to want to risk trying to escape.

The Met officer, DS Milly Grant, who duly attended with an area car about five minutes after an ambulance, apologized, saying that no one more senior had been available. I think the protocol nuance involved with that remark escaped Patrick too. She told us that two witnesses to the drive-by shooting had called the police and another area car had responded to that, the crew seeing the vehicle involved which had been left at a bus stop. They were still taking statements.

'Are those four the same men you encountered in Saint Edwina's?' Grant asked when we had given her an account of what had taken place and the suspects had been removed. More detailed reports would be given to Commander Greenway as soon as possible and Patrick had promised to copy them to her. There was not much else she could do right now as it was the NCA's case and I was hoping that the NCA would now take Saint Edwina's apart brick by brick.

'No,' Patrick replied.

After noting this down, she said, 'Can I arrange for you to be taken anywhere?'

'Just to where we've left our car would be helpful,' Patrick answered, giving her a winning smile.

'That was sexist,' I whispered to him when we were walking back up to the road, a lift having been organized.

'Sexist?' he queried.

'Smiling at her like that. You wouldn't have done that if it had been a bloke.'

'I might have done – if I'd fancied him too.'

Some people are impossible.

Greenway, who had been in yet another, and lengthy, meeting when we arrived, which meant we had to wait, didn't appear to be about to dish out any plaudits and I'm sure Patrick wasn't expecting any. This recently shot-at part-time author – or perhaps one-time now, I thought bloody-mindedly – would have appreciated a smile or even a hint that he was pleased with the news that we had seemingly made a connection with Saint Edwina's and crime. No, nothing. Something had happened.

'I issued a search warrant as soon as you phoned me,' the commander said. 'The Met's still there but so far they've found nothing incriminating. Apparently someone's going to ring me shortly. Someone else made the point, probably rightly, that just because a car driven by people who committed a criminal act was parked behind the place it doesn't mean the mission itself is a den of iniquity.'

'I'm sure they were from the same outfit,' Patrick insisted. 'They were wearing exactly the same kind of clothes, black jeans and sweatshirts with no logos on them.'

'That would hardly stand up in court, and you know it. I have to admit though that it surprises me that the man you spoke to – Yellen, the one you say swore at you – was the head of something purporting to be run on religious lines.'

'He wasn't the head of it – he was some kind of stand-in,' Patrick told him.

'Oh?'

'I phoned my father's friend the Reverend Paul Broadley a short while ago and described Yellen to him. He wasn't the man he spoke to and not the one pictured on their website. I have to confess that I hadn't had time to look at that and Broadley went on to tell me that it's been taken down now for what's described as "updating". The only similarity, it would appear, is that they both look like crooks.'

'What the hell does a crook look like?' Greenway enquired irritably.

'Well, as Broadley himself said, like an old reprobate he once knew who ran an iffy stall in Berwick Street market.'

'And they denied all knowledge of Graves.'

'Of course they did. They were lying. I know when people are lying. It used to be my job when I was with MI5.'

'But it was your clergyman who said Graves had connections with the place.'

'Courtesy of some C of E grapevine.'

'I'm not happy about this, Patrick,' Greenway said after a pause. 'If it gets about that we're raiding religious establishments . . .'

'Yes. Morons on social media will have a field day,' Patrick responded sarcastically.

In the face of what he might have perceived as threatened mutiny, Greenway took a deep breath and turned to me. 'Your opinion, Ingrid?'

I said, 'My opinion is that you're not engaged with this, not interested, can't imagine what it's like to have someone trying to evict your mother from her home, been bogged down in rubbish meetings all morning and haven't had anything to eat or drink since breakfast.'

He hadn't been looking for this kind of opinion of course and there was a short silence. Then his phone rang and he was rescued from making immediate comment. When the call was over – his reactions to whatever someone was saying to him having merely been grunts – he gazed at us, looking grim.

'The place isn't all that large apparently and all that was found other than the people who work there was the accommodation for paying guests upstairs, the usual catering arrangements, a library, a meeting room, a few private rooms for members of staff and the principal and another room used, temporarily or otherwise, as what appeared to be a chapel. That was full of nuns holding a vigil of some kind. I have an idea that, right now, I'm a laughing stock.'

'There *are* four hoodlums who took shots at us still to be interviewed,' Patrick reminded him, knowing as well as I do that Greenway's skin is too thick to be bothered by anything like that for very long. 'You asked us to find evidence against the place and I reckon we found some.'

'But it's not strong enough evidence, is it?'

'A *roomful* of nuns?' Patrick countered. 'Really?'

'The DI did revise that – eight or nine.'

'What about all those doors marked "private"?'

'Nuns' bedrooms – or "cells", as they called them.'

'They had plenty of time to change the scenery. How much do nuns' outfits cost to hire?'

The commander dismissively shook his head. 'Let's get back to practicalities. The Met can carry out the interviews and we'll see what they turn up. But you're not doing it – and I mean it. You're too close to this particular investigation. I want you to concentrate on the Somerset murder case and get that out of the way.'

'And never the twain shall meet,' Patrick said when we were making our way to the exit of the building. 'You know, I actually wanted to knock his block off because that was what he was being – block-headed.'

My sister rang me a little later saying that she didn't want to worry us but Patrick's mother still wasn't at all well. I knew Elspeth would feel very guilty if he left work on her account so I went back to Somerset alone, by train, having told Patrick that I would let him know immediately if there was real cause for concern. What he might do in the meantime – and I was trying not to think about it but couldn't imagine that it had a lot to do with the Somerset murder – was for him to decide. If Graves was in London, or indeed hiding out in Saint Edwina's – or Saint Ed's as we were calling it now – I was sure he wouldn't stay hidden for long.

It had started to snow again.

Sally had arranged a doctor's visit for Elspeth rather than accompany her to the surgery because all she wanted to do was stay in bed. This was alarming and not like her at all. Another doctor, the one she usually saw, Anne, who lives close by, arrived shortly before I got home and made the same diagnosis as had her colleague: Elspeth was suffering from stress, depression and exhaustion. Had she rested? No, for the very good reason that she had escaped from her home as often as possible because she was so worried the Graveses would turn up again and, despite taking the mild sleeping pills, usually found it impossible to do so and relax.

'A holiday,' said Anne, as forthright as ever, finding Sally and me in the kitchen. 'For God's sake, get this lady away from here for a while. I know on the one hand she doesn't want to go because of her grandchildren, but if she stays here any longer while all this is going on she'll have a nervous break-down, or worse. Mrs Gillard didn't go into details, only saying that some kind of local harassment's involved. Frankly, I find that staggering seeing the work she and her late husband put into the village.'

I felt I ought to offer a short explanation as to what had been occurring, adding that there was a warrant out for the arrest of those responsible. Anne was nodding before I had even finished.

'There has been some gossip,' she said. 'A rather odd couple going round the village smiling at everyone?'

'That's them,' I said.

'If I see them do I phone the cops then?'

'Please do.'

Sally said, 'Elspeth can come home with us. I know we have the decorators in but they must have done some of it by now and it's quite a big house. We can go today if she's up to it.'

'Go and tell her,' Anne said. 'Not ask, tell.'

Sally and I don't look remotely alike – I'm dark-haired and she is very fair. This had caused my father, who was an avid follower of horse racing – although he never gambled – and in possession of a wicked sense of humour, once to remark, in company, that his wife must have 'jumped out of the paddock'. She hadn't spoken to him for a full two weeks afterwards but he hadn't cared; he hadn't loved her any more, a fact that was resoundingly her fault. She is still alive, doesn't want to see any of her family, especially for some reason her two daughters, and one day will be one of those elderly people found very, very dead at home. That is why Elspeth is so special to me.

Later, I was able to report to Patrick that she had departed for Sunbury already looking brighter and promising that she would indeed rest. The older children were due home from school at any minute when she left, their absence a good thing as a mass waving-off from all the family would have been upsetting for her. There was also the prospect of course that Patrick, as he had the car, would be able to find the time and go and see her.

I went to put the Smith and Wesson back in the wall safe in the living room and then changed my mind, locked it in a drawer of John's desk instead and put the key under a box of new A4 paper in another. Derek and Sally had said they had not had any trouble from callers other than Wendy Dando – I had warned them about the pair – who had come round on the pretext of asking after Elspeth and been spotted by Derek before she could ring her doorbell.

Another problem arose. Apologetically, Carrie came to me to say that she had been very worried by recent events and wanted some guarantee for her own and the children's safety. I tried to reassure her as best as I could, telling her that I would stay at home as much as possible while Patrick was in London. She already knew that a warrant was out for the Graveses' arrest as Patrick had told her, but how could she be expected to put up with the hostile stares of local people when she was in the village? Horrified that she too was being dragged into it, I said I would do my best to fix that, if nothing else.

This was beyond serious now and I found myself getting more and more angry. Sufficiently angry after brooding for a short while to throw on a jacket and go round to the Dandos' house and hammer on their front door with my fist as the bell didn't seem to be working. Henry Dando, flustered, answered the door.

'We're just going out,' he snapped when he saw who it was.

'No, you're not,' I said, and shoved him out of the way to gain entry.

'I say—' he began and then had no choice but to follow my progress into the living room where his wife was watching television. I snatched up the remote control from the arm of the sofa by her side and killed the soap. She uttered a weird squeak by way of protest.

'I thought you'd like a progress report,' I said, seating myself in an armchair facing them. Without giving them a chance to say a word, I continued: 'Having almost certainly arranged for several unpleasant things to take place at the rectory, including criminal damage, your friends the Graveses broke into our house recently while Patrick and I were out. Despite us not telling her about this latest outrage, Elspeth is not at all well due to stress and has had to go away to stay with relatives. Now, I've discovered that our nanny Carrie has been experiencing hostile behaviour from locals. These confidence tricksters who have won you over via your bank accounts – no, don't interrupt – have, with your help, turned the village against us. Simon Graves served several years in prison for being involved in what was described to me as an "upmarket prostitution set-up". There's a warrant out for his arrest and also for the woman with him. The probable reason for his interest in the rectory is that he's hoping to dissuade my husband from investigating the murder of a man connected with another criminal organization with which we think he's also involved.' I paused to allow that to sink in for a few moments and then continued, 'If you want to check on what I'm saying you'll have to go and see Detective Chief Inspector James Carrick of Bath CID as I doubt whether he'd be prepared to discuss it over the phone – unless he arrests you first for the very good reason that you're both in this right up to your *necks*.'

Their faces had gone the same colour as most of their decor: a sickly shade of pale beige.

'But . . . but . . . but . . . look . . .' Henry Dando stuttered.

A sound. A floorboard creaking, above my head.

I didn't think, just tore out of the room and up the stairs. It was only when I reached the top that I remembered I no longer had the power of arrest. That fact immediately became irrelevant when I saw Simon Graves coming towards me across the landing at speed. I gained the top of the stairs but caught my toe on the top step and went sprawling. This resulted in Graves, who had had a hand raised to strike me, tripping over me and going headlong downwards. I was aware of cries of consternation from the Dandos, who must have followed me out of the living room, and then was viciously kicked in the chest. It completely winded me. I succeeded though in grabbing Natasha by an ankle as she went by, ridiculously noticing that her tights were laddered, and she flew like a bird, screaming, only touching down when halfway to the bottom. They were out of the front door, the woman hobbling, before I could get enough breath to pick myself up, an agonizing pain in my side.

'They – he – he – threatened us,' Dando babbled when I had finally reached the ground floor. 'Yes, that – that's right, threatened us if we – we – refused to let them stay.'

I sat on the third stair, found my phone, which for some reason I had brought with me, and dialled James Carrick's number while the pair stood there like shop dummies, goggle-eyed. I didn't want cops unknown to me in an area car; I wanted him.

The Dandos had both bolted back into their living room by the time Carrick arrived. I had shut the door on them, locked the back door and pocketed the key but couldn't have prevented their escape through the front door as my ribs hurt too much. And when they saw him they made no move as he has the habit upon entering what he understands to be a crime scene of fixing those he reckons might be guilty of something with a look that has the effect of nailing their feet to the floor. After I'd given him the basic story Carrick knew enough about what had been going on to be content to invite them to go to the nick in the area car that had arrived with him. There, a little later, they would be expected to help with enquiries.

'You OK, hen?' asked my favourite Scotsman when the Dandos had been ushered out. 'You look a bit pale.'

'I might have a cracked rib,' I told him from where I was again sitting on the stairs. 'He tripped over me, and she kicked me in the side in roughly the same place.'

'Who, *that* pair?' He waved in the general direction of the newly departed Dandos.

'Sorry, no, the Graveses.' I had to stop talking then; I could hardly breathe for the pain.

He held out his hands and gently helped me to my feet. 'You might need an X-ray,' he said soberly. 'I'll take you.'

'But first put out an alert about the Graveses, eh?'

He found his phone. 'D'you know the registration number of their car?'

'Patrick made a note of it somewhere.' I had to admit to myself that I didn't actually care right now but where the hell had the vehicle been? Not in the Dandos' drive anyway.

'I'll get on to him too.'

Which he must have done, probably on reflection at least twice during the time I was diagnosed as having two cracked ribs. James brought me home and when I had been there for around an hour Patrick arrived which rather suggested that he had broken every speed limit in the south of England. I was on all kinds of pain relief but that didn't seem to be making preparing the dinner any easier. Carrie had promised to help me later with lifting pots and pans in between looking after the little ones. She had also volunteered to meet the older children off the school buses until I felt better.

'I've messed things up for you,' I said, wanting to have a good howl.

'How the hell have you messed things up?' he asked, pecking my cheek on the way to washing his hands at the sink before coming over to remove my cook's apron.

'I should have demanded to know who was upstairs and rung Carrick *before* I dashed up there. They might not have got away then.'

'The idiot Dandos wouldn't have told you – or lied, said it was Great Aunt Agatha.'

I leaned on the wall.

'What's all this going to be?' he went on to ask, gazing at the pile of ingredients on the table.

'Oh, just sausages, cut up new potatoes, ditto red peppers and onions plus herbs all tossed up with crushed garlic and olive oil and then baked. There are some washed greens in the fridge to go with it. It'll have to be ice cream afterwards.'

'I think I can achieve that. The usual small- to medium-sized dish for the three youngest, another biggish one for us and Matthew and Katie a bit later?'

'No, the other way round tonight – the children can all eat together.'

'Go and rest on the sofa – I'll bring you a glass of wine

in a minute.' He turned to grin at me. 'They didn't get away. They were picked up on the motorway near Bristol and taken to a nick there. Carrick's hoping to get his hands on them tomorrow.'

For some reason I then had my good cry.

Regrettably, a little later, I also had more than one glass of wine, the relief that these wretched people would no longer be lurking nearby washing over me like a warm, scented bath. I knew that the euphoria would be short-lived as there were others, criminals, involved in this and we not only hadn't begun to find Mannering's killer but were yet to make a connection between these lines of enquiry. But with my feet up on the sofa, a bag of frozen peas wrapped in a tea towel held to my painful ribs, glass in hand, hearing Patrick singing snatches of an aria from an Italian opera – I had no idea which one – while he cooked was heaven indeed. He even looked in a recipe book and made some chocolate sauce to go with the ice cream.

It went without saying that Elspeth would shortly be told the news – her son would want to do that – but we had agreed that she ought to stay right where she was for at least a week in case there was more trouble while the effect the Graveses and Dandos had had locally was still simmering. I knew that Sally and her husband were planning outings at the weekends and had already promised her a trip on the Thames. Now she would be able really to enjoy her break.

'I'm going to work mostly at home for the rest of the week,' Patrick told me when he joined me while the children's dinner cooked. He fixed himself a tot of single malt.

'You mustn't do that because of me,' I said.

'I can pop out now and again to try to catch up on my wife's tally of locating mobsters.' Then he laughed. 'God, I can't believe those bastards have been arrested.'

'But surely, if they're only going to be charged with assault and breaking and entering they'll be released on police bail.'

'Carrick's going to resist any application for bail on the grounds that there's such a strong suspicion that they're involved with serious crime and Graves has a criminal record.

When they're brought to Bath he can hold them for forty-eight hours for questioning anyway. He told me he'll be rooting through every relevant Met file to discover if there's anything in that bloody man's criminal history that can safely be resurrected. Meanwhile, for at least three weeks, you're going to have to take plenty of painkillers, gently walk about, take deep breaths and cough if you want to or you'll get a chest infection.'

I didn't really need reminding as, not all that long ago, he had been through the same thing himself when he was shot.

Matthew and Katie came thundering down the stairs having seemingly finished doing their homework at the same time. They had been told what had happened.

'I'm starving,' said Matthew, predictably.

'You'd better tell the chef,' I told him. 'Where's Justin?'

'He was kicking his football around in the garden, in the snow, when I saw him a little while ago,' Katie said.

'Please tell him his dinner's nearly ready.'

But Justin wasn't in the garden, nor in his room or with Carrie. Alarmed as it was almost dark, I opened the front door, stepped outside and called him as there was a chance he was playing with his ball in the drive. This is not really allowed as Elspeth has a lot of spring bulbs given to her by parishioners planted at the sides and they were beginning to come up. The bitter irony of this in the present circumstances fleetingly occurred to me.

Then I heard it, the sound of someone small running as fast as their feet would carry them. I called again.

'Mum!' my son's voice yelled – no, screamed. 'Dad!'

I started to hurry up the drive.

Patrick was by my side almost immediately. 'What's going on?'

'He's in trouble,' I managed to get out, suddenly in a lot of pain again.

'Please stay there.'

Realizing that I should have done it before, I went back indoors and switched on the lights at the front of the house. These immediately revealed, but only just as he was at the limit of the illumination, a small figure, Justin, running full tilt towards us, someone right behind him. Whoever it was, a man, caught up with him and made a grab but then shouted out in pain as his shins were kicked, shouted again as they got another quick-fire battering and then turned and bolted. Seconds later Patrick arrived and scooped up his son. It was pointless his trying to catch the man – he simply can't run fast enough.

Justin didn't know whether to laugh or cry, didn't have the breath to do either and ended up with hiccups. He was taken indoors, given a drink of water and we endeavoured to calm him down. This is never easy – he's just like his father. Usually a soothing dose of Grandma does the trick but as she wasn't at home it took a bit longer. It was vital that his parents stayed calm but, inside, I felt as though I was being torn apart. When would this nightmare ever end?

While Patrick reported what had happened Carrie took the first course out of the oven – just in time.

'Right,' Patrick said to Justin, who was sitting by my side on the sofa, Matthew on the other for brotherly support. 'Please tell us what happened and then, when you're calm and quiet, you can have your dinner.'

'I went out on the green with my football,' said Justin. 'There was too much snow in the garden.'

'You're not supposed to go there on your own, especially when it's getting dark.'

OK, I thought, giving my husband a look. Justin knows that. Now is not telling-off time.

'Then what happened?' Patrick continued, having fielded the look.

'A car was sort of cruising around. It stopped and a man got out and said did I want him to play football with me. I said no. He said did I want to go for a ride in the car. I said no, picked up my ball and started to come home. He came at me looking a bit horrible and I threw the ball at him and hit him on the nose. I hadn't meant to do that,' Justin added, looking so contrite that my heart bled for him. I gave him a little hug.

'Then what?' Patrick prompted gently.

'He got really mad and came at me again, fast. I ran.'

'Was he the driver of the car?'

'No, he got out of the other front seat.'

'Can you remember what kind of car it was?'

'No, it was too dark. The car was dark too.'

'A saloon or a four-by-four like ours?'

'Just ordinary – quite old p'raps as it had a rattle. And it had an England flag on the radio thing. Can I have my dinner now?'

A memory. Of a car going away from me up the rough track at The Spinney. In the moonlight there had been a little flutter, seemingly mostly red, on the roof of the vehicle. A flag.

'You're getting police protection,' was the first thing James Carrick said when he called round about an hour later. 'Tomorrow morning. How's the lad?'

'He appears to be completely unruffled,' I told him. 'But you never know with children.'

'Did you put the clothes he'd been wearing in a bag in case there's some of the attacker's DNA on them?'

'Yes, we did. I put it in the hall as you said you were coming round.'

'I've been interviewing those neep heids the Dandos and have a mind to keep them in custody overnight. They're both talking, admitting taking money from that Graves character but they're insisting it was for the church and they passed it on to the treasurer. He seems to have dazzled them with promises of some kind of high positions at this mission in London – doing what, he didn't say. A house, a car, you name it. As I said, neep heids.'

'The Met raided the place and found nothing untoward,' Patrick told him.

'It's not encouraging, is it? I get a bit depressed when I'm up against criminals who are clever.'

Invited to have a dram, Carrick seated himself and then, at the same time as I, spotted Justin who was in the conservatory in his pyjamas looking a bit lost. He was supposed to be in bed, asleep.

'May I have a word with him?' the DCI asked me.

I called Justin, who said he was looking for his best toy racing car, and then realized that the two might not have previously met, our preferred socializing place with the Carricks being the Ring o' Bells across the green and if we invite them round for a meal he's in bed.

The introductions were made.

'Has he told you what I did?' Justin immediately wanted to know.

'Who?' asked Carrick.

'The man I hit on the nose with my football and then kicked his legs. Has he told on me?'

'No, we're looking for him as it seems he tried to kidnap you.'

'Oh.'

'Did you see what he looked like?'

'He wasn't as tall as Daddy and a bit fat. His hair was funny – sort of combed to make him look as though he had some on the top when he didn't. It blew the wrong way and he had a long bit over his ear like a curtain.'

'What was his voice like?'

'That was funny too. But not funny-funny. Spooky like a baddy in a computer game.' The child brightened. 'D'you think there's some of *him* on my football? He was all sweaty and dirty and smelled as though he hadn't had a bath for *ever*. He was really *yuck*!'

Patrick put his head in his hands for a moment after this out-of-the-mouths-of-babes utterance then disappeared to find a torch and went outside. He was back not long afterwards with the football in an evidence bag. It must be said that this long-suffering plaything was so scratched and worn that it probably had the DNA of most of Hinton Littlemoor on it, together with their dogs, never mind the horse manure on the roads.

'Will I ever get it back?' Justin sadly wanted to know.

Carrick said, 'Suppose you and I go shopping on Saturday and I get you a new one?'

Our son then went to bed with a big grin on his face.

'I can go and beat my head on the wall now,' Patrick observed bitterly. 'Just think, when I worked for MI5 and had *carte blanche* I would have sorted it out my way.'

'But that's not an option now,' Carrick pointed out somewhat unnecessarily.

My husband said something under his breath that I guessed was along the lines of 'Bugger options'.

I could have done with taking more painkillers but related to Carrick our night-time sortie to The Spinney following being intercepted there earlier in the day by the man with the shotgun. And our reason for going there.

'It's hellishly tenuous,' Carrick said with a smile.

I continued, 'I came home as Patrick's much better at moving silently than I am. As I did a dark car arrived which I've just remembered had a flag with red on it on the roof. Patrick said that it parked by the house, a lot of security lights came on and several men got out and went indoors. Patrick threw a rock through a downstairs window of the house, an amazing number of alarms went off and men, probably the same ones, ran out. He got away and came back across the fields, which is actually a shortcut. No one reported the damage to the police. Then, tonight, the man who tried to grab Justin got out of a dark car with an England flag on the radio aerial.'

'Well, I suppose it's one way of finding out if folk are in the habit of breaking the law – just chuck rocks through their windows and see what their reaction is,' Carrick commented breezily. 'I'll suggest it to the lads.'

No, Patrick didn't kill him.

Possibly detecting a few less than enchanted vibes, Carrick tossed off what was left of his tot and got to his feet. 'I must go – it's my turn to cook the dinner. I'll be in touch about the football shopping.'

I automatically thanked him and then felt guilty after he'd gone. He's a good friend and the Gillards when not at their best can be downright horrible.

'You look dreadful,' Patrick said. 'Go to bed and I'll bring you your meal.'

I shook my head. I hate eating in bed.

NINE

Persevering over the next couple of days with a rotation of bags of frozen peas when I was seated – no point in wasting good food if they really started to thaw – had the result that the swelling and soreness around my ribs subsided quite a lot. Also, having a theory that drug manufacturers factor in people like me who take painkillers a shade short of the time one is supposed to leave between doses I found that, with Carrie's help, I could cope with just about everything that needed to be done to keep the home running fairly smoothly. But not writing. I simply couldn't concentrate even though armed police, in cars, took it in turns to guard the entrance to our drive and occasionally patrolled through the churchyard on foot as our garden is accessible from there. I had been given a number to phone if there was an emergency.

The Dandos had been released and given an official warning. They had also been told that further investigations might result in their being prosecuted. Carrick himself had warned them against coming anywhere near the rectory, even, if they felt like it, to apologize. They were unimportant, he emphasized in a phone call to me, small fry in the case, just an example of how stupid people can be manipulated by criminals. Inwardly, I added a few more robust descriptions of them of my own.

The Graveses had been interviewed, separately, by Carrick, but he had got nowhere as both had protested their innocence and refused to answer further questions. The DCI held them for as long as was legally possible but was unsuccessful in getting them remanded in custody pending further investigations. The fact that the Dandos had admitted that Graves had paid them money to intimidate Elspeth until she vacated her home did not appear to be deemed sufficiently serious. Any fraudulent activity by both parties in connection with

Saint Michael's Church in Hinton Littlemoor was still to be looked into. Meanwhile, the Graveses were released on police bail, had to hand over their passports and were told to stay in the area.

This was a huge blow.

As he had said he would, Patrick worked from home, mostly on other cases for which he was responsible, only going out for short periods. During the day, with the older children at school and Carrie perhaps having taken the other two to toddler club or play group – she went with a couple of mothers and their children she had met – the house seemed very empty with not even an awareness of Elspeth busy doing something in the annexe. She had not been told about Justin's narrow escape, nor that the Graveses had been released on bail.

My heart missed a beat then the morning after Carrick's call when the doorbell rang. Telling myself I was a nervous fool as all visitors' identities were being checked, I went to see who it was.

'Hi,' said just-call-me-Steve, DI Stephen Potts. 'Just thought I'd pop by on my way to see the boss – Carrick, that is. I think I've had a bit of a breakthrough. Is hubby around?'

Ye gods, he really was the pits.

'Patrick's gone to the post office,' I informed him. 'But you can talk to me about it as I work for the NCA too.'

'So you do,' he acknowledged slowly, as though I'd just revealed the secret location of Oliver Cromwell's head.

I invited him in, vowing that I wouldn't be angry with him on account of being stressed as it can become a very bad habit.

'As you know, there was one hell of a mess in the room that appeared to have been used as a study at Mannering's place,' Potts began, having cast himself extravagantly on to one of the sofas. 'More like a dirty old man's private cinema, taking into account the stuff that was on his computer. Nasty stuff, little kids. Disgusting, actually. People like that revolt me. But there were masses of paperwork, bills, brochures, junk mail, on the floor, in cupboards and drawers – I reckon he'd hardly ever thrown anything out. We rolled up our sleeves and took it away by the sackful. The boys and girls at Radstock have been sorting through it when they've had the time between working on other stuff – I really could do with more staff – and yesterday DC Hemmings, she's a bright girl, found a solicitor's letter dated a while back that's in connection with the purchase of a house in north London. Matey apparently had paid half towards it.'

'What is it called?' I asked.

'Hope House, but for some reason no address was given. We've got the exact location as the letter mentioned covenants in connection with rights of way and fishing rights on a river, named, that runs somewhere close by. We found the river and the house is highly likely to be the mission that I noticed is mentioned as suspect in the case notes – Saint Edwina's.'

I said, 'It's thought that Mannering had been about to buy, or had already bought into criminal gangs.'

'What was the source of that info?' Potts asked with raised eyebrows.

'MI5. Mannering, or Sir Julian as he was then, consorted with criminals and also people in high places, including an MP who lost her seat at the last election. MI5 became involved because there was concern national security might be compromised as the woman had been on several committees, one of which was involved with national security. And now, thanks to your DC Hemmings, we appear to have a real connection between Mannering and this so-called mission.'

Patrick returned just then and I made some coffee. We were drinking it, Potts relating to Patrick what he had told me, when Justin put his head round the door. I had kept him off school as he had had a stomach upset overnight – again, but not grapes this time, perhaps delayed reaction after far too much excitement – and had been allowed to stay in bed.

'Hi, young man!' exclaimed Potts. 'Are you the one who fought off some stinky alien the other evening? Kicked his smelly legs? *Kerrpow!* Zonked him on the nose with your super-whizzo football? *Splat!*' This with appropriate wild gestures, almost knocking his coffee over.

Justin smiled shyly and nodded.

'And then he ran away utterly terrified of you?'

'One of his legs was shorter than the other,' Justin said happily. 'So he ran funny.'

'He shouldn't be too hard to find then. I can see you're going to be a cop when you grow up.'

Justin gazed at me longingly. 'Mum, I'm really hungry.'

'So, we now know that Mannering bought into Saint Ed's,' Patrick said that evening, emerging from my writing room where he had been working and finding me in the living room with Mark and Vicky. 'Or, to be precise, he paid for half the house. I've had a mini-breakthrough myself today. With a view to checking that Graves really was connected with Saint Ed's I contacted the Reverend Paul Broadley again and asked him about the reliability of the grapevine rumour that he was involved. Apparently it's gold-plated. He rang me back having looked into it a bit deeper – that is, phoned a friend. Apparently some time ago Graves went round to the local vicar, introduced himself and said that he represented the place, even produced a business card to prove it, and went on to say that they were about to open as a retreat, run courses and begin doing what he described as "good works". No doubt the visit was to give themselves local credibility. The vicar in question thought him decidedly suspect and added his suspicions to a secure Church of England website, a sort of private rogues' gallery.'

'Have you heard what those four arrested after trying to mow us down are saying?'

'Yes, but they're refusing to say anything. D'you want me to cook?'

'Just the vegetables, please. There's a beef casserole and jacket potatoes in the oven.'

'I could have done that.'

'I know you could. I'm feeling better and Carrie lifted the pot for me.'

'Glass of wine to celebrate?'

I felt I was drinking too much but it helped. When he returned with it he fixed himself a tot, relieved me of Mark and plonked him on his lap. Incongruous really; here we were talking about crime in the company of what Mrs Hedges had described as our 'lovely kiddies'.

Which reminded me . . .

'Did James get someone to talk to the father of Rob Hills,

the youth Mrs Hedges thought might have caused trouble here with her son Nigel?'

Patrick was blowing raspberries on Mark's hands, making him giggle and wriggle. 'Dunno.'

I patiently waited until things got switched on again.

'Oh, yes. The man denied all knowledge of what his son had been up to, said he'd bought the goggles at an army surplus store, given them to him and hasn't seen them since. And, he said, lads go up in woods where they're not supposed to be, don't they? So it's the usual situation with everything that's gone on here – no evidence.'

I must then have looked a bit glassy-eyed, for Patrick said, 'Everything all right other than, as usual, you've taken too many painkillers?'

'Has anyone identified this ex-MP who was suspected of being involved with criminals?'

'Yes, I think so. I'll check.' He went away, presumably to check on an MI5 file to which he still has access. When he came back a few minutes later, he said, 'Her name's Mo Burrwood – no idea what the "Mo" is short for. She was an independent MP for Harlsbury North in the Midlands and lost her seat after her personal life became extremely off the wall and she was prosecuted for driving under the influence of drink and drugs.'

'Is there a photo of her?'

'Er – no, not on what I was looking at.'

'Please see if you can find one.'

He gave me a silly salute, put Mark on the floor and went away again. Mark immediately set off crawling after him, sat up by an armchair and then, holding on to it, hauled himself to his feet. He had been doing this for a few days now and we hadn't swooped on him to take photos or selfies, shriek encouragement or generally behave in idiotic fashion. I then watched, entranced, as he tottered a few steps away from the chair, again going in the direction taken by Patrick, then lost his balance and flopped down again. Deciding that speed was preferable he then crawled out of my sight through the doorway.

I still couldn't get out of my mind the way Graves had said, 'I'm sure you love your family.'

A couple of minutes later Patrick came back carrying his son and my iPad, the latter of which he handed to me. On the screen was a head-and-shoulders photo of the woman in question, possibly a still from a local TV station interview. She had blonde shoulder-length hair, blue-grey eyes and possessed a distinct resemblance to a disgruntled hamster.

'Mark's walking!' I said.

'I was just about to tell you that. He was staggering round your writing room just now and I had to catch him before he ended up in the wastepaper bin.'

'And *this* harridan, now older and perhaps wearing a wig, I'm sure is the female now calling herself Natasha Graves.'

'I had an idea it might be her. I'll let Carrick know.'

'When are you due to get your army pension?' I asked.

'In around two years.'

'We could manage until then.'

'If I chucked it in? I've been thinking about it. But I'd get another job. And we could move; I've had more than enough of this place.'

His mobile rang and he went into the kitchen to talk, presumably to enable him to watch the pots. I told myself it was time I moved around and went to check on the rest of the family. When I returned to the living room it was obvious that Patrick had had some kind of bad news.

'What's wrong?' I asked.

'That moron Potts has arrested Terry on suspicion of killing Mannering.'

'On what grounds?' I asked, horrified.

'Carrick doesn't know yet. But he'd had no choice but to put all the details I gave him about what happened at Hartwood castle into the murder case file, including the names of those present, when Haldane and Mannering, as he wasn't then, tried to kill us all.'

'I thought it was restricted information.'

'It *was*, but because this has now happened I shall get on to Dixon and ask him to send their file to Carrick as I'm damned if Terry's going to be accused of murder when the cops don't have all the background info and evidence. Apparently Potts went all the way to Sussex to question Terry at home and is coming back with him tomorrow. Carrick's insisted he's brought to Bath.'

'Perhaps you could be involved when he's questioned.'

'I have every intention of being present.' Utterly exasperated, Patrick threw his hands in the air. 'Who knows, the idiot'll arrest me next.'

'Terry *might* have killed him.'

'That possibility's been keeping me awake at night. Oh, and those four arrested after we were attacked in London are still refusing to say why they did it or who paid them. But at least they're being remanded in custody as they're no strangers to the local police.'

I got the impression it was unprecedented but Patrick obtained permission for the pair of us to be present, as observers only, when Terry Meadows was interviewed. Carrick himself had had to get official blessing for this from his Superintendent at HQ in Portishead and I could only surmise that *that* senior officer must hold the DCI in high regard. Any regard he might have for his embedded NCA officer and his part-time 'consultant' could only be guessed at. I wasn't bothering myself with wondering about DI Potts' rating as it was a waste of brain-time.

I was quite shocked when I saw Terry as he looked drawn in the face and very tired, as though he hadn't slept properly since we had last seen him. He registered surprise when Patrick and I entered and gave me a tiny smile. The two police officers already in the room were stonily ignored.

Carrick opened the proceedings by introducing himself – although I had an idea that at some stage they had already met – and Potts, added the usual formalities and then said, 'The arrangement is that Detective Inspector Potts, who is stationed at Radstock, the police station handling this murder case, will conduct the first interview. I'm present on account of being the senior officer at this nick and in overall charge and also due to the fact that matters regarding a past MI5 case are involved. So we're regarding it as serious. Other one-time operatives of MI5, whom you know, are present at their request as observers, but might be able to provide some background details if necessary.'

'Good morning,' Terry said to no one in particular.

Carrick turned to Potts. 'I hope you've fully familiarized yourself with the details of this affair in the armoury of Hartwood castle in the file sent by courier from London last night. It's restricted information and MI5 want it back. I don't think we need go through it all again. All witness statements taken by the Sussex force, who were the first police on the scene, tallied and are in the file. It must be borne in mind that the chief intended victim of this crime was the man whose professional name was Richard Daws. He had absolutely no reason not to give an accurate account of what had occurred.'

'The chief?' Potts queried, for some reason seeming to be a bit flustered. 'Because he was titled?'

'No, because he was the chief object of hate by the recent murder victim, you fool,' Terry said scornfully.

I bit the tip of my tongue hard to prevent myself laughing.

Ignoring both question and response, Carrick continued by inviting Potts to make his case.

The DI began by saying, 'I understand from the file that you'd convinced Nicholas Haldane and Sir Julian Hardy, as he was then, that you were on their side. You told them that this was because of the way your one-time superior in MI5, Patrick Gillard, had treated you. You even went to the length of giving him a serious beating to prove your point.'

'No,' Terry said. 'I slapped him around a bit. We used to practise things like that and we're good actors. He pretended to be hurt; he wasn't.'

'You wouldn't call yourself a violent man then.'

'No.'

'Yet you went on to gun down several thugs hired by these two men using a semi-automatic weapon that you'd previously concealed down the barrel of a small cannon in the armoury.'

'I did. The men had been hired by Haldane and he was just about to order them to kill everyone else.'

'I see,' said Potts as though he didn't. He continued, 'I understand that those present, the intended victims, I mean, included your fiancée, now your wife.'

'That's right.'

'Whom you admitted when I spoke to you yesterday had

suffered some kind of breakdown as she's never really got over the affair.'

'Admitted? Is it a crime if your wife is taken ill?'

'I suggest to you that you were furious that your wife was still so affected by this affair and swore to take revenge. You already knew that Haldane had recently been killed because, again, you were present. Again, Meadows? That seems to be a bit of a coincidence. However, you then discovered that the other man, Hardy, was still alive, had been released from prison and had changed his name. I suggest that on the day before the body was discovered you drove down to Somerset after the early-morning meeting you mentioned to me and killed him. After your employment with MI5 you would have had no trouble in obtaining a suitable weapon.'

'I didn't kill him,' Terry said.

Patrick cleared his throat. 'Permission to provide some background detail?'

'Go ahead,' Carrick said before Potts could react.

'Perhaps you didn't read that bit in your own case notes, Steve, but the ballistics people were pretty sure that Mannering was killed with nine-millimetre bullets fired by something like a Browning pistol. Brownings were used until quite recently by the British Army and date back to 1935. Using a weapon like that wouldn't come easily to a comparatively young man proficient at firing Glocks or even Smith and Wesson handguns and certainly wouldn't have been his weapon of choice.'

'And the modern ones would have been easier to obtain?' Potts enquired.

'To a professional killer, yes.'

'Yet I understand criminals are increasingly having to rely on old weapons like Brownings as it's getting more difficult for them to get hold of anything else.'

'That's correct as the police, the Met especially, are getting better at tracking down illicit sources of firearms and under-world armourers. But criminals aren't necessarily pros, professional killers.'

'Do you consider yourself to be a pro?' Potts went on to ask Patrick.

'Not in the way you mean.'

'If Meadows had asked to borrow your Glock would you have lent it to him?'

'No, I'd rather have filled the bastard with lead myself.'

'To get back to present business . . .' Carrick began heavily.

To the DCI, Potts said, 'What's just been said is interesting: weren't the weapons found in the cellar of Mannering's house Browning and Webley pistols?'

'They were,' Carrick agreed. 'But none of them had been recently fired.'

'Then the murderer took it away with him.'

'Or her,' Patrick added absent-mindedly. 'Sorry.'

Terry broke a little silence by saying, 'It really was Mannering who was killed then?'

'I'll ask the questions,' Potts snapped.

'A little further background detail courtesy of the NCA?' Patrick ventured.

Carrick gestured that he should continue.

'Yes, it was Mannering. I'd forgotten to mention it to Ingrid and I was going to bring it up this morning. Commander Greenway contacted me yesterday about the question of identity. He'd asked someone to find out where Mannering had had his heart op and it was at the Royal Berkshire Hospital in Reading. Apparently a patient's DNA is regarded as part of their medical records so it was quite easy, over a matter of a few hours when it was compared to a sample taken from the corpse, to establish that indeed the body in the mortuary in Bath is Mannering's.'

I had been quietly soaking all this up, making a few notes and wondering at Potts' change of manner. This was another, serious, side of him.

To Terry, Potts said, 'You were frank with me yesterday and told me that your wife is blaming you for what happened to her and also for your assault on Gillard. She's having nightmares that the Gillards' little boy was killed and it was her fault as she was their nanny at the time. Despite saying a while ago that she was coming home having been staying with friends, she hasn't. Is she going to divorce you?'

'It hasn't been mentioned,' Terry replied very carefully, and I was grateful that his temper isn't as volatile as Patrick's.

'No? But didn't you have a notion that when she went to Lyme Regis it might be all over between you?'

'No, I didn't. She badly needed a break.'

'Did you have serious rows about it?'

'No, none and I didn't want there to be any as Dawn's four months' pregnant. If you're married with a family you'll know how it can drastically affect a woman's emotional state.'

'I'm not,' Potts retorted stiffly.

Now there was a surprise.

'What kind of car do you own?' Potts asked Terry.

'You know the answer to that already because you saw it. A red BMW 4 Series sports.'

'Yes, I noted down the registration number. I have news for you. It was seen in Great Mossley on the day before Mannering's body was discovered. At Mannering's business premises during the afternoon, to be precise.'

'Is that reliable evidence?' Carrick wanted to know.

'Yes. The driver, male, went inside and asked to speak to Mannering but he wasn't there. Whoever was asking then said he was an old friend of his and wanted to know where he lived. They told him but whoever he spoke to became suspicious and wrote down the registration number of the car.'

'This has only just come to light?' Carrick asked.

'Yes, the day before yesterday. Someone on my team showed initiative as we were getting nowhere with the case and visited both places to make more enquiries. God knows why whoever it was hasn't come forward with this information before.'

Potts should have informed Carrick of this before but I had an idea he'd delayed divulging the revelation to enhance himself.

'Any comments on that?' Carrick asked Terry.

The suspect just looked acutely miserable and said nothing.

'You went to the house,' Potts resumed. 'Perhaps you intended to confront him in some way. Seeing him brought it all back to you and you lost your temper. Perhaps those boxes of weapons were in the room with him and you completely lost it, grabbed one and shot him.'

'There was no ammunition,' Patrick put in, risking being asked to leave.

'There was,' Terry whispered.

I felt as though my heart had turned over.

'What *happened*?' Potts demanded to know.

'I'm up in a corner, aren't I?' Terry mumbled.

'Yes, you are!' the DI cried triumphantly.

'Tell the truth,' Patrick whispered.

Choked with emotion, Terry said, 'I never thought for a moment that it would come to this. And I've one vulnerable woman who is too far away from me right now and it's my fault and another even more vulnerable person who will suffer horribly and that'll be down to me too now.'

'Please explain,' Carrick urged gently, and there was quite a long silence during which Patrick glowered at Potts, daring him to speak.

Finally, Terry sat up straight and said, 'I decided when Dawn went off to stay with friends that I'd try to trace the one-time Sir Julian. Yes, I was angry that she was still suffering. Perhaps I wanted to kill him, perhaps not. Perhaps I wanted to be able to tell Dawn that he was a broken man – to make her feel better somehow. I just desperately needed to do *something* to remedy the whole bloody horrible situation. Having contacted an old colleague at MI5 for any available info on the man I was told he had changed his name to Mannering and *might* be living in Somerset. That wasn't much help but I Googled the name anyway and came up with that car hire business. It was a slim chance but I went to Great Mossley and asked where the boss lived. It wasn't difficult to find – the motor business had his new name plastered all over it.'

He gathered his thoughts for a few moments, then resumed, 'I still thought it was hopeless and it was the wrong man but I heard the shots when I'd just parked the car outside the house. But as you might know the report of a gun being fired from within an old building with thick walls can sound like someone dropping heavy items on to a bare wooden floor. So I wasn't sure and exercised a bit of caution. I went through the gate, which was ajar, and up the slope to what appeared to be the main entrance at the side of the house. That door was open too. There was a cold draught blowing out as though another door was open as well. It was a freezing day and I wondered if the bangs I'd heard was the central heating boiler blowing up after having failed some time previously. Then I heard a sound, like a person crying, and immediately thought that someone had been hurt.'

He then stopped speaking, seeming a bit overcome by it all.

'Go on!' Potts rapped out.

'Shut up,' Patrick told him.

Terry pulled himself together. 'I went into the room where I thought the sound had come from, quite a big living room. I shall never forget what I saw. There was this old, old lady holding a handgun, crying and trembling as though she was going to fall to pieces. On the floor partly to the rear of a sofa was a man, or the body of one, I soon discovered. Then the old lady saw me. "You a friend of his?" she demanded to know. She had a Cockney accent. I told her I wasn't, possibly wise in the circumstances. Then she broke down again and I persuaded her to give me the gun, a Browning – I think. She then grabbed me in a tight hug, still shaking and all I could do was stand there trying to comfort her. I was actually worried that the situation would kill her. After a little while I sat her down on the other sofa, found the kitchen and made her a cup of tea. I had to be careful and kept my gloves on – I didn't want any of my fingerprints to be found in the place.'

Carrick shifted impatiently in his chair. 'Man, if you'd only rung the police *then* you wouldn't be here now.'

'But I had a real motive to kill him, didn't I?' Terry said. 'I had no idea who the woman was and she might then have sworn on everything holy to the cops that she'd found *me* there holding the weapon. Who would have been believed?'

'What did you do then?' Carrick enquired.

'I suppose I panicked a bit. The old lady was going on and on about how he'd been a filthy bastard who'd watch child porn on his computer and he was a filthy bastard in the house and she'd given in her notice. I guessed from that that she'd been his cleaner or housekeeper. While she was talking I wrapped the gun in a tea towel that was in the kitchen and then asked her where she'd got the weapon from. She told me down in the cellar – she'd found them while looking for something. She told me where the key and the door were and I went down there. There were several boxes, one of which had been opened. There was a box of ammo in it which had also been torn open. Thinking that her fingerprints were bound to be on that too, I took it back upstairs, wrapped it in another tea towel and put the key back. Then I asked her if she knew anything about the weapons. She said Mannering was a crook as well as everything else and she'd heard him talking on the phone to someone about them as he was selling them. Then she burst into tears again and said something about how he'd sexually assaulted a local little girl hardly more than a toddler near a play park. Then he'd threatened her mother, who was only a matter of yards away, with the same, and worse, if she told the police.'

'Coffee,' Carrick decided, getting to his feet.

'You covered up for this woman then,' Potts said to Terry.

'Yes, I told her it was up to her whether she confessed to the police or pretended to find the body. She immediately said that she reckoned she'd done the neighbourhood a favour, was damned if she was going to prison and could I chuck the gun and box of ammo in a river somewhere. Then I took her home.'

The DCI had remained in the room so I asked if I could put a question to the suspect. This was granted.

I said, 'How on earth did an old lady like that know how to load and fire a Browning pistol?'

'She did tell me. As I'd already guessed, she was born in the East End. Her father was in the Home Guard during the war. He'd had a Browning issued to him, showed her how to use it in case he was killed "if Jerry came", as he put it. Eventually she married a GI who, it turned out, came from a wealthy family and inherited a lot of money. He ended up losing it all gambling, shot himself, and she had just enough funds left to come home to the UK where she married a man from Somerset. He's dead too now and she still doesn't have any money, except for her pension, so she does cleaning jobs.'

Potts said, 'If this amazing story is found to be true you'll be charged with perverting the course of justice, assisting an offender and wasting police time.'

'Yet another Brownie badge for you then,' Terry responded with a big smile.

'And you'll be remanded in custody,' the DI finished by grimly saying.

'No, he won't,' countered Carrick, who was still over by the door. 'He'll be released on police bail. And if those ex-MI5 personnel present wish to supervise his whereabouts until tomorrow morning when we can talk to him again, that's fine by me.'

The door slammed behind him and then opened again. 'What *did* you do with the gun and ammo?'

Terry said, 'Chucked them in a river somewhere.'

'*Which* river?'

'God knows. I could probably show you where. But, look, this old lady . . . do you know who she is?'

'We do, and please don't worry about her.'

TEN

'Question,' I said that evening, when Patrick, Terry and I were back at home. 'Mannering was killed *after* Graves showed up here so if there's a connection between these people – sorry, criminals – what was their motive then?'

'Well, surely it has to be something to do with the guns in the cellar,' Patrick said. 'How's this for a theory? Mannering had obtained the weapons somehow or the other and they were due to be sent to Saint Ed's. There was just the delicate matter of an agreed price and arrangements for the handover. As I think you suggested, Ingrid, Mannering might have stalled. Perhaps he wanted more money or had received it and was refusing to pass over the goods. Saint Ed's got fed up with him and after threats, or not, put out a contract for him – weeks ago. *That* was the guy who climbed over the wall at the end of Mannering's garden and left strands of his sweater on the stonework. But either his intended victim wasn't there or he found him stone dead.'

'That's perfectly feasible,' I said. 'But you didn't answer the question. Why did Graves come *here*?'

Patrick shrugged. 'All part of an already agreed plan to get at us instigated by Mannering? It has to be something along those lines.'

'I'm trying to work out how I'm not going to get divorced,' Terry said gloomily, having probably not been listening.

It had been bizarre walking round Sainsbury's with him as he helped me with the shopping. He had offered to cook the dinner – he's a good cook – and I had been happy to let him get on with it and buy things accordingly. But at least he had unburdened himself of his secret. Privately, although I was reluctant to say anything to him, I thought it highly likely that Dawn would return if she knew he was in trouble and had been made aware of the details behind it.

'Any ideas?' Terry suddenly asked the pair of us, breaking into our collective reverie.

'Phone her,' I said, throwing away my reservations, sick to death of stalemate. 'Tell her everything that's happened, especially that Mannering is dead. Tell her the truth, that you did it to try to protect someone from prosecution.'

'She'll say I was mad,' he protested.

'You've both been a bit mad after what happened. Patrick and I have been a bit mad too and there have been a couple of occasions when I really thought he was going to murder people on the spot. Go on, phone her.'

We were in our living room and Terry went away, perhaps to do as I had suggested, perhaps not. We had accommodated him in the annexe, which of course was very handy.

Patrick, who had been looking at me a bit askance, said, 'Really?'

'Really. You were within a cat's whisker of killing Graves with your bare hands in the garden, never mind almost gunning down that so-called principal. I think you should find out who's living at The Spinney. Then you can follow your inclinations and conduct a night raid on the place throwing grenades and mow down everyone not killed in the explosions. Then you could do the same at Saint Ed's. Sorted.'

'You're being flippant again,' my husband said accusingly. 'It's not funny.'

'Of course not, but that's the kind of thing that's taken over your mind right now and preventing you from thinking clearly. Violence. Lashing out. Hitting back.'

He stared at me with those wonderful grey eyes.

'The oracle doesn't always say the things you want to hear,' I observed quietly, loving him to bits.

There was another thought-filled silence and, a little while later, Terry came back into the room, his eyes very bright. He reseated himself, just managed to get out, 'She's coming back – tomorrow,' and burst into tears.

Wordlessly, Patrick gave him a pat on the shoulder and a tot of whisky. I left the room to busy myself somewhere else for a few minutes.

*   *   *

The following morning Terry made a formal statement to Potts and Carrick and again was released on police bail. But he was ordered to remain in the Bath area. This resulted in temporary domestic turmoil for me as we immediately invited Dawn and the little one to stay in the annexe with Terry for as long as she wanted to. This meant borrowing a cot, which Carrie organized for us. A further development was the DCI flatly refusing to allow Potts to interview Mrs Smythe on the grounds that in view of her age someone she might find more sympathetic ought to ask the questions. My initial thought was that this would be DI Lynn Outhwaite but Carrick insisted that as the overall investigation belonged to the NCA I ought to do it. In my view this conclusion was a bit wobbly but I wasn't about to argue. It was his nick and, anyway, he didn't like Potts.

'Oh, it's you two,' said Mrs Smythe when she beheld Patrick and me. Patrick was again present as an observer but got the formal business out of the way for me first.

Carrick had offered a couple of guiding points but otherwise left everything entirely up to me. It seemed inconceivable that Terry hadn't been telling the truth but I knew better than to automatically assume she was guilty. Her son-in-law, Brian Cowley, might have done the deed and she'd gone with him as she had a set of keys. He could have quickly hidden himself in the house somewhere when Terry arrived.

'I've been copped all right,' said Mrs Smythe. 'My mum always said chickens come 'ome to roost. Did that young bloke grass on me? I didn't think 'e would, but you can't always tell with fellas.'

'He didn't have a lot of choice,' I told her. 'The police arrested him for the shooting.'

'Go on! What the 'ell for?'

'He hated Mannering too.'

She appeared to have dressed for the occasion and was wearing a rusty-black suit and clutched a huge handbag to match. At first thinking that her hairstyle was rather odd, I realized that she was wearing a grey head-hugging feathered hat, her hair sticking out the sides and back in a wavy fringe. Her work-worn fingers were loaded with gold rings, which perhaps represented her entire worldly wealth. We had been told that she was eighty-five.

'Oh, Gawd,' Mrs Smythe lamented. She brightened. 'But I'll plead guilty and it'll save you cops a lot of time, won't it? Despite wot I said I don't really mind goin' to prison, luv. It'll be warm and there'll be 'ot meals that I don't 'ave to cook. And I'll know I've rid the world of that 'orrible so-and-so.'

I said, 'What on earth made you do it, though?'

'I just boiled over. On account of 'im, and wot 'e'd done. When I told 'im I was leavin' he refused to pay me and gave me a dirty gesture. I won't show you wot it was on account of you bein' a lady. And because 'e assaulted little Fay Bidders. 'Er Mum, Viv, has been too scared to go out in case '*e* was lurkin' around somewhere. But she ain't now.' This last remark was accompanied by a big smile.

'So you'd found the boxes of weapons in the cellar some time previously and removed one of the pistols, loaded it and taken it home with you?'

'No, it wasn't quite like that. The vacuum cleaner packed up and I wondered if there was another one down there. I went down – 'orrible an' dirty it was too but what else should I 'ave expected? That bit wasn't part of my job. I couldn't find another cleaner and then I noticed the boxes and that one of 'em 'ad bin opened. Loo rolls. What would 'e want with that many loo rolls? Then I saw there was other stuff underneath 'em. Guns. That's when I really knew 'e was a crook. There was ammo too. I loaded one just how my pa showed me and put it back in the box exactly as I'd found it.'

I said, 'But that means that you didn't just "boil over", as you put it – you planned to kill him.'

Mrs Smythe looked dubiously at Patrick. 'It wasn't quite like that either,' she said. 'It was before I done that. Can you, a bloke, understand a woman wantin' somethin' 'andy that made 'er feel safe in an 'ouse that was 'orrible?'

The one with a Glock 17 in a holster beneath his jacket smiled gently and said, 'Yes, but you could have resigned earlier.'

'Of course I could! But then I wouldn't 'ave been able to

prove that 'e was a crook and get 'im arrested. Pa went in the Met Police after the war so p'raps I take after 'im. Them guns was a big find but I wanted to know more. But that was before 'e molested poor little Fay. Then I didn't care about the rest of 'em – I just shot the pig.'

A little tingle went down my spine. 'Rest of who?' I enquired.

'Oh, I 'aven't said yet, 'ave I? His weird friends, that's wot. People from London. Mannering used to get me to cook a few bits and pieces when 'e 'ad 'em visitin' 'im. I 'ad to do it at 'ome – I'm a good cook, although I shouldn't say it myself – as the Devil 'imself wouldn't have got me cookin' anythin' in *that* kitchen.'

'You told the man who was arrested that you'd heard him talking on the phone about selling the guns. When was that?'

Mrs Smythe shrugged extravagantly. 'Dunno exactly. A while back – not long after I found 'em.'

'And people turned up shortly afterwards?'

'Oh, it wasn't the first time folk'd come – and I'm only goin' by the number of times 'e asked me to cook stuff.'

'Did you ever actually see anyone at the house?'

'Well, 'e wasn't the kind of person to have folk round for a drink – not locals anyway as 'e thought they was all country thickos. The only time I saw people was not long ago when I was a bit late bringin' 'is sausage rolls and other bits and they were there. 'E was angry that I was late but I'd 'ad to go out and buy more ingredients for 'em, 'adn't I? There was three of 'em, a woman and two blokes. I didn't like the look of 'em at all, I'm tellin' you. More crooks, most likely.'

She didn't seem to be the kind of person to have a wild imagination either . . .

'In fact,' Mrs Smythe continued, 'that was when I took the loaded gun out of the box and put it in one of the kitchen drawers I knew 'e never went in. They'd been talkin' when I arrived and I 'eard one of the men say somethin' like why don't you step up the pressure on that bloody cop or whatever the 'ell 'e calls 'imself if you want revenge. Then 'e said, "Get someone to rough up 'is kids." Honest, that's what 'e really did say. The woman shushed 'im and they went quiet. That was when I felt scared – that they'd get me somehow, knowin' I'd over'eard.'

'Can you describe these people?' Patrick asked, his face expressionless.

She beamed at him. 'When I've 'ad a nice cuppa?'

He left the interview room.

'Thinkin' about it now, I feel bad about not sayin' somethin' about 'im to the cops before,' Mrs Smythe continued in a low voice. 'I mean, the kids might well 'ave got roughed up and I could 'ave prevented it.'

'Some yobs did try,' I told her. 'But the children involved aren't tiny and fought back rather well. No real harm was done.' I resolved to steer the conversation back to what was really my brief to question her about and said, 'Patrick'll be back with the tea in a moment but was that the only time you saw visitors at Mannering's house?'

'Yes, in the flesh, so to speak. I only went there once a week, you know. But there was sometimes more washing-up than was usual for him to make so I reckon he 'ad folk on other occasions. They must've eaten some meals at a pub.'

'He left all the washing-up for you to do?'

'Too right, luv. Just left it all in the sink. Too mean to get a dishwasher.'

'You informed the police on the Tuesday morning that you'd found him dead. Was that your normal day for working there?'

'No, I cleaned for 'im on Mondays.'

'And that's when you shot him.'

'Yus, after I'd done my two hours and said I was leavin' and he gave me a finger.'

'So you had no real reason to go there on the Tuesday morning then.'

'I said to the cops that I went there to get my pay, which wasn't that much of a lie when you think about it. As I just said, he'd refused to pay me the day before but raidin' his wallet 'adn't seemed quite right.'

'He'd managed to get the house in a real mess in twenty-four hours then.'

'As I said, the place was always a pigsty.'

'Oh, I've just remembered – where's the key to the cellar door kept?'

'It's hung on a nail in the coal 'ole,' Mrs Smythe replied as though I should have known that.

She lapsed into silence and I made a few notes.

A minute or so later Patrick returned with three mugs of tea and some sugar on a tray. Mrs Smythe put two heaped spoonfuls in hers, which was of no concern as she was as thin as a heron, and sipped it gratefully, blowing on it to cool it. I found myself liking her enormously.

To me, Patrick said, 'Our visitors are arriving at around four. Dawn is driving up as she has her own car.'

'Now then,' said Mrs Smythe, carefully setting down her mug. 'You want to know what they looked like. One of the blokes, the one who'd said about roughin' up the kids, was big, fat rather than tough, if you get me. 'E was about sixty and had dark quite curly 'air goin' thin on top – very thin, come to think of it – and spoke with a bit of a foreign accent, don't ask me wot sort it was. The other two might've been an item – as they say in the soaps – but I was surprised as far as the woman went as she looked as though she could curdle milk just by lookin' at it. The bloke was creepy so perhaps they made a good couple. 'E was thin – as my mum used to say like a broomstick with the wood scraped orf – very fair and 'is 'air was smarmed down like in the old Brylcreem ads so that it looked polished and shiny. 'E could've walked straight out of an old film – a gangster film.'

Oddly, I felt no emotion but surely these people were the Graveses, together with an unknown male, to use the correct terminology. 'Were any names mentioned?' I asked.

'Not as I 'eard.' Hesitantly, she then said, 'Does me 'elpin' you with your enquiries like this mean someone'll put in a good word for me?'

'I'll do whatever I can,' Patrick promised.

'Scouts' honour?'

'I wasn't in the Scouts. But you have my word.'

Her head on one side like a bird, she surveyed him with her rather beady eyes. 'No, you seem a bloke who would've thought that kind of thing too bloody borin' by 'arf.'

*   *   *

We found James Carrick in his office. When apprised of what we had learned, he said, 'Human nature never fails to amaze me. My main concern is what the hell am I going to do with this old lady? I don't think remand centres are really geared up for the very elderly and if they are they'd be used to them being men. She's *compos mentis*, isn't she?'

'Definitely,' Patrick replied.

The DCI shook his head. 'I'll have to get advice about it. And meanwhile, we have another link in our murder case. I'll get Potts to find out who lives at this place you're dubious about, The Spinney. But as I said before, it's tenuous, if not clutching at straws.'

'Care is needed,' Patrick warned. 'I'd be quite cheerful if someone gave our Steve a good smack round the ear but we don't necessarily want him making a mortuary table look untidy.'

Carrick almost smiled but fought it off. 'Mrs Smythe told you that the other man at Mannering's house was big, on the fat side, and had thinning, dark, quite curly hair. He spoke with a foreign accent but she didn't know what it was. Is it worth asking her to look at mugshots of criminals who fit that description?'

'Anything's worth a try,' I said. 'And don't forget, her dad was in the Met.'

Mrs Smythe was given a light lunch, had a little nap, and then announced herself ready to look at 'photos'. An hour later, after another cuppa, she had narrowed her search down to five, immediately rejected one when told of his height, over six feet, and then another when it was revealed that he had only one arm. The remaining three names were immediately run through Records. It was soon discovered that one was still on the Met's Most Wanted list, his whereabouts unknown but actually thought to be dead, another was in Wormwood Scrubs on consecutive life sentences for three murders, and the third, a Scotsman, had been released from prison and known to be running a bed and breakfast business in the Western Isles.

Patrick and I grabbed a bite of lunch ourselves and returned to the DCI's office. He really seemed to be fired up with the morning's progress. 'This character who's thought to be dead,

Herman Grünberg . . .' he began. 'The grey area is due to a body being found in a burnt-out car, his, in Ilford some years ago. The charred corpse inside it was not only unrecognizable but almost burnt to ashes which meant that extracting DNA with the technology that existed at the time was virtually impossible. He's played dead before, when he was in his thirties, a rather pathetic effort when he left his clothes on Weymouth beach and disappeared. But he turned up again, in north London, when he was positively identified by a snout who used to be in his employ.'

'His specialities are what?' Patrick wondered.

'Running drugs, and forcing vulnerable women, usually illegal immigrants, into prostitution. There are a couple of unsolved murders that happened on what was almost certainly his doorstep. His last known whereabouts were, again, in north London. But, clutching at straws with regard to this property not far from you, there's no word of his having bought a house in Somerset. It would be a good bolt-hole though.'

'Simon Graves was sent to prison for very similar offences,' I recollected.

'Doesn't mean they're best buddies,' Patrick observed glumly. 'I think it's important to get a photograph of who-ever's living at The Spinney – if only to get rid of the doubt in our minds.'

Carrick considered. Then he said, 'From the point of view of eliminating him, or her, from enquiries and in deference, Ingrid, to your powers of observation and intuition I'm willing to give permission to action that.'

Yes, he did sometimes sound as though he was giving evidence in court.

'And I'll do it,' Patrick ventured.

'You won't,' Carrick said.

'I'm trained to do it, I have the camera to do it and abso-lutely none of your local personnel have the experience. So you'd have to call in help from HQ. And if it turns out that a wacky but top-ranking dowager's living there with an obses-sion about security then, because I'm a discreet sort of bloke, it won't be all over the Avon and Somerset force that you've been a silly boy.'

The DCI might have been thinking that his recent slapping down of Potts could result in something along those lines when he agreed, albeit reluctantly.

I went home after this as there was a lot of cooking to do, for five adults and six children, to be precise. Carrie was continuing to eat with us to supervise the youngest and anyway, confessed to preferring my cooking to her own. I could see this becoming a semi-permanent arrangement when we were *en famille* and didn't mind at all. Further assistance soon became apparent when I arrived at the rectory and found Terry engaged in the early preparation of enough food for around twenty. He had borrowed Carrie's car to shop – I didn't ask if he was insured to drive it – and insisted that while he and Dawn were staying with us he would pay for and cook the main evening meal.

Perhaps this, and the police protection, lulled me into a false sense of security.

Snow had given way to rain and slush but by the time night came the rain eased. I knew Patrick wouldn't try to gain entry to The Spinney unless a unique opportunity presented itself but would hope to get what he wanted when whoever lived there left the house. True enough, he went off, taking the Range Rover part of the way as before, about an hour before it got light. I hadn't slept much.

Fully occupied during the day, I had little time to worry about the project. It was really good to see Dawn again but for most of the morning she, Terry and their little daughter, Emma, stayed in the annexe. They had a lot to talk about. Any sensitivities they might feel involving my need for peace and quiet to write was admirable but, needless to say, I still couldn't write a word. During the afternoon Emma played with Vicky, Mark 'assisting', and it became very noisy. OK, I thought, I'll give up on the writing and run a playgroup instead.

Eventually, the youngest children had their dinner and were got ready for bed. Terry knew what Patrick was doing and that I would prefer to be up a tree with him somewhere rather than in the middle of domestic mayhem. A little later, I was assisting him in the kitchen by doing a dessert for the rest of us – he preferred not to be crowded at the stove – when he came over and put an arm around me, giving my shoulders a squeeze.

'He'll be OK, you know,' he said.

Sometimes it's ghastly when you have a good imagination: all I could see in my mind's eye was a body hanging on barbed or high-voltage wires. Where the hell was he?

We waited for him as long as possible for dinner, but at a little before seven with Matthew, Katie and Justin patrolling like starving tigers, we put the food on the table. At that precise moment I heard a vehicle outside and shortly afterwards my husband unlocked and then stumbled in through the front door. Hearing the vehicle, I had already gone into the hall.

'What have you *done*?' I cried.

Patrick flopped on to a settle with a groan and started to remove his boots. 'Fell out of a tree and it took me a while to get back to the car,' he said, wincing. 'It's nothing.'

'Men usually say things like that when their heads are half hanging off,' I scolded. He seemed to have a lot of forest still adhering to him, twigs and leaves sticking to his clothing, his hands and face smeared with mossy earth. Then I realized that was probably camouflage.

Terry appeared and took over removing the boots. 'Hi, boss. Dinner's on the table. Shall I put you under the cold tap first?'

Patrick gave him a poisonous look, got to his feet and limped away. Not far to begin with though, just into the living room where he poured himself a large tot of whisky and downed it practically in one. Then he painfully made his way up the stairs.

'Is that Dad?' Katie, always attuned to the moods of others, asked in a whisper as she sat down for her meal.

I nodded.

'Has he gone to bed in a strop?' Justin asked in a loud voice.

'Eat your dinner!' she snapped at him. 'You don't always have to know what grown-ups are doing.'

Everyone studiously got on with their meal.

Five minutes or so later Patrick appeared, minus the forest, seated himself carefully and said a general hello. Terry took his dinner out of the Rayburn's warm oven and placed it before him, receiving a word of thanks.

'Well?' I said, utterly unable to wait a second longer for news.

'The branch broke,' Patrick said.

'Before that?' I prompted. 'Did you get what you wanted?'

'Eventually. Terry, this is delicious. Did you make it?'

'Yes, I did.'

'What is it?'

'Shepherd's pie,' the cook answered grimly.

Afterwards, time had to be given to the family and it was just before ten when Patrick, Terry and I sat down with a chance to talk. I was aware that Patrick had already made a call to Carrick and as he spoke it became obvious that he had also kept the DCI informed during the day. Dawn was with us too as I had said that it was manifestly unfair to exclude her now as, initially, she had been deeply involved. Her reunion with Justin had been emotional for her, for reasons that he couldn't understand of course, but it was lovely to be able to nullify her nightmares about him.

'The Graveses are there,' Patrick began. 'I got a few good shots of them when they went out in their car and also when they returned. I sent them to Carrick. A lot later, when the light was going and I was about to give up, they went out again with a man who fits the description given to us by Mrs Smythe, although he has a lot less hair than in the mugshot. They went off in his car, a Merc of some kind, and hadn't returned by the time I left. There were other men there and when I did a recce before I climbed the tree I saw a dark blue car parked round the back of the house by buildings that had probably once been a coach house and stables. There's a much older wooden barn there too. The car had an England flag on the radio aerial. There was also the Merc and a black van. Unusually, perhaps, the drive is circular and goes round behind the house so there's vehicle access from both sides.'

'What about that character with the shotgun?' I asked.

'I didn't see him patrolling, which was lucky. He might have been one of the others who I got the impression were living in some of the outbuildings there as they're quite extensive. They were sort of pottering around. One of them had a slight limp so he could be the one who tried to grab Justin.'

'Is Carrick planning a raid?' Terry asked.

'If I get my way it'll be a failed raid,' Patrick said. 'We need to allow them to get away, follow them and hope they bolt for Saint Ed's.'

'That's a real risk,' Terry said. 'They might head for Peru.'

'I know. I don't think James'll go for it.'

'Please tell me again that that ghastly man's dead,' Dawn requested quietly.

'Dead,' Terry told her. 'Think of stones, door nails and dodos. I saw him, on the floor with three bullets in him.'

She was overtaken by tears and he put his arms around her.

The doorbell rang and before I could move Patrick rose, stiffly, and went to answer it. I was pretty sure that he was drawing his Glock as he left the room. He returned with James Carrick.

I introduced him to Dawn who, embarrassed by her tears, had been all for fleeing to the annexe but had been persuaded to stay.

'Delighted to meet you, Mrs Meadows,' he said. 'I'm also happy that you're here so you can be witness to the closure of this appalling case.'

If you're at a loss for a graceful and uplifting remark, consult a Highland Scot.

He said, 'I apologize for intruding but felt I had to come over due to the latest developments.'

'Whisky,' Patrick decided. 'If any situation called for it, this does.'

This was duly attended to, all round.

'They're going in at two a.m.,' the DCI said after taking a sip. 'With back-up from an armed support unit. Patrick, you say you didn't glimpse the individual with the shotgun. Were any of the other men you saw openly armed?'

'No, but obviously that doesn't mean there aren't any weapons on the premises,' Patrick replied. 'My question is what are you going to charge them with? The Graveses haven't really broken their conditions of bail and we have absolutely no evidence to point to the other man being who we think he is. It would be a good idea if you let at least one of them escape and tail him.'

But I could tell that Carrick, still fired up, was having none of it as Highland Scots can be stubborn too. There was further discussion during which he outlined plans for the raid. Some of his tactics were argued against, politely, by Patrick, who not only related everything he had learned about the place during the day but went on to emphasize that he had bad feelings about the plan. But to no avail, and finally Carrick assured him that he would follow all correct procedures and left.

'I really, really hope you're not going on this raid,' I said to Patrick.

'Not a chance. If I can't have a hand in the planning I don't want anything to do with it.'

It would emerge later that the raid had been a disaster. Even before the two squad cars and the armed support unit's vehicle came to a halt at the front of the house there was a blaze of security lights, just as had occurred when we had seen the dark car arrive there. A siren howled. Then, around the side of the house several men appeared and raked the arrivals with fire from semi-automatic machine guns. The armed support unit personnel, now sheltering behind their car, returned fire but two of them had been wounded, one seriously. Two gunmen fell – the others kept on firing until only one of them remained standing. He ran back out of sight.

Up until then it had been impossible for an order to be given to enter the house but before any decisions were made a large black van drove from around the other side of the building. Someone in the front passenger seat of the cab opened fire with another rapid-firing weapon and then the vehicle sped away. At the entrance to the drive it rammed another squad car that was just arriving, sending it hurtling into a ditch.

Two police officers had been killed and five wounded – three seriously, including the DI in charge, Lynn Outhwaite.

A disaster.

ELEVEN

It was a quiet night and Patrick, attuned to such things, heard the gunfire. He leapt out of bed, waking me, put the bedside light on, got dressed – that is, threw on his clothes – and disappeared. A short time later I heard the Range Rover start up and drive away. Wide awake now, I stayed where I was for a minute or so, worried, and then also got up. Would they escape the police and come here?

In my pyjamas I dashed downstairs, switched on a couple of small lamps and took the Smith and Wesson from the drawer of John's desk. Grabbing a blanket from the conservatory, I wrapped it around myself and then curled up on a sofa in the living room, facing the door into the hall but able to see if any of the security lights to the rear of the house came on. Other than windows that could be forced, that was a weak spot. The front door definitely wasn't as it was the original one, a sturdy chunk of English oak with various locks and bolts. We tend to use the conservatory entrance after dark for the simple reason that it is easier.

The room was still warm as the open fire had been alight, the grate behind the guard a heap of glowing wood ash. I got up and put another couple of logs on it. It was very quiet except for the soft ticking of clocks; no one else seemed to have been disturbed by what had happened. If I hadn't felt so raw inside with tension and my ribs weren't aching so much it would have been quite pleasant. It suddenly occurred to me that we would have no choice but to move; there were too many horrible memories here now. But where would we go?

I woke with a start to a whispered 'Ingrid?' and saw Patrick looking down at me. He gently removed the weapon from my limp fingers and then seated himself on the other end of the sofa and put his head in his hands. I realized with a shock that he was crying. All I could do was move closer so I could put the blanket around the pair of us. He was shivering.

'It was my fault,' he finally managed to say.

'Tell me what happened,' I said.

He told me. The bare details but not everything he had witnessed. I could see that all too clearly in my mind's eye: the blood, the suffering, human bodies smashed by high-velocity bullets. This man used to be a soldier but that didn't make it any easier.

'It *wasn't* your fault,' I told him.

'I should have put forward a plan of my own, a proper military-style proven strategy that wouldn't have resulted in them heading into their own bloodbath.' Again, he wept.

'You did try and warn him but James still wouldn't have agreed to it. You know that he can be very pig-headed and although you're friends he sometimes resents having you around as you were so senior in the army and have seriously got in his hair in the past.'

Patrick didn't appear to have heard what I said. 'I don't think Lynn's going to live.'

Neither of us said any more – we just sat there under the blanket until I looked up and realized that it was almost seven a.m. The children would soon be up and I needed to prepare their breakfasts.

'Tea,' I said softly in Patrick's ear as I got up.

He looked up from where he had seemingly been sunk in depression and although he said nothing I knew exactly what he was going to do. Then he left the room, stiffly, still sore from where he had fallen out of the tree.

Carrick had attended what amounted to crisis meetings and the stress of those and the horror of the early-morning raid were mirrored on his face. I had phoned and asked him if he needed our presence in any capacity and he had replied that we were welcome to call in at the nick later in the morning. This we did at eleven thirty.

'God, I could do with a drink,' the DCI muttered as he came along the corridor towards his office.

Patrick, surely of like mind, made no response and the three of us traipsed into the room and seated ourselves. Silence fell.

'I should have taken your advice,' Carrick said.

There was nothing either of us could say in reply to this either and the silence continued.

Patrick broke it by saying, 'It won't help you at all but I have every intention of sorting this out. I shall break all the rules and probably the law but I don't care. While whoever was responsible for that outrage, Graves, that Grünberg character – if it is him – and his surviving lowlife scum are alive, Ingrid, my mother, our children and Meadows and his family aren't safe. That's already been demonstrated several times at the rectory.'

'You might end up losing your job and in prison,' Carrick warned him. 'For a very long time.'

'I could handle that, easily, if I knew they were all safe. They're more important than me.'

I gazed at the boy I had fallen in love with at school and tears misted my eyes.

There was a knock at the door and after Carrick had bade whoever it was enter, Potts came in.

'I think I've discovered something important,' he said, not seeming too happy about it.

Carrick waved him to a spare chair.

'It's not good,' the DI muttered.

'Spit it out, man,' Carrick said.

'I've been concentrating on trying to find the murder victim's – Mannering's – ex-wife,' he began. 'Yesterday – and I won't go into the rather complicated details of how I found her – I succeeded. She's living near Trowbridge running a dog-grooming business from home, more of a hobby than anything else, I gathered. I contacted her – her name's Gloria and she's sticking to Hardy as a surname – and asked her to come and formally identify her ex-husband. She seemed only too pleased – didn't know he was dead and said, "Whoopee!" But it would have to be tomorrow, today now, as she was very busy. She then said that if I arranged for her to be collected and brought back home she'd do it first thing. I did as she asked as it's not that far. It's not him.'

'Not him?' Carrick gasped.

'No, it's his brother, Lionel.'

'Bloody hell,' Patrick whispered.

'Apparently they were always close and both changed their names to Mannering after Julian tried to play crooks and went to jail, her words, as a ploy to avoid the media and adverse publicity. But Lionel was the car-mad one – he had the heart op and drank like a fish so the liver cancer PM finding fits too.'

'But the hospital records show that the man who had the op was called Julian Mannering,' Carrick argued.

'Gloria thinks it very likely they colluded,' Potts continued. 'In her view they've always been underhand and secretive too. Julian was loaded, and could easily have given his brother, who was always broke, a load of dosh to use his name so he himself could disappear without trace.'

'Do brothers have the same DNA?' I asked.

'I went into that a bit too. It appears that they may share DNA markers if the parents of both are the same people so an ordinary test wouldn't necessarily be able to differentiate between individual siblings. Further testing would be required.'

'OK,' the DCI said, reaching for his phone. 'Further testing it shall be. We must be absolutely sure.'

He arranged for it to be done and then, not for the first time that morning, conducted a short debriefing. Of the five police officers wounded, three seriously, one had been discharged from hospital with a hand injury. He had been driving the squad car that had been knocked into the ditch. His colleague was uninjured. Another had been shot in the arm and remained in hospital but his wound was not regarded as life-changing. Of the three seriously hurt, Lynn Outhwaite was in intensive care having undergone surgery and her chances were regarded as fifty/fifty as she had been hit twice. Carrick had asked if he could visit her but this had been refused. Injuries to the remaining two, one a sergeant, were serious but not life-threatening. The DCI intended to visit as many of these personnel as soon as he could after he'd left the nick before he went home this evening. The two dead were a constable in his twenties and another a little older.

It went without saying that a nationwide manhunt had imme-diately been put into operation and the police were hoping that the one wounded member of the ambush who had survived would be a source of information. No one was counting on this – he was badly hurt, might not survive and as soon as he had regained consciousness after surgery gave every impression of being in a semi-vegetative state.

'I'd like to visit the crime scene again,' Patrick said. He turned to me. 'Yes?'

I nodded. 'Yes.'

'That's where I'm heading right now so come along,' Carrick said. 'You might be interested to know that they were squatting there – they'd smashed their way in. I'm still trying to find out who it really belongs to.' He turned to Potts, thanked him for his efforts and told him he was in charge while he himself was out.

Perhaps the DI would have preferred to come with us but if so, he hid his disappointment well.

As one would expect, The Spinney was crowded with scenes-of-crime personnel, the entire area in front of the house cordoned off. This was the methodical, careful – plodding, if you like – work that has to be done. The house represented weeks, if not months, of effort, here, in labs and in offices. All those present would be burning with anger but had to channel it into concentrating on what they were doing.

We had given Carrick a lift and the three of us were able to make our way around the edge of the cordon. To get the full picture the three of us then looked at the exterior of the building, following the circular drive to the rear. It was bigger than at first would appear. On two floors but with several single-storey extensions at the back that were little more than cheaply built add-ons including a collapsing plastic-roofed 'conservatory', the place had little to commend it. I yearned to drive a bulldozer through the whole lot. Among the other outbuildings was a large open-fronted shed in which a Mercedes car was parked. Nearest to the house, a range of brick buildings that looked as though they might have been the stables and carriage house or cart shed mentioned by Patrick were in better condition. This area, he told us, was where he had seen men hanging around. The stables were on two floors, the upper one accommodation in the past for grooms perhaps and from an end window there, he added, it would be possible to see who was coming down the entrance track. They had obviously posted a look-out.

'The house is being searched but so far nothing particularly interesting has been found,' Carrick said when we returned to the front. 'I suggest we take a look inside for ourselves.'

We put on anti-contamination suits and then went in. Lights had been rigged up in some of the rooms, scenes-of-crime personnel working here too. These did not dispel what I can only call the deadness of the place, an almost tangible manifestation of the general gloom and cold. This was indeed an old house and there didn't seem to be much in the way of radiators to heat it. Truly, it was the kind of place that meant I immediately found myself wondering how many people had been done to death here, how many hanged from the gnarled trees of the overgrown and ancient orchard during the political and religious turmoil of England's past.

Carrick said, 'I'm told it's a real labyrinth in here with a much older section in the middle complete with panelled walls and narrow twisting staircases.'

We then maintained a grim silence as we walked from room to room. There was nothing to say as we saw the dirt, dust, rubbish, remains of takeaway food rotting on tables and, in the kitchen, piles of unwashed mugs, empty wine and spirit bottles tossed into corners and evidence of drug-taking.

'Pigs,' Carrick muttered. 'Filthy pigs. It's just like Mannering's place, isn't it? Apparently the outbuildings where the henchmen shacked up are even worse. No toilets over there so they just used corners.'

We drifted apart, the men going upstairs, and I went through a narrow doorway, using my torch, into what must be the even older part of the house, a series of tiny dark rooms with linen-fold panelling and carved, embossed ceilings. One had a large open fireplace with iron firedogs, ashes still in the grate. It was cleaner here – modern low life had perhaps found it too claustrophobic, 'posh', spooky even. This was the original Elizabethan house and, to my eyes, and even without windows – what had happened to them? – it was beautiful. There was no furniture other than an old horsehair sofa with the bottom falling out and, incongruously, a small fridge, not working as there were no electrical sockets.

In one corner of the room with the fireplace a tiny twisting staircase led upwards, possibly set into the thickness of the original walls. I went up trying to ignore the cobwebs. These looked as though they had been around during the reign of Elizabeth the First as well and I told myself that their occupants had almost certainly died long ago of starvation. I didn't search for any survivors though.

Thus do writers' minds wander even during the most serious moments.

I came into the first of what appeared to be two little rooms separated by an archway. This one had a small window, the thick glass having tiny bubbles in it. Through layers of dirt, I looked out. Below was a yard open to the sky that was full of rank weeds and completely boxed in by walls. I could imagine a tiny garden there at one time that had been surrounded, destroyed, when the house was extended.

'Modern planning regulations do have their uses,' I muttered to myself.

The second of the rooms was almost exactly the same as the first, but the window in this was lower and set in an embrasure that had the remains of a padded seat in it. Then, somewhere in the house, there was a sudden commotion, a woman shrieking and the sound of quite a few feet pounding on boards. The whole pantomime seemed to be coming in my direction. Seconds later I heard someone come thumping up the staircase and then the woman I had known as Natasha Graves burst through the doorway I had just come through, applied the brakes when she saw me, staggered for a few steps, regained her balance and then went for me like something demented, yelling abuse.

I do not fight women. It gets very nasty with screaming, hair pulling, nail-raking – seriously horrid. So I just evaded her initial rush at me and lightly clipped her on the jaw, husbandly tuition paying off, and she went down with a crash like a dead donkey. Then I waited for back-up to arrive, which it did very quickly actually.

'I'll have you for assault, you bitch!' the woman shrieked at me when she was hauled to her feet.

Solemnly, Carrick arrested her for being an accessory to murder and took her into custody.

Apparently the room she had been hiding in was little more than a very large cupboard, most of the space being taken up with wooden and cardboard boxes, one of the latter she had obviously been sitting on as the top was squashed down, which also suggested that it wasn't full. It had already been opened. More guns. Modern ones.

Patrick and I left the investigating team to deal with it all.

The experience of being taken to Bath police station again with a much more serious charge against her caused the one-time member of parliament for Harlsbury North, Mo Burrwood, to come clean, sing like a canary, cough, whichever hackneyed expression anyone preferred. This was gratifying to Patrick and me as it meant that those who had been the victims of some of her activities could be present the following morning to hear what she had to say, but again, only as observers.

The woman was fairly neat and tidy, considering, and it was noticeable that the dark brown hair had been dyed and was growing out as it was blonde at the roots. Judging by the redness of her eyes she had been doing rather a lot of crying and I wondered if we were going to get a 'poor little me' scenario. Or perhaps having said that she was about to reveal all would change her mind and metaphorically spit in our faces.

She listened impassively while Carrick dealt with the preliminaries and listed the charges, her gaze flicking over the pair of us when he mentioned the observers, gave Potts a hard stare and her solicitor, a Mr Jonathan Fielding, a stern-looking individual grey of suit, tie and visage, a tiny smile.

No, poppet, he's not going to get you off, I thought.

'Are you married to Simon Graves?' Carrick asked by way of a warm-up question.

'I am *not*,' she snapped.

'You posed as his wife.'

'That was his idea. You can't turn up in backward little

villages in the middle of nowhere saying you plan to live there and expect much of a welcome if you're not.'

'So you lived with him?'

'Only for the purposes of the job. If you're really too coy to ask me if we went to bed together the answer's definitely no, we didn't. I wouldn't have slept with him if he'd paid me.' Another little smile twitched at her mouth. 'It put an edge on his general demeanour, though, the fact that I wouldn't, and made him even more poisonous than he is normally.'

'Why did you operate with him then?'

'Because I was *paid* to,' Burrwood answered as though speaking to an idiot.

'Who paid you?'

'Some character calling himself Herman Grünberg. I've no idea whether that's his real name or not.'

'Did he pay well?' Potts asked.

She looked at him as though he was something she had just found stuck to the bottom of her shoe. 'Very well.'

No, it appeared that she was now going to present herself as the sorely tried ex-public servant from an impeccable background. The effect was of a *very* down-market version of Penelope Keith.

Carrick said, 'Although you didn't know them personally you went to Hinton Littlemoor for no other purpose than to put a lot of pressure on National Crime Agency personnel who lived there.'

'Do we have to talk about this? I admit that. It's irrelevant – just a job.'

'All right. Tell us about The Spinney.'

'Grünberg was squatting there. He said he didn't know who the owner was but I didn't actually believe him as he lied about everything. Perhaps he didn't want to admit to owning such a dump and had lost all the keys. He has quite a lot of drop-outs and other yobs working for him who lived in the outbuildings so the place was convenient. Some of them shoplifted or busked in Bath for money during the day. It saved him from having to pay them too much. Sometimes they all went into Bristol at night and went on mass mugging sprees.'

Carrick made a note of that, no doubt solving quite a few crimes for his Bristol colleagues at a stroke. 'Ms Burrwood, how the hell did you get mixed up with people like that?'

'I needed money and a man by the name of Julian Mannering introduced me to him. And before you ask I'll tell you that I met *him* when I was an MP, at a drinks party – years ago. He seemed to have fingers in quite a lot of pies, some of them not at all legal. That kind of thing has always interested me.'

I was glad that she had forced a change in the direction of the questioning before the ice-capped volcano seated beside me erupted after her statement that harassing Elspeth was 'just a job'.

'Mannering was murdered recently,' Carrick said in conversational tones.

'Was he? I don't know the first thing about that. Among his other activities, I understand he was an arms dealer who had contact with someone in a mid-European country. It might have been a woman but I know absolutely nothing about that either so it's no use your questioning me about it. She, or he, sent over weapons of some kind hidden in consignments of this and that and, again, I wasn't told any details and didn't want to know. The more you know the more dangerous it is in that game.'

'You were sitting on a box of handguns in that box room,' the DCI observed.

'Was I? How exciting,' she said in a bored voice.

'D'you reckon Grünberg could have had Mannering killed?' Potts asked.

'Quite likely. The man *was* being a damned nuisance.'

'In what way?'

'I gather that he kept wanting more money. Or said he couldn't get a consignment when he'd previously said he could. Grünberg was losing patience and once did mention to me that he was thinking of getting rid of him.' She shrugged. 'Perhaps he did want him out of the way, I don't know. He was rather obnoxious.'

'And I suppose you didn't know about the precautions that were taken at The Spinney in the event of a police raid.'

'I knew that some of the men were armed but that's all really.'

Her offhand manner clearly infuriated the DCI. 'Two police officers were killed and five injured, three seriously, yesterday morning, one of whom is on life support. You don't seem to find that of particular concern.'

'Of course it's of concern. But this man's a professional criminal. Such things ought to be expected.'

'But at no stage did you consider it your duty to report what was going on. You just needed the money.'

She smiled at him as though he had finally solved an easy riddle. 'That's right.'

'You don't appear to be feeling any remorse at all.'

'No, why should I?'

'May I put a couple of questions to her?' I requested.

'Go ahead,' Carrick replied. 'As long as they're about the part of the investigation that we're at present discussing.'

'Did you hide or did they leave you behind?' I asked this ghastly woman.

'Oh, I hid. The firing woke me up. I had a sleeping bag in a room upstairs, you know – and locked the door.'

'So other than pretending to be Simon Graves' wife, you haven't actually played a part in any of this.'

'No, that's why it's so monstrous that I'm being charged at all. Pretending to be someone you aren't isn't necessarily a crime and I'm going to fully cooperate with your enquiries.'

'Lovely,' I enthused. 'In that case tell us everything you know about Saint Edwina's so-called mission.'

'That was Simon's side of things. I haven't a clue what goes on there.'

'She's lying,' Patrick said to Carrick in little more than a whisper. 'As someone trained by Army Intelligence to know when people aren't telling the truth I can say emphatically that she's not only lying but played a much bigger role in that criminal outfit than she's making out. I wouldn't be surprised if she isn't running it. I think she hid hoping not to be found when the others bolted for freedom. If discovered and arrested she could play the innocent, or be overlooked and make her

escape when it got light. Free this woman on bail and that's
the last you'll see of her.'

'I object,' said Mr Fielding. 'This man is only present as
an observer.'

Carrick frowned. 'Yes, but I'm at liberty to listen to advice
offered by anyone. Mr Gillard wasn't addressing the accused.'

'I'm *not* lying!' Burrwood said furiously.

'We weren't quite straight with you just now,' the DCI said
to her. 'It was Mannering's brother, Lionel, who was murdered
recently. We think that, temporarily or permanently, he was
paid to assume Julian's identity. But you probably know that,
and about the illegal weapons concealed in the house. Whether
he paid for the house and the car business out of money given
to him by Julian will be part of our investigation.'

'This is all Greek to me,' Burrwood said unconvincingly
with a little shrug.

'Where is this Julian Mannering?'

'Where? How the hell would I know?'

'He's wealthy – very. It's known that he bought into one,
or even two, criminal enterprises. I'm of the opinion that one
of them is Saint Edwina's and the mission it's supposed to
run is a front for serious crime.'

He was on thin ice here as we only had the gut feelings of
a few people instead of evidence.

Scornfully, our suspect said, 'The mission is perfectly
genuine. Anyway, the police raided the place and found absolutely nothing.'

'How do you know that?'

'Oh, er, Simon told me.'

'How did he know?'

'Well, I expect he's in contact with someone there.'

'Grünberg?'

'I expect so.'

'Ms Burrwood, you've just said that Grünberg's a professional
criminal and now it would appear he's involved with the
perfectly genuine mission. Would you care to clarify that?'

'No comment.'

'I'm coming to the conclusion that Julian Mannering is
heavily involved as well.'

'No comment.'

'Is that where they all went when they escaped?'

'I've no idea.'

Patrick sighed loudly and muttered something inaudible.

'You're a real smart arse, aren't you?' Burrwood raged at him.

I wasn't watching him but guessed that she was then in receipt of one of his death's head smiles.

Softly, he said, 'Madam, you're not the first person to throw that at me. The others were guilty as hell too.'

'I want this man out of the room!' the solicitor said loudly. 'He is putting undue pressure on my client.'

Carrick gestured, ton-of-bricks style, that he should leave.

Patrick got to his feet and said to him, 'You might like to ask her why she's wearing the signet ring with a green stone in it that I last saw on the hand of the man then referred to as Sir Julian Hardy. It was at Hartwood castle actually and I noticed it just before he gave the order to his thugs to kill us.'

Amazingly, the woman really lost it and screamed at him, 'And he would have succeeded if it hadn't been for that bastard who ratted on him and turned out to be working for you! I know all about it. He's next, we know where he lives and Julian won't rest until you're all bloody *dead*!'

Patrick turned to give her a lascivious wink and then went out, quietly closing the door.

The once Right Honourable Member burst into a storm of tears.

TWELVE

The accused was given a short break from the questioning and the four law enforcers went to Carrick's office where he presided regally over his coffee machine. I noticed that he kept sliding glances in Patrick's direction. As soon as we were settled, Potts' phone rang and he had to leave as he was needed back at Radstock.

'You have a dreadful effect on people,' Carrick said to Patrick, handing out coffee.

Patrick just smiled wordlessly.

How do you explain the inexplicable? The ability just to sit quietly in a room and make others feel uncomfortable or furiously angry is something that he might have been born with. On occasion, dripping malice while questioning suspects, usually violent criminals, my own husband can be too big, too close and too damned dangerous.

'As it would appear they're in danger you'd better keep Meadows and his wife and daughter under the protection you already have at home,' Carrick then said. 'To be frank, I don't know what to do with him and shall have to get advice. OK, he assisted an offender, he removed the murder weapon and ammunition from the scene of the crime and disposed of them, he wasted police time. Meanwhile, we've discovered an awful lot about the far more important criminal contacts of the murder victim's brother so one can argue that he didn't really waste much police time at all. To bring the man to trial seems counter-productive and another waste of public money. But, as you know, that decision won't be in my hands.'

'And, don't forget,' Patrick said, 'a lot of the background info to the case is covered by the Official Secrets Act and, if we catch the other lot, will be *sub judice* as well until after they've been tried.'

The DCI pondered and then said, 'I'll have to charge the old lady though.'

'Where is she?' I asked.

'A place was found for her in a secured safe house. She's in the company of a couple of young female immigrants, one of whom is pregnant and not very well, their status not known right now, who were arrested for shoplifting.'

We finished our coffee and then the questioning of Burrwood continued. Patrick remained somewhere else but I was permitted to return – we needed first-hand knowledge of what else she had to say, if anything.

'Right,' Carrick said to her. 'You've as good as admitted that you're deeply involved with this criminal set-up and it will help your case if you cooperate. Was that ring you're wearing given to you by Julian Hardy, as he was then?'

Burrwood, who was still sniffing and dabbing at her eyes, looked at Fielding. He said nothing and was probably thinking about lunch. The woman then removed the ring and placed it across the table in front of the DCI. Having related what she had done for the benefit of the recording, he picked it up and examined it.

'It has the initials JWH on it,' he said, again for the recording.

'I'm so glad you can read,' said Burrwood icily. 'Julian William Hardy, only it appears to be Mannering now. We married when he came out of prison after his wife divorced him and I think I've been regretting it ever since. It's why I've reverted to my maiden name.'

For a few moments I had to admit a certain grudging admiration for her – she had her back to the wall and could still bitch. But then again . . .

'You were the woman named in the divorce then,' Carrick said, giving back the ring.

'I was. But she was mad, dog mad actually. Julian can't stand the bloody things and she filled the house with them. He said some of them had worms and used to wipe their backsides on the carpets. I have to say that I've discovered Julian's personal habits aren't really much of an improvement on that.'

Carrick leaned both elbows on the table. 'No more evading tactics. Where did that mob at The Spinney head for?'

'Back to HQ, I should imagine.'

'And where's that?'

'Not a clue.'

I said, 'Detective Chief Inspector, you might ask the suspect why, as she seems to detest her spouse now, she still continues to wear his ring.'

'Yes, why?' Carrick prompted.

'Well, I suppose I just forget to take it off,' said Burrwood. 'Does she *have* to be in here?'

'Yes, she does,' Carrick answered shortly.

'You do realize that she hit me.'

'I gather that was to prevent you from hitting her. You're lying and wasting my time. A short spell in a remand centre might help you to decide to tell the truth.'

There was a knock on the door and it was Patrick. 'An urgent call for you, sir,' he said.

Carrick muttered, 'Damn,' and rose. 'Keep an eye on her, would you? Your assistant wouldn't be able to stop her if she made a run for it.'

'The pair of you are only underlings then,' said Burrwood with a sly smile when he'd gone.

'If you like,' Patrick said, taking Carrick's seat. 'I've been reprimanded and told to not exceed my brief.'

'That fool Dando said you gave yourself huge airs.'

'Definitely a fool,' Patrick agreed.

'And I'm not going to answer any questions you ask me. You infuriated and frightened me last time and I'm glad you've been slapped down.' She turned away from him. 'You won't let him, will you, Jonathan?'

'Er, no,' said the solicitor, looking worried and quite likely thinking the same as me, that she wasn't quite right in the head.

'I have remembered something, though,' Patrick said. 'Funny you should mention the Dandos – who, by the way, have been selling you so far down the river that you'll probably end up floating in the Bristol Channel. What I'm going to say next is right off the record as I'm not officially allowed to mention things that affected me personally and it won't be allowed in a court of law. When you and Simon Graves promised them a house, a car, money and God knows what else to get a certain lady out of her home, he said something about Saint Edwina's being bigger than it looked. When I learned that at the time I took it to be bragging on his part but it occurs to me that some of the premises might be hidden behind false walls or it has extensive attics. Any comments?'

'No,' Burrwood said. 'None.'

Fielding cleared his throat. 'I think, Ms Burrwood, that you ought to consider telling the truth. It will be much better for you in the long run and no amount of losing your temper and crocodile tears will help.'

'Crocodile tears!' she blared at him. 'You're supposed to be on my side!'

'But regretfully, madam, I have appointments with other clients,' came the smooth reply. 'You must understand that I can't help you through a fog of deceit. We can prepare your defence at a later date.'

Weren't these the kind of remarks usually made during private discussions between legal representatives and suspects? I asked myself.

She turned her ire on Patrick. 'All right, nasty little underling. I can't stand any of them and that's the truth. That phoney mission *is* a front for Julian's criminal activities. The building was used by some spy network or other during the Second World War that was discovered and they were all shot, no questions asked. Nothing was ever made public; it was all covered up as things were then. There are old wine cellars and other basement rooms that Julian uses for storing weapons and stolen property. I understand that it's quite extensive.'

'Have you been down there?' Patrick asked.

'No, I hate confined spaces.'

'How does one access it?'

'I'm not at all sure but it might be down through a trapdoor in the old kitchen.' She sniffed loudly. 'I wouldn't be surprised if he isn't doing the same thing. You know, in contact with a foreign power, selling secrets.' She added derisively, 'The idiot probably fancies himself as a master spy.'

'Where might one find Mannering if he's not at this place?'

'I've no idea.'

'You lived with him there then.'

'No! That's an absolute dump too!'

'So where *did* you live?'

'In hotels.'

If Patrick thought this a lie he made no comment, saying instead, 'You were thought to have suspect contacts at one time.'

'It depends what you mean by "suspect".'

'You know what I mean. Career criminals, industrial spies in the pay of other countries, people who used to be referred to as traitors.'

'How the hell did you get to know that anyway?'

'MI5 told me.'

'You'll be telling me that you work for them next.'

'I do – sometimes. And I'm all in favour of people like you being shot, no questions asked. Who knows?'

Her face went the colour of dirty chalk but Patrick didn't witness this as he had got up and walked out.

'That was a good ruse of yours,' Carrick said. 'Is she suffering from what I'll politely call diminished responsibility?'

'Yes,' Patrick and I said together.

'You can call me "sir" any time you like,' Carrick added and then laughed, not something he does very often on duty. 'Oh, by the way, they think Lynn's out of danger. I've just called the hospital and a nurse on her ward told me that although she's very weak she'd welcome a female visitor as she's embarrassed by all the tubes and so forth in places where she'd rather not have them and doesn't want blokes seeing her.'

I said I would go that afternoon.

'Now we have this lead I shall have to get Mike Greenway involved,' Patrick said. 'He's the one with links to the Met if this place is going to be raided again and I need to brief him first.'

'Carry on. I'll get a copy made of the recording from Burrwood's interview and you can send it to him.'

We took it personally instead, travelling up by train very early the next morning. I had made no comment following Patrick's saying that he was still involved with MI5. How

else had Charles Dixon got all that information? It did not
rankle either that he hadn't made the situation clear to me,
for what Burrwood had said about the danger of knowing
too much applied to this too. And I don't care what rabid
female equality wonks throw at me – most men are wired
to protect their women and children and to challenge that is
not only futile but stupid.

Something similar might have been going through Patrick's
mind, for when we had raided the buffet car for breakfast –
coffee and toasted cheese sandwiches – he said, 'Sorry that
you're a bit of a Watson at the moment.'

'It's the way of things now,' I said.

Lynn had obviously still been very poorly but youth and
a strong constitution were on her side. Her parents were due
to travel down from the north of England to visit her but
had been held up by a rail strike at their end. I had left her
wondering whether she would want to continue with her
career in the police. Her recovery time would be protracted
– months.

When we got to his office, Greenway listened to the
recording impassively but I knew he was pleased: if nothing
else, it vindicated both him and his staff.

'D'you reckon she's bonkers?' he said, switching off the
machine.

'Greed, ruthlessness and diminished responsibility on a
grand scale just about sums her up,' I said. 'She's a bit of
a psychopath really.'

There was a short silence during which I got the impression the commander wrestled with either common sense or
his conscience, or even both.

'I'm reluctant to get the Met to raid that place again
without prior surveillance,' he said. 'There might be an
action replay of last time – or even an action replay of what
happened in Somerset. I simply can't take the risk.'

'Then I volunteer to undertake that surveillance,' Patrick
said.

'Not on your own you can't.'

'I can. I reckon I can establish in a twenty-four-hour period
what exactly is going on there.'

To his credit, Greenway didn't argue with this as he is fully aware of Patrick's experience working for Special Forces and MI5. He pondered further, toying with the brightly coloured paperclips with which he makes patterns on his desk when he is thinking. Finally, he scooped up the lot in his big hands and poured them back into the small antique Chinese bowl in which they otherwise reside.

'OK,' he said. 'Twenty-four hours. And for God's sake don't kill anyone or come back in a long box.'

'You're mad,' I whispered as we were leaving the building, having not wished to make any comments inside. After working for MI5 I'm constantly mindful of long ears and hidden microphones. But not in the NCA HQ, surely. No? All right, no.

'It's the only way forward,' Patrick insisted.

'You said your days of pretending to be a fencing contractor or investigating reported gas leaks were over,' I persisted. 'Besides which, you'll be recognized.'

'Trust me.'

We hadn't discussed it in depth but I knew this would be Patrick's last assignment. He would resign. Financially, we could manage and I knew that he would get another job, a boring nine-to-five one if necessary and probably locally, in Bath or Bristol. Gone were the times when we used to set off together to undertake dangerous surveillance; there would be no more creeping around on rooftops, watching the homes of criminal suspects from a building across the street or, later, storm into those houses, firearms at the ready. When the odious Simon Graves and the real Julian Mannering were behind bars the threat to our family would be lifted. What part the 'squatting' Herman Grünberg played was anyone's guess – mine was that he merely hired the lowlife support, perhaps a kind of roving mobster forced into a nomad existence by the attentions of the police.

I went home alone, the thing I dread. I had done it too many times before and there was always the thought that I wouldn't see Patrick alive again, ever. This time though I told myself it would be the last time, we would be a more 'normal' family and he could direct his talents towards the children who were increasingly needing his presence at home more often. I was trying not to think what he would do for the next twenty-four hours and could only hope that what information he did gain could be used by the Metropolitan Police to enable them to conduct a successful raid this time. The existence of cellars was worrying though.

'Any news?' Terry asked when I got home to find yet more snow.

I brought him up to date including the information gleaned from Burrwood's questioning.

'I ought to be there, with him,' he muttered.

'You can't,' I said. 'You'll break your bail conditions.'

'We didn't worry about things like that when we worked for D12 though, did we?'

'But we don't now so you mustn't torture yourself.'

He went away, looking very unhappy.

As usual at such times I threw myself into domestic activities but took both my personal and work mobile phones everywhere with me. It salved my conscience to take over the cooking as Carrie and Terry had been doing it between them. I busied myself all through the rest of that day, jumping out of my skin every time any mobile or the house phone rang. *This is the last time, the last time*, was going round and round in my mind until I felt that I was going demented.

I went to bed later than usual because Katie wasn't well with a heavy cold and earache, and I sat up with her until a hot-water bottle and medicine had soothed her off to sleep. I didn't sleep for hours, wracked with nerves, and when I finally did I was woken at around six a.m. when my personal mobile rang.

'Patrick?' I said, half-asleep.

'No, it's Mike,' said Greenway's voice.

'Please tell me it isn't bad news,' I begged.

'I'm afraid it is – in a way.'

'What d'you mean, in a way? Is he hurt?'

'No, except for a grazed hand. So far I've only had the barest details but it looks as though he got in there, somehow locked most of those there in a storeroom and then shot dead the rest.'

For a moment, my vision greyed.

'Needless to say, he's been relieved of his duties pending investigations,' Greenway went on. 'Ingrid, I'll do everything I can to help.'

'I'm coming back,' I told him.

'By all means.'

'Who reported it?' I asked before we rang off.

'He did.'

I went downstairs and made myself tea and toast.

'You OK?' Terry said, putting his head round the kitchen door as I fed the kittens. 'Sorry, I was wide awake and heard someone moving around.'

I told him what had happened and he swore quietly. 'I should have been there,' he went on to say helplessly.

'In which case you'd be in custody – again,' I snapped and then apologized.

'I'll come with you to London if that's where you're headed.'

'You can't. No, think of Dawn and Emma and the others. I desperately need you here in case there are any repercussions. And we must keep James Carrick on side. He's a friend but also a very good cop and won't hesitate to throw the book at you if you skip bail.'

I gave him a mug of tea and went upstairs to get dressed.

Commander Greenway called me again when I was on the train – I didn't trust myself to drive safely having had hardly any sleep – and said he intended to visit the scene of the shootings. He would give me a lift there if I went to HQ first and I gladly accepted. It was only after the call that I really started to try to work out what had happened. Given what had been going on recently, it made perfect sense. Patrick had said he would 'sort it out', breaking the law if necessary. He always means what he says but that he would take such a drastic course of action hadn't occurred to me. He'd sorted it out then and would probably go to prison for a long time. But his wife and family would be safe. We would move house and wait for him.

I shed some tears and an elderly couple in seats across the aisle gazed at me sympathetically for a moment and then tactfully looked away.

I could imagine news of the incident already blaring from the media headlines: *Cop Goes on Killing Spree. Nunnery Raided by Rogue Cop – Nuns Raped. Mass Murder at London Holy Site.* But I had no time to waste at Paddington to look for a newspaper stand and hurried to find a taxi. That I could discover everything I wanted to know about it from my smart phone didn't occur to me just then – I was too upset and aching all over with tension.

Greenway was waiting for me in the large entrance lobby, understandably looking grim. 'I should have expected this,' he muttered. 'Did he give you any inkling?'

'Almost right from the time I met him I've had alarming inklings about Patrick,' I replied. 'But he did tell DCI Carrick he'd sort it out, breaking the law if necessary, and James warned him he'd lose his job and go to prison. Patrick's been haunted that his family would never be safe while these people are on the loose. As you said yourself, they're his leftovers from MI5.'

When we were settled on the back seat of the waiting car, Greenway said, 'Does he still have connections with MI5?'

'Yes.'

'Do you know if there are any national security connections with this affair?'

'Not to my certain knowledge but the Burrwood woman was on security committees. She said in the interview, if you remember, that she wouldn't be surprised if Mannering wasn't following in the footsteps of people who had a spy network in the basement of the so-called mission building during the war.'

'Who were all shot dead on the orders of the War Office. Yes, I've been doing a bit of research into the incident. If you don't mind my asking, where did you two meet?'

'At school. I was fifteen and Patrick eighteen and about to leave at the end of the summer term. He was head boy. Our fathers knew one another and Patrick was sent round to help me with my physics homework.'

'I call physics homework child cruelty.'

'He did most of it for me but deliberately made a couple of mistakes so the teacher wouldn't guess I hadn't done it.'

And now he had shot and killed a whole lot of people for me too.

I wanted to scream out my misery.

The road in front of the building had been closed in both directions, police cars even parked across the pavements on the approach to it. Greenway and I had no choice but to walk across one corner of the park opposite and, as on the last occasion I was here, we made our way through a thin crust of snow. It probably wasn't doing his expensive shoes a lot of good. We showed our IDs to a uniformed constable at the incident tape cordoned-off area, ducked under it and crossed the road, making our way through an amazing number of vehicles.

Someone recognized the commander and there was a flurry of activity to find the person in charge. This proved to be a DCI Jane Cunningham and she came out to us, a striking redhead who instantly reminded me of Carrick's wife, Joanna. Yes, she too, I thought, will be doing things like this one day.

'Good morning, sir,' said Cunningham.

Greenway introduced me.

'I understand Gillard is one of your personnel,' she said to him.

'Insofar as he's the NCA officer embedded in the Avon and Somerset force,' Greenway said.

She continued, 'At oh-three-hundred hours a report came in of a shooting here and—'

'Reported to whom?' Greenway interrupted. 'Nine-nine-nine? Restricted number? It wasn't reported to the NCA and I received the info second-hand.'

'It was the restricted Met number, sir, asking for support. Nine-nine-nine calls from local residents who had heard the shots followed.'

The one Patrick and I had used when we were besieged in the park.

'OK, go on.'

'Gillard was sitting in the office just inside the entrance and had apparently opened the large metal gates to let in the attending officers. A Glock 17 was on the receptionist's desk in front of him that he said was his. He appeared to be quite calm. A quick look round convinced the crew to call up more support and—'

'Only one car was sent to attend an in-house emergency call?' the commander queried.

'I understand there was another fairly serious incident locally at the same time in connection with a fight with knives outside a club.'

'All right, go on.'

'It quickly became apparent that there were multiple deaths, three in the area hallway beyond the entrance, another three in a room just this side of them and another in a basement that was accessed from a kitchen. All of these people appear to each have been killed with a single bullet.'

'Has the whole place been searched?'

'They're still working down in the cellars.'

'Did you find any nuns' clothing?'

She looked surprised. 'Yes, we did actually, sir – in a room upstairs.'

'Are the bodies still in situ?'

'They are.'

'Show me.'

Greenway turned to me. 'D'you want to come as well?'

I nodded.

'Was he under orders?' Cunningham asked.

'Not from me,' Greenway answered abruptly.

'Where is he now?'

'I don't know. I told him to stay away.'

We put on anti-contamination suits and followed her. I, of course, was familiar with the entrance and the office just inside that had been presided over by Melanie Hunter as well as the room on the other side of the two-way mirror. The corridor beyond, where the usual scenes-of-crime people and photographers were busy, was wide, perhaps once the imposing hallway of the original house, and as the DCI had said, was the site of three deaths. The bodies were lying close together, virtually in a heap. I looked and saw and there was no doubt at all in my mind as to the identity of the person who had fired the shots. In a word: clinical.

'Recognize any of them?' Greenway asked me in an undertone.

'I'm fairly sure they were three of the four who were referred to as security officers here. But I wouldn't be able to swear to it under oath.'

Another officer, busy making notes, had accompanied us but Cunningham didn't introduce him. In the room next to the reception office, to which we had to backtrack a little, a body was sprawled in an armchair I couldn't remember having seen on our first visit. It was of the man who had said he was the principal, Felix Yellen. At his feet another body lay on its back, a look of surprise on the features, a neat hole between the eyes. The third corpse had pitched face down so I couldn't see if I recognized him.

'All male?' the commander enquired of the DCI.

'Several women were all locked in a room in the cellars. There were mattresses on the floor and buckets that they'd had to use as toilets so they might have been in there for a while. I get the impression they were on the premises under duress but most of them are either too frightened to speak – terrified after all the shooting actually – or have no English. Trafficked probably to be forced into prostitution. We've searched upstairs and there are more rooms perhaps used for bona fide purposes as I understand this place offered accommodation. One woman managed to get us to understand that they were rounded up by a man with a gun. Whether that was your man only time will tell.'

'Indeed,' was all Greenway said. 'Lead on.'

'There were no men locked in cellars?' I asked. 'I thought that's what was said.'

'Oh, yes, sorry. Six of them. They weren't hurt. We've arrested them.'

'What about the women?'

'They've been taken to hospital for a check-up as they were all in poor shape. They'll be questioned of course but I can't see them being anything other than victims of whatever was going on here.'

She led the way down the corridor where there were several doors with *Private* signs on them, and then on through various rooms, one a canteen, another with rows of chairs like a meeting room, where nothing much was going on. The place seemed to be a muddle, perhaps because larger rooms had been divided by partitions. Then, emerging into a kitchen – if one can call an area with built-in wall cupboards, a bank of microwaves and a sink a kitchen – we came across more forensic staff emerging through a trapdoor in the floor.

'One deceased male down there, ma'am,' one of them reported.

We went down, Greenway going first so he could offer the females a hand as the wooden steps were damp and slippery, if not rotten in places. The smell of mould and mildew rose to greet us as we descended, and by the weak illumination provided by a single dirt-covered light bulb I could see that the walls were green and running with moisture. I remembered what DI Potts had said about fishing rights in connection with a river. It wasn't far away.

'What a hole,' Greenway muttered.

The corpse was flat on its back about five yards from the steps and if it wouldn't have been an utterly appalling thing to do I would have taken a photo of it with my phone.

'Know him?' the commander asked when I felt that I had been staring at the body for ages.

'Simon Graves,' I said, my voice husky.

Graves had been shot through the throat and there was a lot of blood still trickling that was merging with the small pools of water on the floor. Perhaps this one had not been an instant death.

Other forensic personnel, using torches, were moving around further down the corridor, which was actually more like a tunnel. There was a crash that sounded exactly like a door being battered in and Cunningham asked us to excuse her and went off to investigate.

'Had enough?' the commander asked me.

I had but said, 'No one's mentioned the weapons. There's a handgun near Graves that gives the impression that he was holding it just before he was shot and there are others on the floors near the bodies upstairs. Surely no one's thinking that Patrick brought them with him and tossed them around to make it look as though they were armed. They *were* armed.'

'This wasn't a shoot-out in the usual meaning of the word either – although I'm sure a few bullets that Patrick didn't fire will be found here and there – he just took them out like those cardboard cut-outs you see on firing ranges.'

'We practise in a Ministry of Defence set-up and did so quite frequently,' I told him. 'It's one of the conditions of being permitted to carry a gun.'

'Thought you did,' Greenway grunted.

There was another door-demolishing crash, followed by muted exclamations of surprise.

'I think you should come and look at this, sir,' Cunningham called.

We carefully picked our way down there as the floor sloped slightly and it got wetter underfoot, making me want to hang on to Greenway's arm but I refrained. I found myself going a bit shivery as this reminded me of the cave complex in Wales where Patrick and I had broken up a school for terror-ists. That was run by a bent cop too.

The cellar room at which we arrived was quite large, the extent of it revealed by the lights of the powerful torches. Someone commented that the light switch didn't work, earning a rebuke from Cunningham who told him that he shouldn't have touched it as he could have been 'fried'.

Round the walls of the cellar were a lot of wooden boxes, some in fairly neat stacks, others dropped seemingly at random on the floor. A few were open and Greenway's curiosity got the better of him and he went forward to have a look.

'Weapons,' he reported gravely. 'Guns. God, there must be hundreds of them in here.'

There was another door in a side wall and without any orders being given one of the more beefy cops present tried a handle and then he and a colleague walloped it with their ram. It held.

'Careful! Cunningham shouted.

It gave way at the second attempt and the men staggered in, off balance.

I registered the stabs of flame, the din, the bullets ripping into the walls but my attention was on the man who ran out, still firing wildly. I dived to one side, rolled over, collided with someone's legs and then, from the floor, opened fire, three shots, with the Smith and Wesson that my fingers had been curled around in my coat pocket ever since I had entered this damned-to-hell building. A big man, he thundered face down, his gun clattering along the floor, and lay still.

Like a cardboard cut-out you see on firing ranges.

'Bloody hell!' Greenway shouted. 'Is everyone all right?'

The torches were all on the floor too, as well as those who had been holding them.

Miraculously, it appeared that other than sprains, grazes and knocks, everyone was unhurt. Then, and only then, did attention turn to the gunman. The deceased gunman.

'Bloody hell,' Greenway said again, only quietly. 'Ingrid . . .'

No, he didn't know what to say.

The body was rolled over and I almost threw up. Staring eyes, rolls of fat under the chin, greasy hair, yellowish skin, blood issuing from the mouth . . .

'That's Herman Grünberg or I'm a pork sausage,' said the commander briskly.

Again, I retched. Then, to Cunningham, I succeeded in saying, 'The incident in this house wasn't mass murder, it was a one-man invasion.'

'I'll get Gillard here,' Greenway said grimly. 'I need to know exactly what went on.'

THIRTEEN

A one-man invasion. The words were going through my mind as I left the building in a bit of a daze, desperately needing fresh air before I really was sick, my ribs hurting like hell. As procedures demanded, I had surrendered the Smith and Wesson for official examination but knew I would get it back, probably later in the day. I had left Greenway and Cunningham talking, she saying that she would have to consult with her superiors because, strictly speaking, this was the NCA's case. A little later I discovered that the decision on this matter was predictable: she would carry on overseeing the routine investigations, the NCA would deal with the bigger picture. The NCA had already kicked off by requesting the perpetrator be brought to the scene to help recreate what had taken place.

But we still hadn't caught Julian Mannering.

Patrick arrived around half an hour later, by which time an enterprising snack van vendor had turned up, having driven, nay ploughed, his way across the park, and opened up for business. I wondered if the rest of north London had come to a complete standstill and was standing by the van, cradling a polystyrene mug of coffee, when I saw a familiar figure approaching on foot, again across the park. He had seen me and waved.

No, I didn't dash over and throw my arms around him in a show of affection that, in the circumstances, might have been a bit upsetting for him. I just waved back, finished my drink and then followed. Having shown my ID, again, I found him in the office inside the main entrance and arrived at the moment Greenway demanded to know what had taken him so long. Patrick apologized without offering an explanation. While this exchange had been going on Cunningham had been hovering, looking a bit worried as though the arrival might just gallop off into the sunset and never come back.

To her, Patrick said, 'Have you found the drugs in the safe in here?'

'Not yet,' she replied urbanely.

'A car turned up and they unloaded a whole lot of stuff and put what looked like packets and bags of drugs in the safe. A couple of blokes staggered off towards the back of the house with heavy boxes – at a guess weapons or stolen property.'

'And where were you while all this was going on?'

'Watching. I was in the room, this room, with them.'

'Oh, come off it!' the woman snorted. 'I've been told that you've been here before. Someone would have recognized you.'

For answer Patrick pulled a woollen beanie hat from his anorak pocket, the one he uses when he's working undercover, pulled it on so it covered his ears and almost his eyes, and assumed a ferocious scowl. No: no one would have recognized him as the police officer who had previously visited.

He said, 'I hadn't made a plan, you can't really, I just watched and waited from behind a tree in the park. I came in with the car when the gates were opened praying that I wouldn't be detected by the security cameras. I discovered when I got in that they weren't activated.'

'Didn't anyone challenge you?' the DCI asked, clearly still not believing him.

'Yes, some hairy thug asked me who the expletives-deleted hell I was and I said Mannering had sent me as he wasn't happy with security. When he doubted this I pointed to the blank screens and then boxed his ears. That seemed to convince him.'

'That was a bit of a risk as Mannering might have been on the premises,' Greenway observed.

'It was a risk I had to take.'

'And then?' Cunningham prompted.

'When the men who had gone off with the boxes returned I pulled the Glock and endeavoured to arrest the lot. There were nine of them in total. Three got out of the door and I went after them, threatening to shoot anyone who followed me. In the corridor the three pulled guns and I had no choice but to fire before they got me. Then someone opened the door of the room next to this one and fired at me. Obviously there was at least one armed man in there but I didn't have time to see which one.'

I could imagine this in all its vivid, cold-blooded detail. It would have taken moments, seconds, and unless you've taken part in live-firing exercises you cannot imagine what it's like. To stay alive, you kill *them*.

'And the six males you left in the room stayed where they were?'

'Too right. Wouldn't you have done?'

'And Graves?' the commander asked.

'By this time he was lurking around in the corridor. He had a gun but bolted when he saw me and disappeared through a trapdoor in a kitchen floor. The Burrwood woman had told us about that. I followed him down and was still on the steps when he took a shot at me. I fired back before he could improve his aim.'

'What about the women you locked in a room down there?' one of Cunningham's team asked, the man with the notebook.

'Not guilty,' Patrick said with a shake of his head.

'Graves, perhaps,' I offered. 'They may even have been locked up in there at night to prevent them from trying to escape.'

'I could do with briefing my boss about aspects of this that aren't connected with the Met,' Patrick said to Cunningham with a smile.

I wasn't fooled by the lightness of tone but the man with the notebook was, for he snapped, 'You don't seem to be showing a shred of regret over all these killings.'

'I'm the sort of bloke who sheds tears, if necessary, in private,' was all Patrick said to him.

'Facts are what we're after,' Greenway remonstrated. 'And right now, I'll take full responsibility for my NCA staff and we'll have something to eat before we carry on with this.'

'Did anyone find Herman Grünberg?' Patrick wanted to know as we went out into blissful fresh air.

'Ingrid did,' Greenway said. 'Big time.'

*　　*　　*

There was a Wetherspoons nearby where the men polished off curries and, to their credit, just iced water. I had a sandwich – I was still feeling a bit queasy.

'Confession time,' Greenway said to Patrick over coffee. 'Who did MI5 order you to remove from the land of the living?'

'Nobody. I was asked to arrest Grünberg if I came across him as they wanted to grill him about his other activities. And I do have to point out here that MI5, so far, has not tried to horn in on this case. It's been thought for a while that he'd gone to ground in a London gang and was carrying on with his criminal career. I reckon that's precisely what he was doing but on the side provided henchmen for Mannering's enterprises and that's what MI5 are interested in. This bears out what the Burrwood woman said about connections, real or not, he has with a foreign power. It goes without saying that I wasn't told everything.'

Other than the fact that he was dead and I had shot him, barest details given, they had made no other mention of Grünberg, perhaps on the grounds that I ought to be able to enjoy my lunch after a bloody horrible day so far, which I appreciated. My main concern now was the possibility that Patrick would be tried for manslaughter – they could hardly make a murder charge stick. He had acted without the necessary authority. Whatever happened there would be a lengthy enquiry conducted by the Police Complaints Commission and it wouldn't be the first time his name had cropped up in *that* outfit.

'I'm going to resign anyway – if they don't chuck me out,' Patrick said, thoughts obviously on the same track as mine.

'*Don't!*' Greenway said. 'Not until this is all over or they might think it's an admission of guilt, that you went in there determined to kill everyone in sight. And don't imagine that you'll be hung out to dry. Not by me, anyway.'

'You have your own career to think of.'

'I don't mind picking Brussels sprouts for a few years.'

They both laughed – I didn't.

Cunningham had consulted with her boss again and Patrick went off to make a detailed statement at a police station the location of which wasn't mentioned in my hearing. In truth I expected that it would be the last I would see of him for quite a while. Would he actually be taken into custody? I had to make a statement of my own, to PC Notebook, but this was only a formality as there had been quite a few extremely reliable witnesses to the action I had taken. All very businesslike, no one had actually thanked me for possibly saving their lives and I think I would have felt very awkward if they had.

Greenway arranged transport for me back into central London and I booked into the hotel Patrick and I use that has a couple of reserved rooms on the top floor for NCA personnel. I wasn't going back to Somerset tonight.

I rang Charles Dixon. He said that he was about to go into a meeting and would phone me back later. Much later, as it happened, when I had had something light to eat in the hotel restaurant and was preparing for an early, if another sleepless, night.

'I know what you're about to tell me,' was his opening remark.

What didn't the wretched little man know?

'It was unfortunate that Grünberg had to die,' he continued. 'He was the link to Mannering and might have provided us with some very valuable information.'

Did he want me to apologize?

Ignoring the remark, I said, 'I called you to give you the latest information as a courtesy as my husband might not be in a position to do so. He's already made it plain that he's going to resign if the NCA doesn't give him the sack so I should imagine the same will go for the odd jobs he does for you. I think we've both had enough.'

'Have you spoken to the press?'

'Of course not!'

'Do let me know if there's anything I can do to help,' said Dixon after a short silence.

The line went dead.

He had no intention of being any help.

Anguish is a word I use only very occasionally in my novels and have always thought it a bit over the top. Now I knew what it really meant. I was aware that, nationally, there had been some other prominent cases of late where what had been unfairly described as 'rogue' police officers had acted without orders and/or in the heat of the moment. An apprehended speeding and drunk motorist had been hauled out of his car and punched when he had hurled abuse; the owner of a yard full of starving cattle tossed into a slurry pit when he had attacked the crew of an area car with a pitchfork; travellers on an illegal pitch, actually a school's playing field, which they had trashed, harassed by dog handlers to the extent that one of the caravan owners had been bitten . . .

Patrick would be sent to prison.

Pour encourager les autres?

OK, I would go and find Julian Mannering.

The next morning and having slept surprisingly well, perhaps due to emotional exhaustion, I first took a taxi and returned to the scene of the incident. I refused to call it a crime scene. DCI Cunningham wasn't there but PC Notebook was and took me to the DS in charge, none other than Milly Grant who had headed the response to our call for assistance in the park.

'Miss Langley,' she said warmly. 'Please call me Milly. I'm sure you can assist me with this as you're on the inside, so to speak. I was quite concerned when I heard that it was your colleague who somehow got a bit out of hand here.'

Thinking that either she was being amazingly tactful or this was the understatement of the year so far, I said, 'He's my husband actually and I can assure you that he didn't get out of hand. He came to this place with the sole intention of arresting those here, defending himself if they offered armed resistance.'

'But he wasn't under orders.'

'No. He was only supposed to be conducting surveillance.'

'Is he always like that – acting what some people might think of as rashly but with the best intentions?'

'Nearly always.'

'Umm, that's the impression I got when I first met him.' She gave herself a little shake. 'Have you dared look on social media such as Twitter this morning?'

I shook my head. 'No, I haven't even seen a newspaper.'

'No names were mentioned of course but the story is that

it was a one-man police raid where several suspects were killed. Opinions go all the way from "give whoever it is a knighthood" to "hang them from the nearest lamppost" – rather a lot of the latter unfortunately.'

This didn't bother me that much as people who have reasons to hate the police are always the noisiest. I then donned an anti-contamination suit and walked Milly through the relevant areas, telling her exactly, *exactly*, what Patrick had said. I had no reason to doubt his word – he had made his intention clear and done it.

'But who would have released it to the media?'

I told her that I simply had no idea. I didn't.

'Do you know anything about the possible whereabouts of this Mannering character?' she asked me when we were standing in the cellar where I had shot Grünberg and I had told her about that too.

I said I'd been hoping she could give *me* a lead on that.

'In the case file it merely states that he's suspected of being involved here, was thought to have been murdered, but the body was subsequently discovered to be that of his brother. We haven't had confirmation about that yet from further DNA testing.'

I gave her the whole story, which took several minutes. The NCA hadn't received confirmation either.

'You say he had, or has, friends within the Establishment?' she queried. 'Whatever that means these days.'

I said, 'According to MI5 he did. They included a woman who used to be an MP, Mo Burrwood. She told the Avon and Somerset force that she was his wife, having married him when he came out of prison. She'd been posing as Simon Graves' wife, which was all part of the job, as she put it. She said she loathes Mannering now.'

'She might know where he is then.'

'She said they lived in hotels.'

'Was that believed?'

'I didn't believe her and I don't think Patrick did either.'

'You know, I'm very angry about this. What a waste if he's sent to prison. Why the hell didn't he get back-up?'

'You wouldn't understand.'

'Try me.'

I took a deep breath. 'We're talking about a man who left the army as a lieutenant colonel, where he served with Special Forces. He then worked for MI5 and now the police. With Special Forces you have tremendous responsibilities for those who serve under you as their lives are put in enormous danger. This was a similar situation and he's never trusted police procedures in such matters – they simply aren't good enough. Not only that, his boss vetoed any action taken until more was known as he didn't want a similar result to what happened in Somerset where Grünberg and his gang were squatting in an old mansion.'

Milly went quiet. Then she said, 'I just want to help. Forgive me, but he's my kind of bloke.'

That smile Patrick had given her seemed to have gone to her head. I could identify with that.

I went outside, got on to James Carrick, told him what had happened, and asked him if, or when, he was going to question Mo Burrwood again as I hadn't gone for her living-in-hotels story. He told me that he hadn't either and planned to talk to her that afternoon. I still had no wish to dash off back to Somerset so asked him to see if he could find out from her where Mannering was. If she hated him so much why not tell us? Then the thought popped into my mind that she might hate him but not his money. If she really was his wife she might have access to it and would high-tail it off to wherever. I had an idea she was the sort of woman who would plead that she'd accidentally got in with a nasty bunch of thugs and hadn't really done anything wrong. A bit retro these days but worth a try perhaps.

On an afterthought I suggested that James got someone to ask the treasurer of Saint Michael's Church PCC if any money had been handed over to the Graveses as a donation to the 'mission', and also find out if he'd received the money the Dandos had said had been given to them. With regard to the latter I thought not. I did add that I wasn't trying to teach him his job, just felt helpless, to which he assured me that he didn't think I was doing any such thing.

Another reason for my wanting to stay in London was that I was hoping to see Patrick, not just from a personal point of view but thinking that something positive might come from it. When I reasoned that the commander was not still in one of his early-morning meetings, I rang him. He told me that someone very senior in the Met had requested that Patrick be ordered to disappear for a while on the grounds that the shootings were their case. Greenway was furious about it. I only discovered the details at a later date; he had a blazing row with the someone over the phone, culminating in his going to New Scotland Yard and bawling that someone out. His argument, I gathered, was how could the NCA conduct the overall investigation if the one person with all the background knowledge, including details that were still covered by the Official Secrets Act, was banished on account of trying to arrest a bunch of lowlife single-handedly? After the smoke had cleared a little some phone calls were made and the order was rescinded. Needless to say, I went straight to HQ when the commander let me know that he'd been successful.

Privately, I thought all this confusion over responsibility – and let's face it, posturing – disgraceful.

Patrick was on his own in Greenway's office, standing pensively looking out of the window when I entered, the usual occupant having apparently 'been delayed'. This might be, I reasoned, to allow us to have a few private moments together. We had a long hug during which I had a little cry and when we stood back and regarded one another I saw that he had shed a few tears too.

'There was no other way,' he said softly.

I didn't want to argue, just stood on tiptoe and kissed his cheek.

'But that other bastard's still out there somewhere.'

'He'll be caught,' I assured him.

'I hope you're going home soon.'

'Yes, today – now I've seen you. But what are you going to do?'

'Dunno. But Mike wants me to stick around.'

'I've been thinking about the man who accosted us with the shotgun at The Spinney.'

'What about him?'

'Was he one of those who got away in the van, do you know?'

'Carrick's more likely to know about that.'

'What about those you shot?'

'There was no one that old. They were all young men.'

Just then my private phone pinged a text and I'd just read it and shared it with Patrick when Greenway loudly cleared his throat from somewhere outside the door and then came in. He dropped into his black leather revolving chair then stared at the pair of us unnervingly. 'What the *hell* am I going to do about this?' he demanded to know.

'Well, someone's made a start by releasing the story to the media,' I said.

'Who, right now, I could chop into very small pieces,' he retorted.

Patrick said, 'Ingrid's just had an unofficial text from DCI Carrick to say that personnel from an anti-terrorist unit – it used to be Special Branch – are commandeering Mo Burrwood and taking her off for questioning. That means that the undercurrents in this do involve national security. As you know, Burrwood said when she was interviewed in Bath that she wouldn't be surprised if Mannering wasn't in contact with a foreign power and, as she put it, "the idiot probably fancies himself as a master spy". But she was the one who used to be on the security committees.'

Greenway pulled a face. 'The entire investigation might be pulled out from under my feet to prevent the NCA poking around any further.'

'That's possible,' Patrick said. 'And also bearing in mind that the NCA was inveigled into handling it in the first place. A big political scandal might be in the offing and MI5 won't want anyone involved to be scared off before they're arrested. But that won't stop Complaints from making a case against *me*.'

The next morning, after the identities of some of the men he had shot were made public, the media made much of a few bricks being thrown at a police patrol car in the East End.

'With one exception they already had criminal records and that one had been cleared of GBH when the victim refused to testify,' James Carrick said in business-like fashion, his attention on his computer screen. 'And I ken that part of London was bothersome before the Romans arrived.' He gazed at me with the icy-blue gaze that had no doubt wowed Joanna. 'Are you OK?'

'As well as can be expected,' I replied.

'And it has to be borne in mind that he may go to prison.'

'He knows there's no point in him fighting it – he's going to plead guilty.'

'To what though? Did he go in against orders?'

'The idea was that he'd only find out what was going on there.'

'And I thought your Richard Daws recruited him to the NCA mainly because he was a loose cannon.'

'Absolutely,' I said dryly. 'The man also said he'd probably end up behind bars. As you must know the police have been getting it in the neck lately after a series of unprofessional encounters they've had with the great British public.'

'I know,' the DCI said wearily. 'And I've a bit of bad news for you – Burrwood stuck to her story about living in hotels with Mannering. I simply couldn't shake her out of it. But the woman *was* at The Spinney.'

Having got back quite late the evening before I had called in to see Carrick the next morning on my way to go shopping in the hope that he had good news for me. He hadn't yet asked someone to talk to the treasurer of the PCC either, so there was nothing else to be said. After just about filling the car with groceries I then paused at an estate agent's office and made an appointment for them to value the house, something I felt we needed to know if we decided to put it on the market. Remembering then that we needed cheese, which I buy from a farm shop, I called in there, stopping for coffee as by this time I was running out of energy and for some reason James hadn't offered me any. The morning had gone.

What to tell Elspeth? There was every chance that she knew of course as although no names had been mentioned as far as the media 'leak' was concerned, the episode had her son's *modus operandi* stamped all over it. This quandary was weighing heavily on me as I let myself in through the front door of the rectory. The house was very quiet.

I unloaded the shopping, put the perishables in the fridge or freezer and then had a walk round the ground floor. No one was in, not even in the annexe. It was a cold, damp day with remnants of snow still in corners of the garden so it was unlikely anyone was outside. Then, with a slight shock, I realized that neither Terry's, Dawn's or Carrie's cars had been parked at the front. They had all been there when I had gone out and now they weren't. Where the hell was everyone?

I had another look round but no one had left me a note and it was in something approaching panic that I dashed upstairs. Children's toys were strewn on the landing, perfectly normal, and there were clothes on the floors of their bedrooms, also nothing to worry about. The bathroom had every appearance of the last occupant having been a water buffalo, also the usual state of affairs on a day when no home helps, of which we employ two, were due, it being a Saturday. I popped my head into Carrie's room in case she had been taken ill and Terry and Dawn had taken the children out for the day but that and the little nursery next door were also empty.

The room I share with Patrick though had a man in it, a fully dressed, unshaven and actually a little grubby man who looked as though he had walked through the door, fallen asleep on his feet and, with great fortune, landed on the bed. I checked that he was breathing. He was. I left him there, attacked the bathroom with various cleaning agents, tidied up and then fixed myself some lunch. There was a big question to be answered, nothing sinister I felt, but I forced myself to be patient as the man in my life was utterly exhausted.

'Where is everyone?' was my first, and obvious, question when he appeared in the living room around two hours later.

Patrick collapsed into an armchair looking as though he was about to go to sleep again and said, 'Sorry, I did try to contact you but your phone was off and I was too worn out even to leave a message.'

I apologized to him, saying that I'd turned it off when I called in to see Carrick. Mobiles can be too, too intrusive.

'Terry rang me. I gather you'd told him that I'd been relieved of duties but not actually banged up – he was concerned by what he called more "happenings" here. Yesterday, Dawn caught Henry Dando peering in through their bedroom window and although she called Terry, who saw him off, it rather frightened her as she had no idea who he was. Then Dando's wife rang the annexe doorbell that evening when she was putting their little girl to bed and demanded to know who she was. Quite nasty apparently. After her recent traumas Terry decided to take them home – the whole lot.'

Fleetingly, I wondered how big their house was and then remembered something. 'Which means he's jumped bail!'

'No, he went about it properly and contacted Carrick who amended the terms to don't leave the country. He already had the man's passport anyway. He sent someone to the Dandos' house but it appeared to be deserted. They must have kept an eye open and nipped round when the crews changed watches. And cops can't be here every minute of the day.'

'I thought Greenway told you to stick around,' I said after a little silence.

Patrick smiled just for me; he didn't feel like smiling. 'I got the impression "stick" could be more flexible than it sounded and didn't want to get into an argument with him, just caught a train. I'd remembered what you'd said about that character with the shotgun. He bothers me.'

'Could he be Mannering?'

'It's possible. That character had a scruffy grey beard and was overweight. The man we knew as Sir Julian was bordering on obese but that was some years ago. His voice was rough but he could have disguised it. I don't have any answers to that but for God's sake check that all the outside doors are locked.'

He went off to have a shower and shave.

'Did you have to hand over your Glock?' I called to a closing door.

'Yes, I did – might not get it back either.'

I went to fetch some more ammunition for the Smith and Wesson from the wall safe and put it with the gun in my bag. Then, on reflection, returned to get the harness and put the whole lot on the chair where Patrick had been sitting. The first thing he did when he returned was to give it back to me.

*   *   *

The house was horribly, horribly quiet – so quiet that I jumped when the phone rang. It was Greenway.

'Is he with you?' he asked without preamble.

I said Patrick was.

'Thought so. But you haven't just confirmed that – I don't know where he is and I don't want to talk to him. You'd probably like to know that they got someone to open that safe in the office at Saint Ed's. Patrick was right insofar as there were drugs in it, including cocaine – I don't know the street value yet but judging by what someone's just told me it's megabucks. And they've been removing the boxes of weapons from the cellar and found another door concealed behind them. In a small room beyond was a cache of booze and cigarettes. This was crime on an industrial scale.'

'What do you want us to do?'

'Nothing. Lie low for a few days.'

'If we do by some chance happen upon Mannering neither of us will be able to arrest him now Patrick's been relieved of duties,' I pointed out.

'Then if you think you're likely to happen upon him take a cop with you.'

I was beginning to think that modern-day policing was as convoluted as working for MI5.

FOURTEEN

The current situation didn't preclude one of our regular 'debriefings' at the Ring o' Bells with the Carricks, which we 'attended' that same evening. In the meantime and wearing my NCA hat I had gone to the home of the PCC's treasurer, who Patrick had told me lived in a cottage up a lane behind the pub, and made enquiries about any possible exchange of monies. He was emphatic that no 'donations' had been given to him by the Dandos either from them personally or on behalf of anyone else. Nor had the church given to the London mission. He was sufficiently concerned about the whole situation to show me the accounts. I had absolutely no reason to doubt his word as John had always spoken very highly of him.

'You wouldn't find prison that onerous,' Carrick said after we had brought the pair of them up to date. He went a bit pink. 'No, sorry, what I meant was—'

'The fact that I've survived serving in Special Forces and God knows what else since it would be a walk in the park,' Patrick interrupted. 'Yes, you're right.'

'You're being dreadfully pessimistic!' Joanna accused her husband.

'He's not,' Patrick said. 'I have to face facts. And other than the obvious and awful effect it will have on my family I shall at least know that they're safe. We'll sell the house and they can go somewhere else as this village has turned against us courtesy of a man with a grudge and a twisted mind. That's my last job, to find him.'

'You have no authority now,' Carrick, ever the stickler to rules, reminded him.

'I shall take a cop with me.'

'Who?' James and Joanna asked together.

I said nothing, I already knew who he had in mind.

'Greenway. After all, he told me to.'

It shocked them into silence for a few seconds and then Carrick said, 'Does he know?'

Patrick chuckled. 'He phoned for the second time today just before we came out and has volunteered. I'm not sure that's the right thing for him to do and said I'd let him know but I admire him tremendously as the last time he got involved personally a mobster shot him in the shoulder. There's a lot of wanting to grab Mannering under the noses of the Met too – you'd be surprised at the one-upmanship that goes on.'

'I don't think I would actually,' the DCI observed dryly. 'But you're right, it isn't what commanders are supposed to do.'

'No, but don't forget he came from the Met and probably got the job because he was a commander who did things he wasn't supposed to.'

Thought about like that they were two of a kind.

'Look,' Carrick said. 'This is my case as well, you know. Right back to when Lionel Mannering was shot by Mrs Smythe and then the raid when members of this force were gunned down, killed or wounded, at that bloody ruin up the road.'

'And your point?' Joanna asked impatiently.

'You want to retain overall command?' Patrick enquired of him.

'It's my case,' Carrick repeated stubbornly. 'And I want to be on board whatever you're planning to do.'

Joanna tossed her long titian hair, on duty worn in a tight bun, off her face. 'It would give credence to any further lurking around Patrick undertook in that bloody ruin up the road, I suppose.'

I felt she would make DCI *at least*.

The men stared at her.

'Isn't that what you're planning to do – to see if Mannering's skulking there?' she asked. 'I would.'

'Are we?' her husband asked Patrick.

Joanna didn't wait for him to respond. 'Well, for a start it wouldn't appear that the man with the shotgun Ingrid and Patrick came upon has ever been explained or located. You showed me the case notes, James, and it would appear that he's middle-aged or older. No one that old was among the men who were arrested or wounded and from what Patrick's just told us about those who resisted arrest or tried to kill him in London he wasn't present there either.'

Patrick gave her a little wave for having worded that so nicely.

'Can't you just order a raid on that house?' Joanna continued. 'It's supposed to be empty, isn't it? Cordoned off? Still an official crime scene?'

'I can't,' said Carrick. 'Even I have to get official approval and I don't think the super would give it to me without evidence. There's nothing to suggest that anyone's there as the house and outbuildings were searched and new locks put on the doors. The place is kept an eye on by passing patrol cars. Raids are expensive. You know that.'

I said, 'I don't care what anyone does. I'm going to have a look round there tomorrow. Everyone seems to have forgotten that I'm the one who's going to have to explain to an elderly lady and five children why they won't see Patrick for several years. Elspeth might not see him again, ever, unless she visits him in jail and I don't think she could bear to do that. Obviously, I shall resign when Patrick's fired from the NCA so this will be a final effort on my part to rescue something from the whole appalling business. If nothing comes of it at least I'll have tried.'

As well as a declaration of intent, and I meant it, this was intended to focus male minds. From what followed it would appear that I'd succeeded.

'Tomorrow's Sunday,' Carrick said musingly. 'First light?'

Patrick drained the last of the beer from his tankard. 'Greenway did say that he fancied some fresh country air. I'll get him to come down tonight.'

'No, you don't need Greenway. You don't want a desk cop, you have me.'

First light on this particular overcast end-of-January morning was at just before eight thirty a.m., a faint greying of the blackness visible through the bare branches of the oak trees on the far side of the churchyard. Patrick and I had been outside for a few minutes huddled into anoraks while we waited for the Carricks. Joanna had insisted on being present – they have a live-in nanny – although I was sure she would be sent to a safe distance by her other half if things got difficult. OK, I know all about women being equal but when there are little children involved, it's different. Little children or not, I was in the unique position of being the only one present permitted to carry firearms, the Smith and Wesson snuggly in its holster beneath my jacket. And, yes, I would hand it over to Patrick if I thought it necessary or he asked me for it.

When they arrived, Patrick said, 'As far as reaching this place is concerned, I know the way and we're going across country. I suggest we keep silence unless there's some kind of emergency. And if it all comes to nothing we've had some good exercise.'

How we would proceed was decided: I followed after Patrick, then Joanna, with James bringing up the rear. We began by going through the little gate into the churchyard, a historic access that permitted the incumbents of old and their families to attend church without encountering the mud of the lane or any unwashed peasants. The path leading to the church door forked left, another, much narrower, which we took, meandered between the graves and ended by a lower section of the boundary wall. At this stage we could use torches, small ones, vital as some of the old graves were just grassy humps in the ground.

Having climbed over the wall, it was just possible to make out this ancient way as it continued across the field beyond, still used by ramblers and sheep, a flock of which was in the field. I heard Joanna utter a squeak of alarm when one that had been grazing under the wall bolted away, just a vague bouncing grey shape in the gloom. The smell of them and crushed grass wafted over us on the cold breeze as we walked and somewhere in the distance an owl hooted to be answered by another.

Patrick had said he would walk a short distance in front to avoid anyone cannoning into him if he stopped suddenly and did just that, probably listening. As arranged, nothing was said and a few moments later he set off again. The winding path led gently downhill, the dark mass of a row of large trees that I guessed was on one of the boundaries of the field just becoming visible in the distance. We reached it and there was a fence with a gate that was tied with wire at both ends to keep it in place. Although the original granite posts were still there the hinges and other fittings had rusted away leaving just holes and dark stains on the stonework.

We climbed over it with only a muttered expletive from Carrick to break the silence after catching a foot in something and almost losing his balance. We went on through the trees, still following a path of sorts, careful not to trip over roots or walk into low branches. Thankfully, Patrick hadn't yet asked us to switch off our torches. I wondered if these were the woods that were part of the grounds of The Spinney but then reasoned that they couldn't be as we were still quite close to home. Coming to the end of the trees we encountered another fence with a gate, which opened, after a fashion, and carried on walking having turned sharp left to follow the boundary. To our right was the invisible expanse of another field.

Patrick stopped again and whispered that it was time to kill the lights, adding, 'It's comparatively flat for a while but the grass is a bit tussocky so pick your feet up.'

After quite a walk we reached a corner of the field where the fence was replaced by a brick wall. In the slightly improving light it was possible to see that it was old and broken down in places. Bearing right, we went through one of these gaps, clambering over the piles of bricks, and into more trees. Then blackness seemed to swallow us – these were mostly ever-greens. I think we all went to switch on our torches but Patrick got us in a huddle and insisted that he light the way with his and we walk in his footsteps, carefully. He had come this way before and hoped he could remember where the overhanging branches were. I think we all did.

I heard Carrick whisper something just after we set off again that I think included the words 'fools' errand'.

'Hold hands,' Patrick irritably suggested, no doubt worried that one of us would kill ourselves blundering off into a tree.

That said, he held one of mine and Joanna held my other having grabbed hold of her husband's and like a purblind caterpillar we made our way through the wood. There were a lot of brambles that caught in our clothing and saplings that whipped our faces and we had to pause sometimes to step over and duck under the aforementioned branches, some of which looked extremely dead and likely to crash down at any moment. The journey seemed to go on for rather a long time and I was beginning to wonder about Patrick's 'shortcut' when I saw a dim light through the trees ahead of us.

He stopped and switched off the torch. 'We do *not* split up,' he hissed. 'And if anyone has a problem such as an injury we abort.'

He was probably wishing he was on his own; we were an encumbrance to him. Carrick probably still wasn't happy either, not relishing being the 'token cop' even though he had volunteered.

Slowly, we moved forward until we were on the far edge of the trees. The house was at an angle to us from this point across an expanse of what I already knew was rough grass, the various outbuildings to one side of it merely darker shapes. We turned right and went in that direction, walking to the rear of them and, quite quickly, they blocked out our view of the house and therefore prevented anyone indoors from seeing us. I was wondering if Patrick had a plan and thought not; he sometimes prefers to think on the hoof.

There was a path of sorts to the rear of these buildings but it was strewn with rusting relics of the buckets, car wheels, tractor tyres and agricultural bygones variety. At one stage the remains of a strange hand-driven machine blocked our way and for some reason I immediately thought of that device straight from *Cold Comfort Farm*, a mangelwurzel chopper. Then I walked straight into my husband, not for the first time when on surveillance sorties, and even in the half-light felt his chilly gaze on me. Somehow, I slew the giggle.

There was no incident tape remaining in place here. An ancient manure heap was stacked up against the wall of a long, low building, obviously at one time a cow byre or stables. A large rear door was ajar. Picking our way carefully through a bed of nettles, not without their retaliation as far as I was concerned, we went over to it. Patrick opened it a little wider, having signalled to us to wait, and went inside where he quickly shone around his torch. He came back shaking his

head, the draught of his movement bringing with it the stench
of stale urine and worse.

We carried on, going the length of the row of outbuildings,
none of the rest of which had doorways that opened on this
side. When we reached the end of them, and without looking,
I knew that we were now at the rear of the house. In front of
us and to the right of the rough drive that encircled it was
what appeared to be the remains of a narrow vegetable patch
but the trees were encroaching on it, saplings growing within
yards of a car that was parked near the rear entrance. There
was a light on in a room with a small window to the right of
it, a thin blind pulled almost down.

'We put tape right round the house and it should still be
here,' Carrick moved forward to whisper.

As far as I could see it wasn't.

Patrick urged us forward and we went along the side of the
building now nearest to us, seemingly a barn, turned sharp
left and went in through the open, and wide, doorway. It was
pitch dark inside. Now, only the width of the drive separated
us from the house. A sudden movement inside the room with
the light on, a shadow falling across the blind, caused us to
jump to one side into concealment and for the second time in
so many minutes I collided with someone.

Who was dead and still warm.

The rope the body was suspended by creaked as it swung
gently. In a spasm of shock I clutched at whoever was nearest
to me – as it happened, Carrick.

'Sorry,' I gasped.

'What's wrong?' he whispered.

'There's a body,' I managed to get out. 'Sorry, I can't get
my fingers out of your coat.'

Back-up arrived and Patrick, having prised me free, risked
a quick look with his torch, shielding the light from outside
with a hand.

'I think it's him,' he said in an undertone. 'That's if the
man with the shotgun *was* Mannering.'

I didn't want to look and fleetingly wondered if his death
was suicide or murder.

'Decision time,' Patrick continued. 'If whoever's indoors is

one of his mobsters he'll almost certainly be armed. Are there
others?' Without waiting for any responses to what was actually a hypothetical question, he continued, 'I suggest that we
get him, or them, to come to us.'

'Failing a loud-hailer . . .' Carrick said and must have given
Patrick a nudge.

So, in his parade-ground voice, he bellowed, 'Armed police!
You're surrounded and under arrest! Come out with your hands
in the air! Now!'

The door opened, slowly, what dim light there was within
silhouetting a portly figure.

'Please don't shoot, I'm quite unarmed,' said Charles Dixon
in his whispery voice, sounding just a little worried.

Patrick told Carrick who he was.

Carrick went forward. 'Are you alone?'

'Yes, but feel free to search.'

'Are, or were you, part of the set-up here?'

'Good Lord, no. I merely led the team who discussed certain
matters with him a little earlier.'

'Mannering?'

'Of course, who else?'

To Carrick, Patrick said, 'Sorry, James, but you can't touch
him. We found Mannering here, dead – and that's all.'

'Are you giving me orders?' the DCI belligerently asked him.

Dixon said, 'No, Detective Chief Inspector, he's merely
anticipating what your superiors will tell you a little later.
As a friend. But please ignore that for the moment and carry
on as normal; you have an unexplained death to report.'

The initial statements and other formalities took all the rest
of that morning and part of the afternoon. There were questions from Carrick's superiors, to whom he had given an *exact*
account, as to why Patrick, who had been relieved of duties
pending an investigation, had been permitted to be present. I
understand the DCI replied that he had only accompanied us
in order to act as a cross-country guide. This seemed to be
acceptable. Patrick had immediately contacted Commander
Greenway, also telling him *exactly* what had happened and
from that point on everything became very strange.

As Dixon had intimated, the next day MI5 slammed a lid down on the entire investigation. Everything: Lionel Mannering's murder, Terry's attempt to save Mrs Smythe from prosecution, the attack on Patrick and me after our visit to Saint Edwina's and his subsequent one-man raid. Carrick was also ordered to put a hold on the inquiry following our sortie to The Spinney, which he had had no choice but make official, resulting in the finding of Julian Mannering's body.

'Do *you* know what's going on?' I asked Patrick after he'd had a call from Greenway with the news. 'I mean, it was absolutely mind-blowing that Mannering was found hanged there.'

'No, I don't. And I've never dealt with Dixon in the ordinary way. I simply have no idea how he fitted into all this but he must be far more senior than I'd given him credit for.'

No one, outside MI5 anyway, has so far discovered the background behind Mannering's death. He had been hanged in what was thought to be 'traditional' fashion – that is, his neck had been broken as the result of whatever he had been forced to stand on kicked out from beneath him.

I suddenly remembered something. 'What about that man whose photo was on the website of Saint Ed's but who we never came across and Felix Yellen was standing in for him?'

'I think the person able to answer that, but no doubt professing ignorance, would be Dixon,' Patrick replied. 'There's been a lot more going on than we'll ever know about.'

'D'you reckon either of them leaked your raid to the press?'

'Possibly. It threw any blame of a possible screw-up back to the cops, didn't it?'

The Dandos had been discovered 'cringing', as Carrick put it, in their house. They were also hungry and shivering as they had not dared to switch on their central heating or go shopping in case they were detected. Both had wept copious tears when they were taken back to Bath police station. There, after consulting with their victims, the DCI had given them an official warning, and went on to demand they handed over any 'donations' they had received from Simon Graves as it might be needed as evidence. If, eventually, this proved not to be the case he would arrange for it to be given to Saint Michael's Church. I gather that he had made it perfectly clear to them that he was much too busy to bring charges against 'neep heids' – which they might have needed to look up in a Scottish dictionary. A couple of days later they had put their house on the market.

Meanwhile, the family had come home. Those four simple words cannot describe the happiness of that day and those following. Almost immediately Elspeth took several long calculating looks at her bedraggled, snow-flattened garden and then phoned a local landscape contractor who had worked with a designer at the Chelsea Flower Show. She had in mind a general refurbishment and a knot garden together with a little grove of *Jacquemontii* birches and told us that if we did decide to move it would be a good selling point.

A couple of weeks later there was a press release, a very muted one, to the effect that several members of a House of Commons security committee were being questioned by officers from an anti-terrorist unit, at one time Special Branch. This was in connection with information covered by the Official Secrets Act being leaked, through a criminal organiz-ation, to North Korea. The kingpin had been a one-time knighted banker, name not revealed, nor that he was now dead. Other than that there was a continuing deafening silence about the entire affair and I suspected there were ongoing enquiries of an exceedingly secret nature.

'End of story?' Patrick queried. 'Or do I have the threat of being banged up for manslaughter hanging over me for the rest of my life?'

'I suggest . . .' I began.

'What?'

'Nothing, the oracle's shut up shop. From right this minute.'

A few days after this Patrick was called to London for a series of debriefings, one with the Police Complaints Com-mission. He told me afterwards that due to secrecy imposed by the Home Secretary they had been rendered, as far as this case was concerned, toothless. Concern was raised but it was deemed not to be in the public interest to proceed further with the matter. As far as other meetings went there was more of the same. The Met and the NCA had all the details, facts, reports and the history behind what had happened and that was all they appeared to be interested in. On that same day Patrick handed in his notice to the NCA, which was accepted.

The Lionel Mannering murder case was finally cleared, mostly, of restrictions and Mrs Smythe appeared in court charged with shooting her employer. She had stuck with her decision to plead guilty. She was permitted to be seated in the dock but was so short in stature that she disappeared so M'lud permitted her to sit in the body of the court and she was assisted there. I was wondering what would happen about the missing murder weapon as, with Terry's help, a police diver had found it, but not the ammunition, on the bed of the River Rother beneath a bridge near Pulborough. But as far as he was concerned nothing happened – the censorious hand of MI5 again? – and she pleaded guilty therefore there was no trial where he would have been required to give evidence.

After various statements had been read out, one by James Carrick, Mrs Smythe was asked to stand. The judge informed her that he was minded to send her to prison but because of her age and medical opinion having suggested her action had had a possible link with senile dementia she would get a two-year suspended sentence plus a hundred hours community service. She thanked him and said that her son had told her there was a part-time vacancy for a cook at a local 'old folks 'ome' and could she do that for 'nuthin?' She was told any decisions would be made by the probation service but that's what eventually happened.

We decided to stay in Hinton Littlemoor for the time being, mostly on account of the children's education. This author finally got on with her novel, discovering that the little she had written in the past few troubled weeks was absolute rubbish. The garden was redesigned, and Elspeth was very happy with it. Out of three offered to him, Patrick took a safe, somewhat dull job based in Bath as an insurance claims invest-igator and the inhabitants of Hinton Littlemoor once again smiled and looked us in the eye.

But MI5? What next, if anything?